LIONBOY
THE
CHASE

Books by Zizou Corder

LIONBOY

LIONBOY: THE CHASE

ZIZOU CORDER

LIONBOY THE CHASE

PUFFIN

PUFFIN BOOKS

Published by the Penguin Group
Penguin Books Ltd, 80 Strand, London WC2R 0RL, England
Penguin Group (USA), Inc., 375 Hudson Street, New York, New York 10014, USA
Penguin Books Australia Ltd, 250 Camberwell Road, Camberwell, Victoria 3124, Australia
Penguin Books Canada Ltd, 10 Alcorn Avenue, Toronto, Ontario, Canada M4V 3B2
Penguin Books India (P) Ltd, 11 Community Centre, Panchsheel Park, New Delhi – 110 017, India
Penguin Group (NZ), cnr Airborne and Rosedale Roads, Albany, Auckland 1310, New Zealand
Penguin Books (South Africa) (Pty) Ltd, 24 Sturdee Avenue, Rosebank 2196, South Africa

Penguin Books Ltd, Registered Offices: 80 Strand, London WC2R 0RL, England

www.penguin.com

First published 2004
1

Set in 14.5/17.25 pt Perpetua

Typeset by Rowland Phototypesetting Ltd, Bury St Edmunds, Suffolk
Made and printed in England by Clays Ltd, St Ives plc

British Library Cataloguing in Publication Data
A CIP catalogue record for this book is available from the British Library

ISBN 0–141–38052–7

LIONBOY: THE CHASE

is dedicated to Julius and Grace Flusfeder,

because we love them

ACKNOWLEDGEMENTS

Thanks again to Fred van Deelen for his beautiful maps and diagrams, and to Paul Hodgson for presenting the music to match.

And thanks to all the Puffin ladies with their continuingly beautiful footwear, especially Sarah Hughes, Adele Minchin, Kirsten Grant, Elaine McQuade, Shannon Park, Lesley Levene and Francesca Dow. And the Puffin gentleman Nick Stearn for consistent top-notch covers.

And the agents: Linda Shaughnessy, Rob Kraitt, Teresa Nicholls, Anjali Pratap, Sylvie Rabineau. And Derek Johns, the perfect agent, sine qua non.

Special thanks again to Robert Lockhart for writing us a gorgeous evocative soundtrack. If you want to hear them all, or learn them on the piano, there is a book of the tunes. They are quite easy – even I can play them – and come with a CD of the music played by a small orchestra, so you don't even have to play it yourself. It is called
Music from Zizou Corder's **Lionboy**,
by Robert Lockhart, and published by Faber Music. You can get it from music shops or online from www.fabermusic.com.

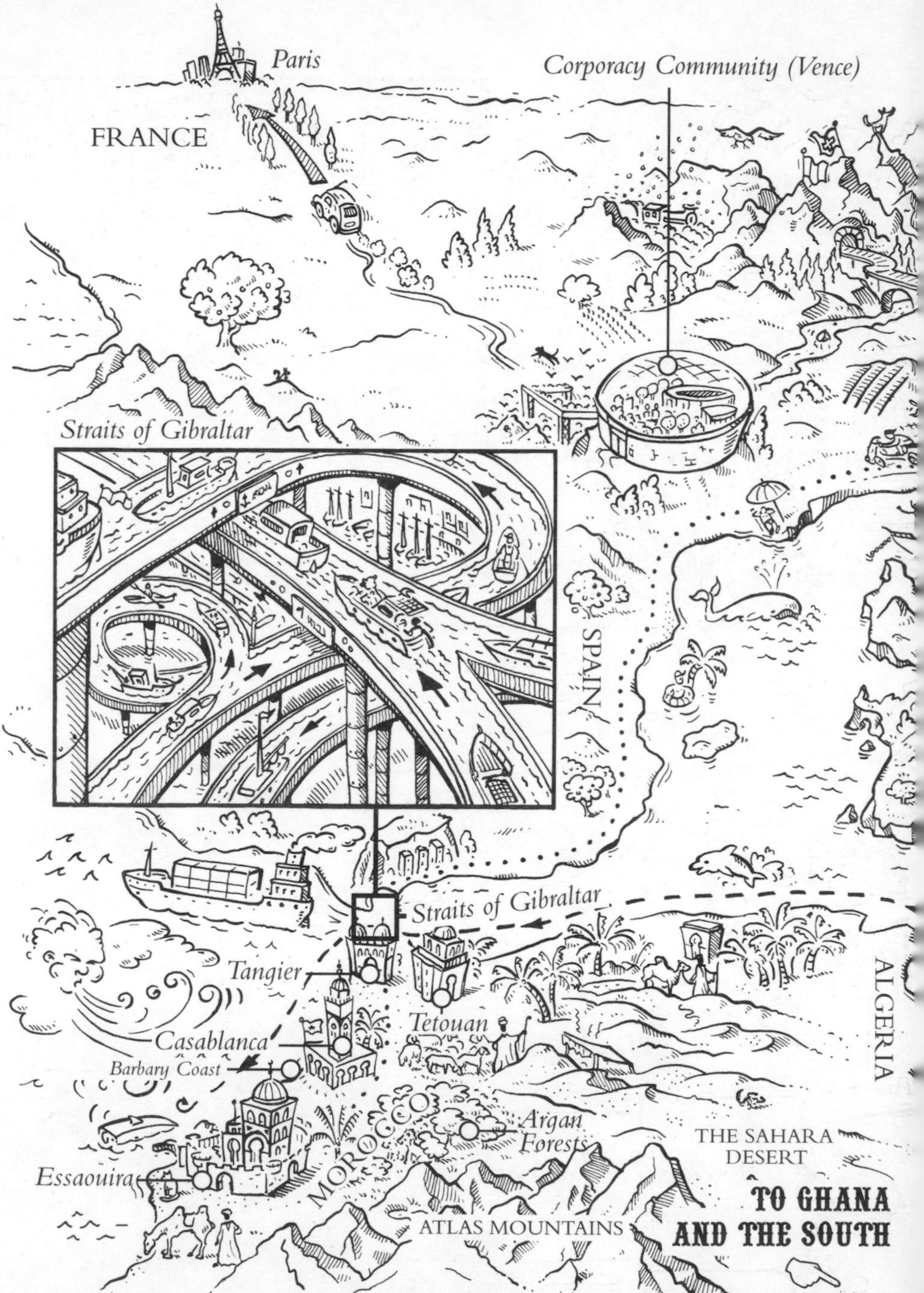
Paris
Corporacy Community (Vence)
FRANCE
Straits of Gibraltar
SPAIN
Straits of Gibraltar
Tangier
Tetouan
Casablanca
Barbary Coast
ALGERIA
MOROCCO
Argan Forests
THE SAHARA DESERT
Essaouira
TO GHANA AND THE SOUTH
ATLAS MOUNTAINS

Venice Station
THE ALPS
Venice & the Lagoon
TO ISTANBUL
AND THE EAST
ADRIATIC SEA
ITALY
MEDITERRANEAN
SEA
SICILY
N
Pantelleria
Western Mediterranean
& Morocco
SCALE:
from here to here
= A LONG WAY

CHAPTER ONE

It is a curious thing for a boy to be stuck on a train in an Alpine snowstorm, in a bathroom with six homesick Lions and a huge unidentified sabre-toothed creature. More curious still to know that bustling around next door in his purple silk dressing gown is a friendly Bulgarian king called Boris, and his security chief, name of Edward, who makes a point of knowing everything there is to know, and perhaps a little more.

If you were a boy whose parents – clever scientists – had been stolen by a villainous lad from your neighbourhood in London, on behalf of you're not sure who, but almost certainly because they have invented a cure for asthma, you might be happy to think that these Lions and this king were on your side. If you and the Lions had run away from a Floating Circus and a nasty, mysterious Liontrainer, you might take the chance to relax for a moment, knowing that neither he nor the villainous lad – who has anyway been savaged by one of the Lions – could make it through the snow to get you.

If the Oldest Lion said to you, 'We are warm and dry, and we have eaten, and we are together. Someone else is going to mend the train that will roar us through this mysterious dangerous weather to the place where your parents are, closer to our home. But now – now we are safe' – if he said that, you might feel warm and cheered up and happy.

This is exactly how Charlie Ashanti felt. Charlie felt as close to safe as he had felt in weeks. The beautiful Lions were lying in a pile around him: the three Lionesses resting after their chase, the Oldest Lion calmly triumphant at their escape, Elsina the young girl Lion still weak from their adventures on the train's roof but so excited to be out in the real world, and the Young Lion, Charlie's friend, fast asleep with his head in Charlie's lap. Next door was King Boris in his glamorous carriage, promising help when they reached Venice. Rafi Sadler and Maccomo the Liontrainer were safely stuck in Paris, and the snow was covering the train like a huge snuggly duvet.

'Now,' Charlie said to himself, 'is the time to sleep and eat and relax, so we will be fit and strong for the troubles ahead.' Because, without a doubt, there were going to be troubles ahead.

Charlie's parents, Dr Aneba Ashanti and Professor Magdalen Start, were in big trouble already. You wouldn't necessarily think it, to see them sitting at opposite ends of the social club in the Corporacy Gated Village Community. The Club Room was long and low and comfortable, with a glass wall looking out over a beautiful subtropical garden, full of palm trees and huge rounded rocks with a stream trickling over them. At least, Magdalen had thought it was beautiful until she noticed that every rock was the same shape exactly, and made of some kind of plastic. She peered carefully at the trees. Were they fake too?

She was sitting with a group of women all talking about how fat they were. They had dishes of crisps and glasses of wine in front of them. 'Oh no, I shouldn't,' they cried, as they stuffed their faces with food that was bad for them. A lot of them were smoking, too.

'You'll get wrinkles from smoking,' said one.

'Clare's got fabulous skin,' said another. 'Don't you hate her?'

Magdalen wondered why you should hate somebody just because she has pretty skin. She wondered why these women were worried about getting wrinkles from smoking but not about cancer. She wondered why they could only talk about how fat they were, when they weren't particularly fat anyway, and if they were really worried about it why didn't they stop eating the crisps and drinking? And if they wanted to eat crisps and drink wine, why did they keep telling themselves off for doing so? Why not just enjoy it?

She felt very tired. She couldn't quite remember how

they got here, to tell the truth – Rafi Sadler tricking them had faded from her mind somehow, and so had the long journey to this place by submarine and boat and truck. She didn't think they'd been here very long. She knew she didn't like it. She wanted to be left alone, to not listen to this rubbish. She wanted to see her son and be with her husband and get some work done. Her brain was turning to mushy gunk here. She knew she was meant to be somewhere else, leading a different life. She felt very tired. I just thought that, she thought. What's wrong with me?

Looking up, she caught a glimpse of Aneba across the room. He didn't look very well. His skin, normally gleaming black, had an ashy tinge to it. The whites of his eyes were a little yellow. His big muscular shoulders, normally so broad and straight, seemed to have sagged.

'You've put on a bit of weight yourself, haven't you?' said one of the women to Magdalen.

At the other end of the room, Aneba was watching football on television with a group of men. Aneba liked football, but this was the fourth match in a row. The men were complaining about how bad the players were, and the managers, and the referee, and the linesmen. They were drinking beer and eating peanuts and saying they could do much better themselves. Under the cigarette smell there was another flavour in the air. He half recognized it. Didn't like it.

After one of the matches, the news had come on. The Empire soldiers had had to shoot up a city in the Poor World, and lots of civilians had been injured and there were no medicines available. There were pictures of children with dirty bandages on, looking terrified and hungry. The men looked up briefly, and said, 'That's terrible,' then went back to complaining. 'Nothing you can do though, is there?' said one. Aneba could see that the man felt bad, and liked him for it.

'Never mind, mate,' said a second man. 'Have another beer.'

Aneba knew there was something else he ought to be doing but he couldn't really remember what.

Looking up, he saw Magdalen on the other side of the room. She didn't look very well. Her red hair wasn't curly and chaotic as usual. It had gone flat.

Soon they'd be due back at the Wellness Unit for their Motivational Management Therapy.

'Cheer up, mate,' said one of the men. 'Have a drink.'

Aneba tried hard to remember what he was normally like.

If Charlie had seen his energetic, intelligent parents like this, he would have revised his opinion that they were not in any immediate danger. He would have been shocked.

Trouble had already announced itself at Thibaudet's Royal Floating Circus and Equestrian Philharmonic Academy (also known as Tib's Gallimaufry or The Show). Major Maurice Thibaudet (pronounced Tib Oh Day), the Boss, Ringmaster and Maestro of the Circus, had been lounging in his cabin on board the giant circus ship *Circe*, wearing a pale-green robe that matched the carved panelling, and drinking a glass of brandy and soda. The Show's opening night in Paris had been fabulous, and everybody had said so. Major Tib and most of the circusguys had stayed up late afterwards, drinking and congratulating themselves. The others were all still in bed with bad heads (except for Pirouette the Flying Trapeze Artiste, and the Lucidi Family of acrobats, who always got up early to practise, no matter what). Major Tib himself was too tough for hangovers, but even so he didn't really expect to be entertaining visitors at such a moment. His visitor, a gentleman from the French Railway, was a little embarrassed.

Major Tib smiled a pale, elegant smile and took a sip of his brandy.

'The Lions!' he drawled in his lazy Southern Empire voice. 'What do you mean? Ain't no problem with our Lions. Mighty early in the morning to come round complainin' about something that ain't a problem, don't ya think?'

'Monsieur,' said the visitor delicately. 'Last night a very peculiar tale emerged. There was an English boy trying to stop the *Orient Express* from leaving the station. He was very wet and crazy and saying there was Lions in the train;

stolen runaway Lions and a young thief who has stolen them. He said that one of the Lions has attacked him, and that the Lions are from your Circus, and somebody throw him in the Canal St Martin down by Bastille . . . Obviously this is nonsense and he is very crazy, so we send him to the secure hospital. But in the dawn the hospital calls me and says this boy has serious hurts on his arm and shoulder like some big thing is bitten him. Big thing. No mosquito, you know. The boy is bloody and angry and wet and crazy but, yes, he has this big bite on him, and the hospital says, well, it could be Lion bite, most likely dog or something, and maybe he get rabies and that's why he so crazy, but you know . . . the boy said the Lions are from here, belonging to your famous trainer, Monsieur Maccomo. So I have to check. I am sorry. You understand.'

'You're saying I've let crazy Lions with rabies escape from my Circus and bite people?' said Major Tib. 'That what you're sayin'? You better be sure, Monsieur, because that's pretty serious.'

'I say let's go to check the Lions.'

'Sure,' said Major Tib. He leapt to his feet, his robe flashing out behind him. He was very tall and thin, and crossed the cabin in a second to fling open the door. 'Come on!' he said, with a grin.

Major Tib strode across the deck, the Railway Gentleman scurrying along behind him. 'Morning, Sigi!' he cried, to the father of the Lucidis, upside down in the rigging between the Big Top and the funnels. 'Seen Maccomo this morning?'

'No, Major Tib,' Sigi called back. 'Not last night neither.'

The Lioncabin was on the same deck as Major Tib's, the other side of the *Circe*'s on-board Big Top. It took them only a moment to get there. And only a moment to fling open the door, and less than a moment to see that all the Lioncages were empty. Where six Lions should have been dozing or gazing, there was nothing. Where Maccomo should have been sleeping, rolled in his beautiful cloth, there was nothing.

Major Tib sucked his teeth swiftly, and frowned for a split second.

Then: 'Probably in the Ring, exercising,' he declared, with a flash of reassuring smile. He knew they weren't. They never exercised till mid-morning, when they'd had a chance to warm up. Pirouette would be in the Ring at this time, and the Ringboys clearing up after last night. 'Why don't you go wait in my cabin while I locate Monsieur Maccomo?' he suggested. 'I'll send you over a coffee.' He was still smiling.

'I go with you. Thanks,' said the Railway Gentleman.

Major Tib's smile wore a little thin.

'As you wish,' he said, and belted out of the Lioncabin to the ropelocker just next door, where the boys slept.

'Charlie!' he roared, as he flung the door open.

Julius the clown's son and Hans the boy who trained the Learned Pig leapt up in fright, and each bumped his head on the shelf above, and each cried out.

Charlie, of course, was not there.

'Where is he!' roared Major Tib. 'Where is Maccomo! Where are my damn Lions!!!'

Julius and Hans stared.

'Haven't seen them,' quavered Hans.

'Julius?' said Major Tib.

'Maccomo went out last night,' said Julius. 'He went for dinner with Mabel Stark. The tigertrainer.'

Major Tib yanked his telephone out of his robe pocket and punched in a number.

A moment later he spoke.

'Mabel, my dear,' he said suavely. 'I'm *so* sorry to call you *so* early on this beautiful mornin', and I do hope you don't find my inquiry indiscreet, but do you happen by the slightest chance to have the slightest idea where Maccomo might possibly be?'

There was a murmur on the other end.

'Well, *no*, of course not, Ma'am, and I'm sorry to . . . Mabel, honey, he ain't here, and his boy ain't here, and I'm just a little perturbed . . .'

The voice at the end perked up no end.

'OK, honey,' he said. 'You call me. OK?' He clicked the phone and turned to the Railway Gentleman.

'Says they had dinner last night and she ain't seen him

since . . . There been any other reports of Lions being seen?' he asked suddenly.

'No,' said the Railway Gentleman. 'Of course, I consulted the police.'

'Get up, boys, and search the ship,' cried Major Tib. 'Find Charlie. Find Maccomo. Find the Lions, or any sign of where they've been. Get the Ringboys out to help. Any sign.'

All this took place while Charlie had been meeting and making friends with King Boris, during which time the snow had begun to fall and the poor Lions, riding (for purposes of discretion and not being spotted) on the roof of the train, had been caught in the snowstorm. They had nearly caught their deaths of cold before Charlie went up on the roof in the dreadful gale and brought them down. At just about lunchtime – the time when Charlie slammed the trapdoor shut on the eddying, whooshing, icy snowstorm outside, and started to warm up the poor frozen creatures with hot water and his mother's Improve Everything Lotion – Maccomo walked up the *Circe*'s gangplank.

He looked very different from the calm, enigmatic man whom Charlie had first met weeks ago, the man whose calmness spread over everybody in his vicinity like a numbing sludge. Now his white African pyjamas were scuffed and dishevelled after his night out, his unshaven chin showed nubs of white stubble against his dry, grey-looking dark skin, and his hands were shaking. Nevertheless, anyone could see that he was still a man of character, with his barrel-like chest and the curious flash in the depths of his eyes.

He went straight to Major Tib's cabin.

'Major Tib,' he said.

The Ringmaster knew how to shout – of course he did. So he shouted, for about ten minutes.

At the end Maccomo said simply, 'I resign.'

'You're creakin' sacked, Maccomo – you're sacked! And you won't be working again in Circus, don't imagine you will. And don't think you'll be paid – you've lost me a valuable asset here –'

'The Lions are mine, sir,' said Maccomo, with the flash in his eyes more like his old self.

Major Tib laughed. 'Then you'll be facing the police charges about letting them run off? And you'll be paying the fine? And what will you be doing about my reputation, Maccomo? How you going to make up to me for making my Circus look so bad? You gonna go round tellin' everybody it was your fault and your mistake? You gonna tell the police that?'

The Railway Gentleman sat quietly. 'The police are on their way,' he said mildly.

'You gonna take responsibility for Charlie, then? He's disappeared too. And what about that English boy they savaged?'

Maccomo sat up. 'What English boy?' he asked.

'Rafi Sadler,' said the Railway Gentleman.

Maccomo blinked.

'I must go and look at the Cabin,' he said. 'See how they got out.'

The Railway Gentleman went with Maccomo to the Lioncabin. Calmly Maccomo looked around. He gathered together some things in a bag. 'The police will want to take me, I suppose,' he said. The Railway Gentleman didn't really know what to say.

'Excuse me,' said Maccomo, gesturing to a small door at the back of the Cages. 'I should look . . .' He pulled a lever, the door opened, and he peered through. The Railway Gentleman smiled politely.

Maccomo was down the Lions' special secure tunnel to the Ring before the Railway Gentleman even realized the door led anywhere, and he was off the *Circe* and heading for the station by the time the Railway Gentleman got back to Major Tib's cabin, where he told the police and Major Tib what had happened. By the time they had put out the message to apprehend him, Maccomo, like Charlie, was hiding out in a train bathroom, where he shaved, changed into a suit, and put on a smart hat and glasses. He looked a different man.

'Charlie Ashanti,' he murmured. 'Rafi Sadler.' He didn't know which of these two Englishboys had stolen his Lions. He had been about to sell Charlie to Rafi! So had Rafi stolen the boy and the Lions? But Rafi had been savaged, and the Lions certainly weren't with him now . . . He wished he had had more time to find out what had happened.

He could understand Rafi wanting to steal the boy and the Lions. That was Rafi's line of business: stealing people and selling them. But what if Charlie had stolen them? Sentimental Charlie would be trying to help them. Charlie the Catspeaker. Maccomo's mouth tightened.

He pushed his dirty pyjamas into his bag. As he did so, he felt the big bottle of Lionmedicine that he had grabbed as he left. For a long time he had used this medicine to keep the Lions docile in the act. He had brought it with him when he fled because it was illegal and he didn't want the police finding it.

What he didn't know was that for weeks now Charlie had been feeding this medicine to him, instead of to the Lions. While the Lions' heads had been clearing, preparing for escape, Maccomo had been growing more dim and confused, weakened.

He opened the bottle and sniffed it. His body had grown used to the medicine and liked the smell of it. He shivered, and poured a glass of water from the little basin, and scattered two or three drops of the medicine into it.

Part of him knew that he shouldn't take it – knew it would do him harm in the long run. But his body wanted it, and his mind was already too weak to resist.

'It's only a bit,' he told himself.

He drank it.

He seemed to feel better.

He sat back on the loo and closed his eyes, while the train rattled him south towards Spain.

Where were they all now, he wondered, those foolish creatures who thought they could get the better of Maccomo?

Rafi Sadler was lying on a narrow hard bed in a cold tiled room in the secure hospital. The ceiling was too high and the walls were pale green. A tough nurse had washed him and taken away his clothes, including his leather coat, which, although it was damp and scummy with green slime from the canal, was still his leather coat, and he criking well hoped he was going to get it back. An uninterested doctor had put on a pair of rubber gloves before coming over to treat him. She had taken one look at the circle of deep cuts around his shoulder, red against the yellow and grey bruising on his skin, and stepped back again.

'*Qu'est-ce que –!*' she had said.

'Says he's been bit by a Lion at the Gare d'Austerlitz,' said the nurse, who was keen to end her shift and go home to bed.

'Ugh,' said the doctor, and poured some more antiseptic over the wounds. She lifted Rafi's arm gently.

Rafi screamed.

'*L'épaule s'est cassé*,' she said. 'Shoulder's broken. You can set it, nurse, drain the wound and give him a rabies jab, HIV jab, smallpox and feline encephalitis, arnica, antibiotics . . .'

'Can't you talk English?' said Rafi. 'I need someone to talk English.' His face was greyish-white and he was still cold, though they told him he had a fever. It's true he was sweating. He looked hardly any better than when he had been yelling at Charlie through the carriage window as the train drew out.

The doctor stared at him. Still these English people couldn't be bothered to learn any language other than their own. Pathetic.

'And painkillers,' he said. 'I'm in a lot of pain here. It hurts. IT HURTS. OK? Hurts. PAINKILLERS. *Quelque chose pour le PAIN*.' He made a face of pain and tried to put on a French accent. Unfortunately for Rafi, '*pain*' in French means bread.

The nurse, who, like the doctor, spoke perfect English, rolled her eyes.

'And some mandrax,' said the doctor.

'Have they found the Lions yet? Did they stop the train?' he said.

The nurse was preparing the medicines.

The doctor hummed a little tune.

'That little sniking graspole!' Rafi shouted. 'That . . .'

'Be quiet,' said the doctor. '*Tais-toi*. You're making a disturbance.' She'd been working all night too.

Rafi lay back. His head was swimming and his whole torso throbbed. The nurse sat him up again and started to feed him pills. Then she turned him over and gave him his injections. Rafi lay with his head in the thin pillow, muttering filthy threats against Charlie. After a while he fell asleep, a tossing, restless, sweaty sleep in which he dreamed that he was very small and everybody was laughing at him.

Outside the hospital Rafi's horrible big dog, Troy, lay thin and miserable on the dusty earth beneath a municipal shrub. Though Rafi was a mean owner, Troy was a loyal hound, and it didn't occur to him to do anything but wait.

Not far away, a mangy black and white cat with a bald bottom was having a dreadful fight with a bunch of bigger cats who had called him names. He had been lurking by his new den in the bins at the back of a restaurant, quietly enjoying the remains of a thrown-out lobster, when they had come up behind him, circling him, and making comments about how of course a scrawny bald-bottom like him would have to eat out of bins because no decent humans would keep such a horrible specimen . . .

The mangy cat stared at the luscious morsel of lobster

for a moment. He was a peaceable cat as a rule – gobby, given to insulting people and not known for saying nothing, but he was not violent. He detested violence.

So he turned round and let rip in words. I'm afraid I can't tell you what he said because it was mostly swearing, but it included a lot about their cathood, their lovability (or lack of it), their ignorance, and how they were a bunch of festering bliddy sniked-up graspoles whose own mothers would pay to have their whiskers minced. And worse. Luckily, because this was a North of England cat with a deep Northern English accent, these Parisian cats didn't understand everything he said. But they got the gist of it. And they all jumped on him.

Now the cat – his name was Sergei – may have detested violence, but that didn't mean he wasn't any good at it. He was, it has to be said, very good at it. He fought them off by all the dirtiest means – biting, scratching, leaping, coming up and under with his fangs agape. And he made the most appalling noise – caterwauling, shrieking, wailing like a banshee. Although there were four of them and they were bigger than he was, the Parisian cats really didn't like the way he fought back, particularly when the chef, Anatole, stuck his head out of the kitchen door and joined in the shrieking. The Parisian cats ran off.

As they ran, one turned back and shouted out something that was not a simple insult. He yelled, 'Yeah, you think you're so clever, but at least we know where your precious scientists really are, which is more than you do, nyaaah . . .'

That stopped Sergei in his tracks.

What exactly did he mean by that? The scientists were in Venice somewhere. That's what he'd been told. Admittedly he'd got the information off a cat who hadn't really wanted to talk to him (snobby twagglers, these Paris cats). He didn't like the sound of 'where they really were'.

Sergei sighed.

It didn't take him long to catch the cats up. They'd stopped for some more scavenging beside a restaurant in the next street. Sergei waited, and after a while the group broke up and the cat who had yelled moseyed back up the street.

It was the work of a moment to jump out, land on his back and pinion him to the ground, hissing in his ear, 'OK, then, where are they?'

The cat who had yelled yelled again. Sergei showed his claws, and described what exactly he would do with them if the cat yelled any more. The cat shut up.

'OK, then,' said Sergei again. 'If they're not in Venice, where are they?'

The cat hiccuped. 'Vence,' he squeaked.

'Vence?' Vence! Sounds like Venice – had he just misheard? 'Where the snike's Vence?'

'In France. South,' said the cat. 'Down – south.'

Sergei was pretty sure he hadn't misheard.

'Why was I told Venice, then?'

The cat was so scared that he blurted out his answer: 'Proper cats don't like Allergenies,' he said.

'Proper cats,' said Sergei dangerously, 'aren't prejudiced bigots. Now – are you lying to me?' With this he tweaked the cat's ear.

'No!' squeaked the cat.

'Because if you are,' said Sergei, 'I'll get a gang of Allergenies to come and show you exactly how proper they are – you don't mind fighting four to one, do you? No, I didn't think so. Or do you mind when it's them that's the four and you are the one? It's different then, int'it?'

The cat agreed that it was, but by then Sergei was just fed up and rather sickened by the whole thing, and he let him go. The cat ran off with his tail down, looking back every now and then to see if Sergei was following him.

He wasn't. He headed back to his den outside Anatole's and just sat there, still shivering a little from the exertion and feeling sick and cross with himself for having got into a fight, and cross with the cat for being so stupid and small-minded, and, above all, sick at heart that he might have sent Charlie to the wrong place.

His piece of lobster was still lying there, greasy and pink in the gutter. He sniffed it, and ate it, but he didn't enjoy it much.

Ever since the Catspeaking boy had tucked that note

into his collar, he had felt changed. It had taken a little time to find out where the Humans were, but he had found them, and got the letter to them. That had felt good. If only those big lugs hadn't been there, carting the humans off, he could have hung around and got a reply off them to take to Charlie.

He wouldn't be feeling sick and cross if he'd managed to do that.

Through the kitchen door, open and emitting delicious fish smells from the wood-grills, he could see Anatole in his white apron and check trousers, working hard.

Sergei remembered how carefully Charlie had written his letter, almost in code, so no one but his parents would understand. He thought Charlie was very brave and tough. He thought his parents very clever. Their cure for asthma would help all cats, and above all it would help the Allergenies. And now he, Sergei, had loused things up for them.

At that moment Anatole shouted at someone inside, and seconds later a bucketful of water came shooting out of the kitchen door into the street, right on top of Sergei, along with some concise French insults, along the lines of 'Get out of here, you mangy useless cat', only a lot ruder.

Sergei spluttered, his whiskers frisking. He had had enough of being a mangy useless cat. In the time it took for that bucket of water to soak him, he made up his mind. He was no longer going to be the kind of cat who people throw water over.

'All right,' he said. 'I get the message.'

He couldn't just go to Venice and tell Charlie – he might be sending him on a wild goose chase. He would go to Vence, and find out for himself.

Back on the frozen train, stuck and swaddled in snow, deep in the mountains, Charlie and the Lions were approaching King Boris's private carriage. This meant Charlie first smiling nervously at King Boris's immense bodyguard (His Majesty had a constant fear of assassins) and then knocking smartly on the polished panelled door. (The Lions, of course, were not scared. They didn't know how to be.) If the bodyguard was surprised to see six Lions arriving to visit his master, he was far too well trained to show it.

'Come in, come in!' cried an excited voice. The King was so looking forward to meeting the Lions that he didn't even wait for Edward to get the door; he just bounced up and flung it open himself. And then bounced back into his seat with shock.

'My word,' he said.

The Lions came trooping into his ornate and formal saloon carriage, their noble profiles high, their strong delicate feet pacing along his beautiful Persian carpet. Only a dim, greenish light made it through the iced-up windows. The effect was most peculiar.

'Golly gosh,' said the King. He was staring and staring.

'Oh my. Magnificent. So quiet. Extraordinary. Extraordinary.'

The Lionesses settled themselves on the floor, arranged around Charlie's feet like the train of a queen's long dress. The Young Lion and Elsina sat upright, one on either side, and the Oldest Lion stood by, proud and quiet like an old emperor. They stared at the King, at Edward, and then the Lionesses laid their heads on their huge paws and pretended to go to sleep. Charlie found himself rubbing the Young Lion behind his ears. Edward goggled. Charlie quickly removed his hand.

King Boris was shaking his head.

'Magnificent,' he said again. And then something in Bulgarian. It took him a moment or two to compose himself. Edward, meanwhile, observed the scene from the corner of the carriage, watching quietly, looking from the Lions to Charlie with great, if well-disguised, interest, trying to maintain his mask of really not taking much notice of anything. He had had lots of practice at this over the years but never had he found it so difficult.

'Why don't they . . .' said the King, searching for words and not finding them because they were a bit too scary.

'They are trained,' said Charlie. Though King Boris was largely in his confidence, and knew all about the escape from the Circus, and the kidnapped parents, there was one thing that Charlie had not revealed. He had not mentioned that he spoke fluent Cat. He had always, instinctively, kept this fact quiet. He just somehow knew that people might be odd about it. He mightn't believe it himself if someone said they'd been scratched by a wounded leopard cub as a baby, and in the swapping of blood they'd somehow swapped languages too.

So as King Boris didn't know that Charlie and the Lions talked to each other, he couldn't know that they were true friends who had been through a lot together and were travelling together now as allies and brothers, bound to help each other and loyal through thick and thin.

'Very well trained,' said King Boris faintly. 'Are you sure it's all right?'

'It's fine,' said Charlie. 'Honestly. They're sensible creatures. They don't eat their friends. Anyway, they've had their tea.'

King Boris took in their smooth, tough skin, their long tails, their calm eyes. He looked at the Oldest Lion's shaggy, wild mane, and the Lionesses' long, strong bodies. The Lionesses, he realized, were slightly different colours: one silvery, one more bronze, and one definitely with a yellow sheen to her fur. He noted the determined flick and twist of the Young Lion's ears, and Elsina's big floppy paws. He knew that retracted inside those paws were claws the size of a man's finger, sharp as knives.

They were so beautiful. And whatever Charlie said, they were wild. King Boris was not stupid. He could see that they were wild.

He breathed out a long, happy sigh.

'I would be honoured,' said the King, 'to offer you the hospitality of my little pad on the Grand Canal, and the services of Edward and my staff there, for the duration of your stay. I think it's fantastic. Look at them. Can I take a picture?'

Edward was dispatched to get His Majesty's camera and take some shots of the King with his arm, finally, after much nervousness and 'Can I really?' and 'Are you sure?', round the Young Lion's neck.

He was blushing with pleasure. The Lions, Charlie could see, thought it all rather foolish – at least the Oldest Lion and the Lionesses did, but the Young Lion and Elsina thought it was quite funny and got the giggles. Charlie could see that these two youngsters were itching to play around (they *had* been stuck on this train for a long time now), to tickle the King or do some other naughty thing. He gave the Young Lion a reproving look, and the Young Lion gave him a very cheeky look back. Then the Young Lion murmured, 'I think – Yes, I think I'll just flick this King's bottom with my tail . . . Just a quick little flick . . .'

Charlie snorted, but he couldn't exactly say anything.

'Go on, then, Charlie,' said the Young Lion – to the other humans it just sounded like a little mrowling noise. 'Go on, tell me off – ha ha, you can't! Because they'd hear!'

At this Elsina started rolling about and stuffing her paws in her mouth.

'I'd better get them back, Your Majesty,' Charlie said. 'They're still tired from being stuck on the roof in the storm.' (As if! They'd perked up no end once they'd eaten and rested a little, and had some of Magdalen's medicine.) Giving the Young Lion a *very* stern look behind the King's back, Charlie ushered them out.

CHAPTER TWO

You may have noticed that only six Lions went to visit the King. The immense sabre-toothed creature who had, in a mad rush, joined their escape from Paris, stayed behind. This creature, they all knew without even talking about it, was something too strong and strange to be just shown to people. Besides, he was very tired and needed to sleep.

When Charlie and the Lions went back to the bathroom, Charlie found himself staring at him again. How *very* strange he is, thought Charlie.

First there was the size: half as big again as the Oldest Lion. Then the flat-topped head, the massive shoulders and long flat neck. Then the strong short back legs, the feet small and stiff compared to the Lions', with their long flexible ankles and wide-spreading paws. The stumpy tail. And then there were the teeth. The Lions' teeth were quite big enough, but these – these were astonishing: huge, gleaming, curved, sabre teeth.

But he was clearly a Lion. Charlie found that he was

shaking his head as he looked at him: he had never ever seen such a creature. What was he? Charlie wasn't the only one to wonder. The Young Lion and Elsina, though they had spent more time with him, were wary too.

As Charlie was staring, the creature looked up. His eyes, still sad, had a little gleam of pity in them.

'Ask, boy,' he said in his rough low voice, like old leather and tattered soot. 'I will tell.'

Charlie was immensely curious, but even with the creature's permission he felt shy to ask. This creature had a story, he could see – reasons why he was the way he was. Charlie realized that he was still scared of him.

Which is bigger, he wondered silently, my curiosity or my fear?

'What are you?' Charlie asked.

And for a while time stood still, as the creature began to talk. In the steamy, misty, ornate bathroom, with its pink frills and shepherdesses, and the snow outside, the strange animal told its tale.

'I am *Smilodon fatalis*,' said the animal, in his smoky, leathery voice. 'I have no reason to be here. Until I met my – cousins –' he gestured to the Lions as he said this – 'I did not know my name, or my purpose, or my nature. I did not know my family or my self.

'I should be dead. I was dead. I have always been dead. Personally. Personally, I don't exist. God did not make me. Nature did not make me. My mother did not bear me – I have no mother. I have no father. I am dead. And as a member of my family, I am – I am extinct.'

He stopped for a moment. Charlie half-expected him to sigh, but he didn't. He simply stopped for a moment, as if to consider the enormity of what he had just said. The Young Lion and Charlie glanced at each other.

'I have learned this in those past hours on the roof with your friends, who are so like me and so unlike me. Your friend –' here the creature gestured with his eyes to the Oldest Lion, who bore an expression of deep concern on his grizzled face – 'has told me this. I am glad to know the name of my family. I am *Smilodon fatalis* as you are human. But no mother gave me a name of my own.

'But you see me before you. I exist, I breathe, I speak. You ask yourself, how can he be dead? I ask myself a similar question – how can I be alive? And I answer myself. I do not know.

'I opened my eyes in a bright hard room. I lived behind a hard, invisible wall. I was fed by distant hands. No one spoke to me. No one touched me. I had little space. I was warm, my food was sufficient. I grew. I had a . . . a memory of something else. Of a larger, open place. I had an idea that things could be different from this hard place. Many things were done to me: humans came, all the time, not many but very frequent, and they put things in me and took things out of me. They stuck me with needles, and they wrote down everything I did. They never spoke to me. There was no one else like me. I don't know how I can talk. I feel blessed to talk now, like water after a long thirst.

'Everything was wrong. *I* was wrong. It seemed to me I could be right if I were somewhere else. I left: I flew through the invisible wall, it shattered before my hard head; it hurt me but I hurt it more. I ran through where the humans came in and out, and I burst through again. I felt no pain. I climbed stairs and I came to a chamber filled with bones, many many bones, clean and arranged, stood up as if they were alive, the shapes of animals, all motionless, in rows, just the bones. There were Lionbones there. There were invisible walls with dead creatures behind them: some just as if they were alive, some in liquid, taken to bits, half an animal, an animal opened up, grey, floating . . . it was a terrible place. I ran through. I hid. I burst through invisible walls again. I hurt my hard head and could no longer think, so I lay beneath a tree under the big sky and, though I was hurt, I felt more right. The big sky and the tree felt right.'

Charlie knew where this was. It must be the Natural History Museum, just by where they had first encountered the creature.

The Silvery Lioness had lain herself down close to him. Her eyes were narrow, but her presence seemed to warm him.

'I hid, and I didn't know what to do or where to go.

Beyond the trees lights raced through the darkness and there was a dreadful noise, rushing and coming and going like many great creatures racing and droning. I lay under the tree. I would have wept . . .'

But Lions don't weep.

'And while I was there I smelt . . . among the minerals and dirt and little creature smells . . . I smelt something, something like me. It was these – my –' and again he hesitated – 'my cousins. I roared and howled. I knew no better. Their smell was the first thing I found that I had known. When they came, they fought me, then they chased me – you know what happened. I saw you. You let me join you.'

He dropped his huge head.

'I am grateful,' he said. Then: 'Your friend knows the history of Lions, of the days when Lions lived all over the planet, different Lions in different places, with our different sizes and colours and teeth. He recognizes me, and he tells me that all my people have been dead for long long years. Lions used to be wild here in Europe – no longer. And me? I am American – Lions no longer live where we lived.'

There was a moment of silence in the steamy cabin.

'I am extinct,' said the Smilodon, and his curved teeth gleamed. 'I became extinct on the other side of the world, in the dawn of mankind, which was my people's dusk. Why am I here? I am extinct.'

Charlie could not say a word. He was shocked. The

Lionesses were looking down and away; they could not bear to see the Smilodon's sadness. Only Elsina looked at him, and her large eyes were even larger. The Young Lion sat fidgeting nervously behind Charlie. The Oldest Lion seemed to send out waves of pride and warmth to the Smilodon.

The Smilodon was their ancestor. He was an ancient, extinct, prehistoric creature. Charlie remembered sabre-toothed tigers from his lessons. And here was a sabre-toothed, ancient Lion, standing before him. A huge tenderness rose up in Charlie's heart for this terrifying, terrified creature, who had been so brave and gentle helping to bring the cold, suffering Lions down from the roof of the train during the snowstorm. He wanted to comfort him. He wanted to help him.

'It is a strange, strange thing,' said the Oldest Lion. 'The Smilodons lived many thousands of years ago. My grandfather in Africa used to tell us tales of the tales he had heard, long ago, of the old Lions, the Lions of Alaska and China, of Italy and Spain, the British Lions, the Arabian Lions, the Lions of the Americas. Many families remain but many more have died away. *Smilodon populator* from Argentina was the biggest, twice my size and strong, huge, they were the best runners . . . The Tasmanian Tiger left us only a couple of hundred years ago, a funny little creature but our cousin all the same. The Snow Leopards from the Himalayas had beautiful thick coats, and fur between the pads of their feet to protect them from the cold and prevent them falling through the snow, and they never roared . . . Far back in time, known only by faded story, were *Homotherium*, *Barbourofelis*, *Thylacosmilus*. Now there remain very few. We are all Felids. We have been Felids for thirty-six million years. The Smilodon is our brother from the past. He is our father. Though we cannot explain his presence, we are honoured by it.'

Charlie could see that the Oldest Lion did indeed feel honoured, but he himself could feel only the sadness that came rolling in waves off the prehistoric beast. He looked so strong, yet there was a deep weakness in him. Even his teeth, so huge that he could not really close his mouth, were like a symbol of his wrongness.

Charlie determined to help him. However the Smilodon's existence had come about, Charlie would help to put it right.

He didn't stop to think about how something whose very existence is wrong *could* be put right. If he had, he might not have been so determined. But he was thinking about something else. At Brother Jerome's one time, a boy had come for lessons. He had turned up lost at one of the Railstations, a refugee or an orphan or both, frightened and speaking poor English and not knowing where he was from or what had happened to him. The monks had taken him in and looked after him and had given him a name: Ralph. He had refused to answer to the name and grown angry. In the end Brother Jerome, who spoke so many languages, was able to find out from him that his name was Justice, and that Justice was all he would answer to.

Charlie remembered the difference it had made to this boy to have his own name used; and he remembered Brother Jerome saying that the boy's parents must have been good people to call their son Justice. Brother Jerome had laughed sadly to think that Justice – the thing Justice, as much as the boy Justice – was lost and wandering, unable to speak, and alone in the world.

'What kind of names did the Smilodons give themselves?' Charlie asked, of the Oldest Lion and the Smilodon equally.

The Smilodon did not know. The Oldest Lion said, 'That detail of knowledge did not survive – do you know what the ancient men, the Neanderthals, called each other?'

Stig, thought Charlie, remembering a brilliant book he had read about a caveman who lived in a dump, and a boy called Barney made friends with him.

'No, I don't know,' he admitted. 'But I was thinking . . .' Here he turned to the Smilodon. 'I was thinking, if you had your own name, it might make you feel better.' He wanted to call him Sir. Something to show him some respect.

The Smilodon narrowed his eyes and blinked very slowly. 'Thank you, Lionboy,' he said. 'A name would be

. . . welcome. My cousin shall name me.' And he looked to the Oldest Lion.

The Oldest Lion gazed at him with his big lustrous eyes.

'An honour,' he said. 'I name you Primo. It means First.'

'I was not the first,' said the Smilodon in his low rough voice. 'But now that I am here I might as well be. Thank you. Now I should sleep.' He turned round in the small crowded bathroom and lay on the floor again, even his huge shoulders tired.

Maccomo stood, suit a little crumpled by the train journey but still the picture of a respectable man, on the deck of the little ferry from Spain to Morocco. The channel of the Straits of Gibraltar, where the Mediterranean Sea meets the Atlantic Ocean, was not wide, but it was home to an extraordinary feat of engineering.

The sea here did not just lie in its bed. It had been divided up into channels like lanes of a motorway. Some lanes were at sea level, but many of them were raised above like flyovers on tall legs, forming a huge, impossible-looking spaghetti junction of aqueducts and high canals. Along these channels passed all the ships, moving in different directions through the narrow waters between Europe and Africa, the Atlantic and the Mediterranean. Ships heading for Portugal sailed on a bridge high above other ships heading towards the north coast of Morocco; still others passed between them going towards the Balearic Islands. You had to get in the right lane or you could be sent to completely the wrong place, and there was no turning back at this most complicated of junctions. There was order to it, but it looked a lot like chaos, and it was always very busy, because it was also a security boundary, with Europe on one side and the Poor World on the other. Refugees and other people from the Poor World often used the crowds and confusion of this area to try to break in to Europe – the Rich World – where they believed life would be better for them. Though he was African, Maccomo had European papers, so he was not worried about Immigrationguys. He could go where he liked.

The ocean sun was high and hot, and the smell of Africa came through the salt and cool sea smells, in shocks of woodsmoke, dust and spice. Africa. Maccomo smiled.

Maccomo was not a young man. He was not impatient. Rafi could not have the Lions, so they were either free (though it was unlikely they could remain so for long, on their own) or – more likely – with Charlie. And Maccomo knew where the Lions wanted to go. Lions want to be free, and they want to go home. Those beasts would head for Morocco, for the sparse and scrubby Argan Forests of Essaouira. Sentimental Liontalking Charlie would help them to get there, and Rafi would be after Charlie. Rafi would need to take Charlie to those people who'd hired him to steal the boy's parents. Plus Charlie had made a fool of Rafi, escaping from him in the first place, and then getting away from him again in Paris.

Maccomo was not worried. He would go to Essaouira, and he would wait.

He took out the medicine bottle. Just a drop or two.

Maccomo knew now that Charlie must have been drugging him. Why else would his body crave these drops?

Oh, that Charlie. Thinking he could trick him. Trick him out of his Lions, out of his payment from Rafi . . . Oh, that Charlie.

Well, he'd stop taking the drops soon. He'd just have a couple now, that's all. He'd spend a few days in Casablanca, thought Maccomo, then he'd go down to Essaouira, to that pretty town – so pretty that its name in Arabic means 'The Picture' – and those lovely forests, where the goats stand in the low trees to eat their shoots, and the white camels from Mali carry you to and fro, and the clever Lions lie in the shade, in the long golden grass . . . He knew just where the Lions would go, because he'd bought them from the Lioncatcher right by where they'd been caught, not fifteen miles from Essaouira.

They'd all be along in due course. And Maccomo would be there. Waiting.

'Mabel? Maurice Thibaudet here.'

'Hello, Maurice.'

'Wondering if you'all still don't have an idea where Maccomo is.'

'No, I don't. I'm sorry.' She sounded a little cold, as if Maccomo was humiliating her by being somewhere that she didn't know about.

'He came back here around one o'clock, and now he's run away,' said Major Tib. He paused a moment. 'Same as his Lions did last night.'

'What?' Mabel sounded truly shocked

'His Lions weren't here this morning, Mabel, and once I had explained the situation to Maccomo he seems to have decided to disappear too.'

'You know, Maurice, I know nothing about this,' she said hurriedly. 'I saw him last night for the first time in a year. He was relaxed and cheerful. It was nice to see him. I had no idea . . . I'm sure he had no idea . . .'

'His Lionboy has disappeared too . . .'

'Yes – you said. Could – I don't see how . . .'

'And that young guy Maccomo was talking to last night – with you, I might add. Rafi Sadler. Good-looking young guy in the leather coat. Sitting beside you for the second half? He's telling everyone he was savaged by one of the Lions as they ran away.'

'What! But how did they get out? Where are they now? Surely six Lions can't just disappear . . .'

'Sadler says they were on the train to Istanbul. As if. And anyway that train has been searched and there's no sign. They think he might have rabies . . . Who is Sadler, Mabel?'

'Some guy. I don't know. He and Maccomo were – oh, I don't know.'

Major Tib thought perhaps she did know. He sat silent for a moment. Then he changed tack.

'So I've got a big hole in my show, Mabel,' he said. 'A big ole hole where your ole boyfriend has let me down. I've told everybody they'll see the best Big Cat act in the world. And all I've got is a big ole hole.'

Mabel smiled. 'You should never have called Maccomo's act the best in the world, Maurice. You know my show's the best in the world.'

Maurice smiled too, thinking about Mabel in her white leather catsuit playing with her tigers. 'It is, isn't it?' he said, laying on the sugar. 'So what d'ya say? I know you're free at the moment. Three weeks, the Paris engagement, at least, and more if you want it.'

'Pay me twice what you were paying him,' she said.

Major Tib tutted silently. This woman!

'Sure, honey,' he said. 'Hundred dirhams a night.'

'That's half what you were paying him,' she said. 'Don't be silly.'

'Three hundred, then,' he said.

'Four hundred, or I'll make it five hundred.'

Major Tib had no choice. He needed a Big Cat act by that night and Mabel was his only option, Normally, he wouldn't want a woman like her in the show – too beautiful, too bossy – but for now, he had to agree.

Mabel clicked off her phone, lay back on her white furry chaise longue and wondered.

Why would Maccomo call her for the first time in a year, then disappear? And as for losing his Lions – that she could hardly believe. Mabel loved her tigers more than anything in the world. She had run away to join the Circus when she was fifteen, specially to be with tigers (and, well, for another reason too, one she never mentioned). She had her marks, the scars from when she'd misjudged a tiger's mood and been attacked. She'd suffered for them and it made her love them even more. She had been working with this troupe for seven years now and she adored them. She would do anything for them. She had been pleased to see Maccomo again, she wasn't going to deny that. She – well – she respected him, she told herself, she respected him as a great Liontrainer. That's why she was so genuinely surprised and disappointed to think he would be so careless with his cats. It didn't seem right at all.

CHAPTER THREE

It was evening when the snowploughs arrived at the *Orient Express*, too late and cold and frozen for them to plough through anything. Outside the train's iced-up windows a peculiar warm orange light – very out of place against the greenish snow – glowed where the braziers were burning alongside the line to stop the switchgears from freezing solid. Inside, it grew colder and colder.

During the day Charlie had played backgammon with the King, with Edward looking on down his long straight nose. During the night Charlie and the Lions slept all together in a pile, like kittens in a basket, and they were snug as could be.

Then, on the third morning, the sun peeking out through rips in the grey sky began to thaw the green layers on the train's windows, and the world became visible again. It appeared through the drips and rushing wetness of the thaw like islands rising from the sea. Rattling and banging and hissing sounds told of busy activity outside, the solar panels started to recharge the engine, and a boosterwagon arrived bringing extra power. The heating started up again: breakfast would be served, a little late, but hot, with eggs and coffee. The huge sigh of relief that rose off everybody on the train merely hastened the melting.

By the early afternoon the line was clear. Soon after, the warmed-up train resumed its journey, chugging gently at first and then faster and stronger through the great mountains, visible now in all their high and snowy glory; chuffing across the Alps, through the tunnel at Simplon, and down the wide broad slopes on the other side to Italy and Venice.

Charlie asked Edward for some bandages: 'One of the Lions has hurt his jaw. We think it may be broken,' he lied. For a moment Charlie feared that Edward would say a doctor or a vet should see to it, but he said nothing. This was one very good thing about being the Lionboy – no one else could ever have an opinion on what the Lions should do or have done to them. Only for Charlie were they guaranteed to behave (and maybe not even for him, although no one ever wanted to put it to the test).

Charlie took the bandages back to the bathroom and wrapped them carefully round Primo's jaw and head, tucking the ends in. The result looked like a cross between bandages and a turban. It reminded Charlie of pictures from ancient Egypt, of a mummy-headed animal. But at least Primo's magnificent, terrible teeth were hidden. It would be a to-do unwrapping him when he needed to eat, but it was necessary.

'I just don't want people having heart attacks at the sight of you,' Charlie explained. 'Or getting too excited and wanting to . . .'

He didn't finish. Primo was quite sad enough without being reminded of how interesting he was to human beings who wouldn't treat him right. He didn't mind being in disguise, which was just as well. He just held his head patiently while Charlie furled and wrapped and pinned.

It was impossible to believe, on the Italian side of the Alps, that there had ever been a snowstorm at all. The sun was shining bright and golden, the blue sky was clear and clean and hot, birds sang, and olive trees rustled their silvery leaves in the light breeze. The plains of northern Italy spread out on all sides around the train, wide and fertile, with broad rivers meandering across, and fields of maize and tomatoes and vines sprouting under the sun. King Boris opened his windows, and a smell of warm dust and cool water washed in. He took off his jacket, and smiled, and said, 'A Campari Soda, please, Edward! And a granita for the Lionboy.'

Edward brought a tall pink drink for the King and a small strawberry ice in a glass for Charlie. Then he stood behind Charlie's chair and raised his eyebrows at the King, who put his feet on the stool in front of him and, leaning back, said, 'So, Charlie. Unfortunately, I have important business in Sofia and I cannot come with you to Venice. But you will be met by a boat, and taken to my little place, and Edward will help you. All right?'

All right? Charlie wondered if it was all right. But he realized that it really made no difference if he thought it was all right or not – it was what was going to happen.

Rafi thought he felt a little better. The ache in his shoulder was still heavy and deep, but when he opened his eyes he could see more clearly, and his head seemed a little clearer. He was still in the same room.

'Nurse!' he called. He thought he was shouting but his voice came out cracked and small. 'Nurse!' He was thirsty, and hungry.

'NURSE!' he yelled. Owww. His throat hurt. Wincing from the pain of the shout made his shoulder hurt. The natural physical reaction was to hunch his shoulders against the pain, but that of course made it worse. He couldn't get comfortable. His sheet was knotted up beneath him.

'That sniking graspole,' he murmured. It was all Charlie's fault. Rafi flung his head back as best he could and tried to breathe. He felt dreadful.

When the nurse came in, his face looked green and clammy, his neck was ringed with bruising and, to be honest, she thought for a moment he was dead. She was sorry – he had appalling manners but he was very handsome, with his gorgeous eyelashes, and too young to die. She started to wipe his forehead with a cool cloth.

Rafi came to suddenly, his arms flailing and his eyes wide. He walloped her – not on purpose, but quite hard.

'Get off!' he rasped. Ow – his throat.

The nurse held her face where he had slapped her. 'Ouf,' she said.

'Well, leave me alone, then, you stupid cow,' he said, in the sandpapery voice which was all that could creep through his swollen throat.

'You look like you've been strangled,' said the nurse. 'It wasn't me – though frankly I'd understand anyone getting the urge. Oooh –'

She poked the dark marks that had appeared at the base of Rafi's pale neck. 'Deep bruising,' she said. 'Nasty.'

'I'm hungry,' whispered Rafi coldly. 'Bring me food.'

She looked at him. He threw up. It hurt a lot.

She cleaned him up, treating him as if he were a small baby who had dirtied his nappy, and telling him that he would be given nothing to eat for twenty-four hours because he'd been sick. After she'd gone, he decided to cheer himself up by ringing Charlie.

He left a message. In his delicate, painful voice, it sounded even worse.

'Hello, Charlie. Rafi here. I'm in pain. Did you know? I've been bitten, Charlie, by some dirty wild animal that will be put down the moment it's caught – which won't be long. The police are on the case. I caught a nasty fever and I keep throwing up. I've nothing much to do here except get better – and wonder, of course, how you will take the pain I'm going to inflict on you as soon as I'm up and about. Wondering who I'll get to bite you. I've been thinking about snakes . . . And what freezing water I'm going to push you into. How long I'll keep you there. Under the surface. What poxy doctor I'll get to look after you – if you survive . . . What I'll feed you, to make you throw up. Interesting subjects. It's making me feel a lot better, to tell the truth.

'Anyway, just thought I'd catch up. I know where your train is going, I know where your parents are, I know you're a really stupid kid . . . oh, and I know you won't be able to hide all those Lions for very long . . . Do you honestly think no one's going to notice? Do you think Maccomo's going to just let you stroll off with his Lions? . . . So, anyway, the police'll be doing all my legwork while I'm in here, and I'll catch up with you later. OK? Bye, then!'

He was pleased with himself for ending in that cheerful tone. That'd scare the kid more than his shouting and ranting on previous messages. He thought it sounded quite sinister and mature. Then he couldn't think any more because his temperature went up and he started retching again, even though there was nothing left to come up.

*

Outside, Troy lay silently. He'd been catching rats to eat in the hospital grounds, and lying low, and waiting. His houndish nose told him that Rafi was still there, and his houndish nature told him to stay until his master wanted him.

The road and the traintrack across the lagoon to Venice were long and thin, like a piece of cobweb stretched over a puddle. At the station there were crowds of people, busy and hurrying. Charlie saw them by peeking through the curtains of King Boris's windows as the train pulled in.

'Get back,' said the King. 'We don't want anyone to see you.' He had arranged for his section of the platform to be cordoned off, but even so they had to be careful.

They were met by four men with a large shiny black covered cart. The Lions – including Primo – slunk into it, pouring off the train straight into the cart like long dollops of golden syrup. They curled up on the floor and waited patiently, as if to say, 'We'll do this for now, but don't push us.'

'Goodbye,' said the King. 'I wish I could come with you. I hope to see you again. Good luck.'

His black-olive eyes had a sadness in them, which looked almost peculiar in such a cheerful man. He went back into the train and Charlie's heart felt a pang: their kind, funny protector was gone. But then – they had never expected to have a protector in the first place, and they were still under his protection anyway, because Edward was with them.

They came out of the station. There, down the wide steps and across the pavement, where the road should be, was water.

Even though he was expecting it, it made Charlie blink. Water! There was no street – no cars, no traffic lights, no horses, no tarmac . . . just swishy green water. And boats. The city was riding on the sea. The city was the sea. The sea was part of the city. Across the water was a pink hotel, the Hotel Carlton Executive, and a green dome covered with a web of scaffolding. And somewhere out there were his parents. His heart lifted.

A long low black boat was waiting for them round the corner on a quiet canalside. Charlie knew what it was – a gondola. Its high curved metal prow rose way up in the air. It was much bigger than he'd expected. Getting on, and looking up, Charlie nearly fell over backwards. It was so high at the ends, and so low in the middle.

The Lions poured from the cart to the gondola. There was no one there in that out-of-the-way corner and in the dusk they seemed invisible – even to the gondolier, a blond, broad-shouldered, snaky-backed young man in sunglasses who needed a shave. Charlie looked at Edward and realized that people working for King Boris – or for Edward – would make a point of not noticing anything they weren't meant to. The boatman gazed serenely ahead into the evening sun, which was burnishing the surface of the water till it looked like liquid gold. Charlie and Edward sat back on low black leather seats; the Lions lay in a pool of darkness on the floor. How easy life must be when you are rich, Charlie thought. How kind of the King to give us the benefit of his wealth. How glad I am not to be skulking through the back streets of this strange and crowded city, looking for a quiet place.

'To the Doge's Palace, Claudio,' said Edward in his quiet way. 'A delivery before we go home.'

Claudio, when Edward wasn't looking, raised an eyebrow that suggested he didn't think much of the Doge, didn't much care for going to his palace and thought delivering him a letter was a particularly tasteless idea.

Charlie, however, was impressed. The Doge was the ruler of Venice! They were certainly not skulking now – far from it. They were swanning down the Grand Canal in a beautiful lacquer-black gondola, pushed along seemingly without effort by the gondolier's twisting oar. The smooth waters dimpled and eddied beneath them and the great city of Venice crowded up on either side. Charlie, for one, was goggling.

There was no pavement here: just old old palaces built of white, grey and pink marble, rising directly from the golden waters, with great striped poles set in front of them, blue and white and gold, for boats to moor at. Each building seemed soggy to the knees, like a hem that has trailed in a puddle. A great many had scaffolding around them; some were completely covered with enormous cloth hangings, bearing a picture of what the palace beneath was meant to look like, and would look like again when the builders had finished restoring it. And all around them, around their balconies and gardens, their tall walls, and rows of arches, was the water.

Charlie had known, of course, that Venice had canals instead of streets, and that it was built in the middle of a broad, shallow, muddy lagoon, and was made up of islands. But he had expected it to look more like islands (with beaches and trees and fields) and less like a city. It was as if the city swamped the islands, spilling over the edges, encrusted over the top like icing on a cake. He liked the image: lots of fantastically iced cakes crammed with grand icing buildings, set in a shallow sea and joined by bridges.

Just as he thought it they came to what he could only call an iced bridge: the Rialto. It rose up in an arch over the canal, and it was covered, all over, with buildings – little shops, on both sides, full of pretty stuff to buy, and busy people buying it.

Charlie knew that hundred of years ago Venice had been one of the greatest cities in the world, with art and wealth and architecture beyond compare. Every merchant who came was required by law to bring something beautiful for the Doge's personal chapel, the massive five-domed Cathedral of St Mark, so the city was full to the brim with statues and paintings and ancient wonders, jewels and mosaics, marbles and gold, jasper and alabaster, bronze horses and stone dragons, columns and arches, silver lamps and roofs of gold. As well, there were the works of Venice's own artists and musicians, and of all the artists who came to see and experience Venice's beauty.

Brother Jerome had explained to Charlie how the first buildings of Venice had been built like seabirds' nests, half on islets and half on wooden platforms over the muddy waters of the wide lagoon. Later brick houses and marble palaces had been built on top. Eleven rivers gushed into the lagoon from the north, and the sea swept up into it from the south, stirring up the mud and rotting the wooden foundations. Charlie had learned how, as the world had got warmer, the water levels had got higher, swamping the thick, tufty salt marshes which used to protect the city from the sea's big waves. After that, the winter storms had rushed in unchecked to hurl huge waves at the old buildings, battering their delicate carvings, scouring their balconies and washing them away, bit by bit. Men had taken natural gas from mines beneath the city, which made the city itself sink down further into the mud. A greedy businessman had been allowed to build a huge oil refinery by the lagoon, which attracted immense dirty ships and spat all its filth out into the waters.

Gradually the great buildings of Venice had started to

tip and totter, to subside and sink. The bell tower of St Mark's had fallen down – they'd rebuilt it. Rats and sea salt and mankind's pollution had eaten away at the buildings. At high tide beautiful white churches sat helpless in filthy water, the grey-green dampness creeping up them till they looked like rotten teeth. Arched stone-stepped bridges rose directly from the surface of the water, leading from nowhere to nowhere. Ornate doorways that used to lead on to white marble quaysides now led straight into the water, and the water stank and overflowed into marble-tiled courtyards, and grew strange and revolting algae. Charlie had seen photographs of St Mark's Cathedral standing at the end of its long, wide piazza, with a great flat mirror of water in front where usually there was paving. The *venditori* who sold pigeon food and postcards and ice cream now sold wellington boots and inflatable boats as well. The Venetians put out long wooden walkways to get across the floodwaters. They had to be careful to see where shallow flooded pavement ended and deep canal began. The surface of the water looked the same and a person could easily fall if they didn't watch out.

He'd learned about the Great Wall that had been built in the twenty-first century: a floating wall with seventy-nine gates that could open or close when a ferocious tide was coming in, to divert the worst waves away from the canals and buildings. He'd heard about the floating artificial islands

TO THE ALPS
Railway Station
GRAND CANAL
GRAND CANAL
SCALA:
Da qui a là
= LONTANO
THE GIUDECCA

The Rialto
SAN MICHELE
Doge's Palace
TO ARSENALE
BACINO
Piazza San Marco
San Giorgio Maggiore
TO THE LIDO AND AFRICA
Venezia
Palazzo Bulgaria

which, though they would not stop the tide or the great waves, would calm them a little before they unloosed themselves on the beautiful, sinking, drowning city.

And he knew what everybody knew: that this hadn't worked. Venice had finally fallen, tumbled into the mucky lagoon. Most of the island called the Giudecca, and the island of San Giorgio Maggiore, lay in piles of white rubble in the greenish depths, and the Venetians and art historians and engineers and musicians and architects and tourists had stood in rows and wept.

Charlie knew about all this, but he had never seen Venice and, as the boat brought him down the Grand Canal in the low golden light of that spring evening, he gasped.

The buildings became fancier and fancier, carved into rows of arches, cut-out circles and flowers, vines running along between columns, balustrades and peacocks, balconies and exquisite doorways, niches and inset panels and birds on the corners, buttresses and windows, angels and spandrels, traceries and pinnacles, lions – lots of lions – but all very flat, as if made of plywood. Or carved from ice cream . . . These beautiful buildings rose straight out of the water like teeth from a gum.

It all looked so clean. How could it be being destroyed by dirt and pollution? (The answer, of course, was that it was being scoured away bit by bit, by polluted wind and rain, and the scouring made it clean as it destroyed it.) Small, dark canals led mysteriously off the big one, between tall buildings. Clean washing flapped gently from lines strung across them. Gondolas rode high and shiny in the water; the striped mooring poles stood proudly. Charlie caught a glimpse of the great Cathedral of St Mark as they passed by, and the two tall columns on the waterfront. On one stood a statue of a noble, ancient lion, holding an open book, great wings on his back.

'Look,' he hissed to the Young Lion, who was gazing up from the depths of the gondola in uncomprehending wonder. 'A lion!'

The Young Lion smiled and nudged the others, who all looked up, saw their relative, and twitched their whiskers.

The gondolier, Claudio, without looking at Charlie, began to speak.

'The Winged Lion of Venice is the Lion of San Marco, whom you call St Mark,' he announced. 'He holds a book which read: "*Pax tibi, Marce, evangelista meus. Hic requiescat corpus tuum.*" In English this mean, "Peace be with you, Mark, my evangelist. Here shall your body rest."' He peered suddenly at Charlie. 'Evangelist means person who goes out and about to say the words of God to people who don't know about it,' he said. Then he continued: 'A long long time ago San Marco, who was the friend of Jesus and wrote one book of the Bible, was returning to Rome. He sheltered for the night on the Venetian lagoon because there was all enemies everywhere for him, and an angel appeared to him and greeted him with these words, "Peace be with you" etcetera, which was very nice for San Marco because, you know, he was pretty tired and hungry.

'Then a long time later after San Marco was dead and buried in Egypt, in year 828, two good Venetian men went in there to that tomb and stole the body. To smuggle it past the guards they hide it in with a lot of pork, which they knew the guards don't touch because they are Muslim and for them pork is very dirty.

'So. They brought San Marco back to Venice and presented him to the Doge, and the Doge builds the church for the body of San Marco, and Venice is very happy because we have a real saint, a big saint, all for ourself, and Venetians start to put lions everywhere, for San Marco. You will see them! But then, when they rebuild the church in year 1063, they hide the body because they think maybe somebody will come to steal it, because in those days they think a saint's body can make miracles, and so they hide it very well. In the end too well – it is lost, and no one knows where it is. So when the new church is ready and they give a service in the church for dedicating the church to God, and – OH! – in the middle of the service – BOUF! – out of a column burst the arm of San Marco! Break right out of the column, with a golden ring on his finger.'

'Good timing!' said Charlie.

'Yeah!' said the gondolier. He was manoeuvring his boat up to one of the mooring posts in front of an immense pink palazzo. 'Some people say it was all planned on purpose to look like a miracle.'

Charlie smiled. Faking a miracle! 'But why a lion for St Mark?' he asked.

'Is in the Bible,' said the gondolier. 'Is a winged lion, six wings and all covered with eyes. Is because Mark says always how God is magnifico like lions.' He gestured up to the Lion on the column. 'This one here he is bronze, his eyes agate, he weigh 3,000 kilos, has been there 1,200 years. Probably he come from the Middle East like Jesus, but he is older than Jesus. Or maybe he is Chinese. Maybe his wings don't belong to him at first but arrive later. No matter. In time of war the Lion is shown with his book shut – no "Peace be with you" then. You see him like that at the Arsenale, where the ships are made. Napoleon – you know Napoleon? French guy, short, invaded everywhere? – he changed the words on the book. He wrote: "The Rights of Men and Citizens". You see, the Lion of San Marco is everywhere in Venice. We like lions.'

Claudio looked down at the Lions in his boat and an expression of wonder and affection crossed his face. Charlie warmed to him. The Lions seemed to as well. The Young Lion was kind of trying to peer over the edge of the gondola to see what Claudio was talking about. Charlie made a face at him, as if to say, 'Don't draw attention to yourself!' The Young Lion showed just the tip of his tongue and said, 'It's all very well for you – but I want to see this Lion with six wings too!'

Charlie had to swallow. It was funny when the Young Lion talked to him in front of humans, but it was difficult too because he wanted so much to respond to him, and he couldn't. The Young Lion was smiling up at him with his cheeky face on. Charlie gave him a stern look and turned away, whistling. He gazed at the palace and the Lion on his column, and then he turned to look the other way. They had reached the end of the Grand Canal, the area called the Bacino, where the waters open out and other islands come into view. But the view was all wrong.

There, beyond the old customs house, where there should have been the island of the Giudecca, and the churches of the Zitelle, the Redentore, and the island of San Giorgio Maggiore, was a roiling, chaotic, mess. It was a cross between a marine ruin and a building site, a shipwreck of a view. There were cranes on boats and pontoons laden with salvage equipment, massive rusted metal sheets standing like walls in the water, and great glass tunnels, half visible under the water, meandering between the piles of ruin. From time to time the tunnels came up out of the water, like gigantic glass caterpillars, climbing over the heaps of marble and brick, carvings and statues, shattered domes and broken pediments. All around them were the tools of the people still trying to pull up and rescue bits of building from the water: massive chains, engines and generators, little submarines and tugboats, piles of rubber boots and oxygen masks, slings and maps and lists. One or two areas of the lagoon bed had been sectioned off and the water pumped out of them, so that a great empty tank, like an empty lock, stood gaping. One of these contained the tumbled remains of the church of San Giorgio Maggiore. It looked like a pile of bleached bones, with workmen moving about on it like flies. Sprouting from the gap, an immense pump was working away, constantly pumping out the creeping sludge and dirty water, like a huge heartbeat. You could hear it.

Charlie gasped at it.

'They are making a museum out of Venice, under the water,' said Claudio, glancing up as he deftly tied the gondola to a mooring post. 'They put these big glass tubes to rest in the mud, and the people will walk through them, gazing out at the underwater ruins. Like fish in a fishtank, with their mouths hanging open. They will put big lights so you can see all the seaweed on our ruins. All the algae, like poisonous slimy cobwebs. So everyone can see nice and clear how the sea has beaten Venice and pushed her down in the mud.'

The Young Lion's jaw dropped. 'I want to go!' he cried. This time he was not doing it to tease Charlie, he was just so excited about the idea of walking on the seabed, he couldn't stop himself. Luckily it just sounded like a soft snarl to Claudio and Edward. Claudio glanced at him, before winking at Charlie and stepping out of the boat. As he did so, Edward, who had been listening carefully to the conversation about Venice, but not letting it show, handed him a small package.

As Claudio headed towards the pink palazzo, Edward, leaning back with his eyes closed, had a very thoughtful look on his face.

Charlie remembered something he hadn't thought of for ages: his parents had come here to Venice on their honeymoon. That's why he knew the view was so wrong. That photo of them smiling with their arms round each other, the photo on the kitchen dresser at home, had been taken somewhere right near here. He recognized it. And he could see that half of that view no longer existed. He could tell from the remains.

He felt sad to think how they would feel about this mess. They would be sad to see it.

So where were they, then? He opened his eyes wide, and started to look out for cats. Cats had brought him information ever since he had left home: all down the Thames in London, and up the Seine to Paris. Cats are such dreadful gossips. He must get chatting, as soon as possible, to a cat.

CHAPTER FOUR

King Boris, it turned out, owned a small palazzo – a palace – on the Grand Canal. It was called the Palazzo Bulgaria, which because this was Italy was pronounced Palatso Bulga-Ria. They'd passed it earlier, and now turned back. Charlie was glad to be out of view of the tumbled remnants of the Giudecca.

Claudio brought the boat alongside a set of wide stone steps that led directly from the water to a tall, elegant doorway in one of the ice-cream buildings. The bottom of the door was ragged with rot; the sides of the steps dripping with bright-green weed. Looking up at the front of the building, Charlie noticed that the balcony on the first floor was supported by carvings of lions. It felt good to know the story behind them. He smiled at Claudio, who gave him a wink.

The heavy wooden door in the great arched doorway slid open. Claudio held the boat steady, and the Lions coiled out, up the steps and into the dim shade of the building. Charlie followed, and behind him came Edward, very upright.

The chamber they entered was high and cool, with dark-red faded walls, and a smooth dark-red floor like one enormous tile, and an air of ancient damp. Charlie felt he had never been in an older place. The curtains at the tall windows on either side of the door were made of heavy dark-red velvet that looked hundreds of years old, held in swags by tassels made of golden wire, which was tarnishing and unravelling. If you were to touch the curtains, the cloth might fall to crimson dust under your fingers. In the distant vault of the ceiling a massive glass chandelier shimmered: just an idea of many pale jewel-coloured drops of glass, heavy with dust, golden candlelight reflecting and refracting from the multitude of surfaces. Staring up at it, Charlie thought he could make out birds and flowers up there, and entwining vines, all with the same low, watery gleam.

Mingling with the smell of damp was a sweet heavy flower smell. A stone tank almost as tall as Charlie stood on one side of the chamber, full of crimson and white lilies. They gleamed like ghosts in the half-light. There was no other furniture. Way down at the other end of the chamber he could just make out another arched doorway, with a great curved stone shell on the wall above it.

Charlie wondered if the whole place was going to be like this.

At that moment another figure entered the room: a long, fair, rather droopy woman with a very long face and pale wide-set eyes, wearing a pale-blue housecoat, denim high-heeled sandals and heavy gold earrings. She looked like a sort of mermaid. She stopped still, gave Charlie a rather rolling-eyed look that made it clear she didn't think much of him, and then, to Charlie's surprise, gave Edward a kiss on each cheek.

'Signora Battistuta,' said Edward. 'What a pleasure.'

But she had turned to the Lions, and her jaw fell open. Her rolling eyes filled with fear, but her wide mouth full of long teeth smiled a big smile.

'*Bellissimi*,' she drawled, through her nose. '*Bellissimi! E questo qui, mio Dio!*'

Primo in particular caught her eye. '*Che bello*,' she said, looking at his size and his strong shoulders. What a beauty. She inquired about why his head was wrapped up, and Edward explained in Italian. The long-faced woman expressed a great desire to see the big Lion's head. Charlie said nothing. His Italian was just good enough to work out what they were talking about.

'So here are our honoured guests,' said Edward in English. 'The creatures can no doubt be made comfortable in the *cortile*, the child in perhaps the Chinese room. Dinner in half an hour, please. There's no luggage.'

Cortile. Cor-tee-leh. Charlie wondered where and what that was.

Signora Battistuta, ignoring Charlie, and still casting loving glances at the Lions, shrieked, 'Lavinia! *Vieni!*'

At this a small pale child of about six appeared, dressed in some kind of peculiar smock. She took Charlie by the hand to lead him across the immense chamber to an equally immense staircase, up several immense flights of stairs to the top floor, where an endless corridor, red-floored still, and painted with the ancient dark-red paint, brought them to a tall dark doorway. Inside was a different world: a pale-green room with curly furniture made of bamboo, and golden pheasants and silver chrysanthemums painted on the walls. For a moment Charlie thought they were real, that he had burst into some Oriental garden, with dangling fronds and pale-crimson flowers. But it was all painted – even the bamboo furniture wasn't actually bamboo, but wood carved and painted to look like it. The effect was a little peculiar: as if, if you sat down, you couldn't be sure the chair was really there. You couldn't quite be sure, for example, whether a wall was a wall or a long view down over a Chinese park from 300 years ago. Charlie, using his common sense, decided it would be unlikely for there to be a 300-year-old Chinese ornamental park inside this Venetian palace . . . though, actually, so many astounding things had been happening lately that he couldn't be sure.

From the window, there was a clear, immediate view of the chaos of the drowned Giudecca. The last drops of the evening sun blazed fiercely down on the scene, shining hotly back off the surface of the water, so it resembled nothing so much as a hell of molten metal, populated by busy, pointless people. Charlie stared and stared.

'*Maledetta Venezia*,' said the pale child. She also talked through her nose.

'Sorry?' said Charlie, turning round.

'*Maledetta, la città*,' said the child. '*Maledetta!*'

Charlie worked it out: *Male* = bad, *detta* = spoken; *maledetta* = cursed. The child was saying that Venice – *Venezia* – was cursed.

Charlie stared out of the window. It was strange how when something beautiful becomes ugly, it is uglier than something that was ugly all along. It was horrible, the sight outside. It did look cursed. It looked like a body with tiny cannibals crawling on its wounds.

He turned away.

'*Bagno*,' said the child. Pronounced 'Banyo'.

'Eh?' said Charlie.

'*Bagno*,' said the child again, pointing out of the door. She seemed to want Charlie to follow, so he traipsed after her down the corridor before being directed into a small room lined entirely with tiles, and with a big showerhead where the light fitting might normally be.

'*Bagno*,' whispered the child again. '*Adesso*.'

Charlie realized that he was meant to wash, so he steered the child out of the room, with a look, and undressed and gave himself the best wash he'd had since leaving home.

The water was hot and strong, and because the whole room was tiled he didn't have to worry about not getting the water on the floor or anything dull like that – in fact he could splash about as much as he wanted, and sit down, or lie down even, under the shower, which was a lot of fun when he put his face absolutely under where the water came out. So then he started singing all his favourite washing songs ('Splish splash I was taking a bath!'), and thinking, and wondering if it was disloyal that for once he was glad his mum wasn't about, as she would make him wash and comb his hair. He hadn't actually washed it properly since leaving home all those weeks before. It was starting to go into little dreadlocks as it grew, and Charlie supposed that he should try to remember to twiddle the clumps so they went into decent locks. He'd always wanted locks. His dad wouldn't let him have them though.

Charlie splashed around some more, aiming the showerhead out of the window to take his mind off his absent parents. He was just wishing he had a friend there with him so they could have a proper water fight when the small voice of Lavinia came through the splashy steamy rumpus he was making. He turned off the water and peeked round the door. The child stood there with a pile of towels in her arms, over which she could only just see. Her eyes were quite pale.

'Thank you,' said Charlie, taking a towel. The child stepped back, waiting.

Bother, thought Charlie, seeing that he was meant to come out of the shower now. Was this child going to follow him everywhere, telling him what to do?

'*Sono bellissimi, i Leoni*,' said the child. '*I Leoni. Bellissimi. Piacciono ai Veneziani, i Leoni.*'

Charlie gathered that the child liked the Lions.

'*Sí*,' he said, with a smile, not thinking about it. Everyone seemed to like them here.

He wrapped the towel round himself and trotted back along the corridor, dripping. He hoped the King kept as good food in his palazzo as he did on his train.

Charlie needn't have worried. The dinner was completely delicious. First there was a dish of salami and ham: delicately spiced and quite the best he'd ever had. He was happily stuffing himself when he noticed Signora Battistuta's eyes on him and slowed down. Perhaps this was a first course and he should keep some room.

Then there was pasta carbonara, Charlie's favourite, cooked with egg and bacon and cheese, very like how his dad made it. Then there was some fish, white and clean with a pungent green garlicky sauce that looked a little scary but was so delicious Charlie thought he might squeak. Then there was some asparagus. Then there were artichokes. Then there was chicken, fried with rosemary. Then there were potatoes and green beans. Then there was a slice of veal with tuna fish and mayonnaise. Then there was green salad. Then there was a pause . . . Then there was cheese, then there was tiramisu with its layers of cream and biscuits in coffee and chocolate, and then there were pears cooked in sweet wine, and then there was chocolate, and Edward and Signora Battistuta had tiny glasses of a clear shining drink with a coffee bean floating in it, which they set on fire.

Charlie could hardly move he was so full. He felt safe and all right, and as soon as he could leave the table, he'd be out finding cats and getting news. Would Edward give him a key, he wondered – or perhaps he would look for cats first on the roof . . .

Then Edward said, 'So, Charlie.'

The words were heavy, like being pulled back in to finish your homework when you thought you were free to run out and play football. Charlie's sense of well-being stopped in its tracks.

'Your parents' asthma cure.'

Charlie said nothing.

'Do you know anything about it?'

Charlie felt a little peculiar. It was Edward who had confirmed that the asthma cure was why his parents had been kidnapped. Edward was King Boris's trusted security chief, and King Boris was Charlie's trusted patron and helper. But Charlie did not want to talk to Edward about the asthma cure. His inner voice said, quite clearly, no.

'No,' he said.

This was only partly true. He didn't know much about

it, and didn't understand how it worked or what it was based on, but he . . . well, he had the cure written down in his mother's blood on a parchment in his bag upstairs. She had written it down months before, and told him to take it with him 'if he had to go anywhere'. That was the first thing to have happened in this whole drama. She'd fallen off the ladder that day, and hurt her leg. Thinking about it now, he had a sudden, piercing wish for her. He blinked.

He must take care of that piece of parchment. It was valuable.

Edward was watching him, not unkindly.

'Well, never mind,' he said. 'We don't need to know about that to find your parents. I'll get on the case and we'll find where they are in no time!'

He was talking like a nursery-school teacher. And while Charlie was glad to have the assistance of the Bulgarian Royal Security Department, he didn't quite like the idea that Edward was going to find his parents. He, Charlie, was going to find them.

Or was that just him being proud?

Of course it didn't matter how they were found, or who by . . . he just wanted them, that was all.

But it did suddenly seem rather out of his power, and he didn't like that.

Signora Battistuta clapped her hands and the child Lavinia appeared again. Signora Battistuta rapped out an order and the child again took Charlie by the hand to lead him away. He bade the others goodnight politely, then as they left the room he thought of the Lions.

'Lavinia,' he said. 'I must go and see the Lions and say goodnight to them.' And discuss developments so far, how to contact Mum and Dad, travel arrangements and so on, he thought, but didn't mention.

The child stared at him blankly.

'The Lions,' said Charlie. '*Leoni*,' he said, trying to imitate the way Lavinia had said it. '*Leoni*.' Lay-ony.

'*No*,' said Lavinia, and turned on her heel.

What? Don't be daft.

'Er, yes,' said Charlie, pulling away from her grabby little hand.

'*No*,' said Lavinia, twice as firmly.

'Yes,' said Charlie, twice as firmly as that.

Lavinia burst into a tumble of words in Italian, the main sense of which seemed to be No, Charlie was not going to see the Lions.

You can imagine how Charlie felt about this. He felt like the Three Musketeers – he and the Lions were all for one and one for all, and not about to be kept apart by a girl.

'Let go of me,' he said. 'I'm going to my friends and I don't want to have to hit you.'

The child stared at him from her pale eyes and began to make a thin, small noise: a slow, rising wail as if the saddest thing in the world had happened to her.

'Oh, shut up!' said Charlie.

He was confused. Partly, he hated when girls cried. The only thing he could think to do was hug them, but what if it was someone you hardly knew and didn't want to hug – Lavinia, for example? And he didn't want this child's caterwauling to bring Edward and Signora Battistuta out from their dinner to make a fuss.

'Quiet!' he said again to Lavinia, urgently, making 'calm down' gestures with his hands. 'OK, OK. Just be quiet.'

The child whimpered to a halt and gazed at Charlie, fear in her big eyes, her lower lip sticking out and trembling.

Charlie sighed, and held out his hand for her to take.

'Go on,' he said, though he knew she didn't understand. 'Take me off, then. Wherever you want.'

It was his best bet. All he had to do was remember his way around this huge building, and then, when Lavinia had gone, he would just sneak out again and go to find the Lions himself. So what was a *cortile*? Perhaps there'd be a cat there to talk to.

From the window of the Chinese room, strings of electric lights and high flares illuminated the scene around the ruins of San Giorgio Maggiore. It looked more like hell than ever in the dark: swamped, flooded, ruined, industrial, and scattered with fragments of destroyed beauty. Charlie didn't look for long.

On the window ledge he noticed his phone, which he'd put there earlier to recharge in the last rays of the sun.

The message icon was flashing.

Since he'd been away, this sight had come to mean nothing but nastiness for him. Only one person had been ringing him.

He stared at it, and then out of the window again.

But he couldn't leave it. He was a curious boy, and he couldn't leave it.

'Goodnight, Lavinia,' he said firmly, and pushed her gently out of the room.

So that was how he got Rafi's message.

Listening to it, his heart sank slowly and steadily. A lot of what Rafi said . . . Police. Train. Maccomo. His parents . . . Oh, lord. There was a lot of danger out there for him and the Lions. A lot of powers gathering against them . . .

He bit his lip.

But now I am here, he said to himself, protected by Edward and King Boris. Nobody is going to find us if we stay here and keep quiet. I just have to make sure that I find my parents quickly, and move on before Rafi gets better and before the police work out that King Boris is hiding us. And keep my head down.

He was deeply grateful that they had this safe, comfortable place to hide.

The people sat in circles on big fur-style cushions on the polished wooden floor. (At least, the floor looked wooden. In fact it was a particular type of material made out of wood, that looked quite like wood, but was guaranteed to wear out more quickly. In many parts of the world this kind of material had been banned because it was a waste of good trees. But the Corporacy had invented it in the first place, thinking they could sell it all over the world and make huge profits because people would have to keep buying more, so they had lots left over. They didn't want to lose money on it, so they used it to furnish their Communities around the world.)

They were eating and drinking, and breathing the sweet cool air of the Corporacy Community Education Centre.

'It's true money doesn't make you happy,' intoned a melodious and sympathetic voice. 'How could it?'

The people smiled at each other. They all knew that money didn't make you happy. Of course it didn't. They were more intelligent than to think that.

'But how much more comfortable it can make you!' said the voice happily. 'What makes you happy? Your loved ones. And how much happier you can make them if you are comfortably off!'

The people thought complacently about their families. Most of them lived here in the Corporacy Gated Village Community. They thought it a wonderful place, with its genuine fake-grass village green, a school just for Community children, shops (selling only Corporacy products) and, best of all, a high wall around it so no scary poor people or foreigners or outside children could come in to disturb Community life. Of course there weren't any really poor people even outside the walls, because the really poor people lived in the Poor World, but sometimes poor people were let in from the Poor World to do the jobs nobody in the Rich World wanted to do, and it was those people who were not allowed in (except to do the dirty jobs, of course). If they tried to get in, the security guards would see them off.

There were lots of Gated Communities. Some of the most popular banned children as well as poor people. Older people could go and live there and never be bothered again by bicycles and football games and pop music and laughing and yelling. Some banned foreigners or different-coloured people – they had to lie about it though, and pretend it was something else they were banning. They all found ways to make sure that only people exactly like the people already there were allowed in. 'Scared pathetic people with no heart, no brain, no imagination and nothing to recommend them at all,' Charlie's mother called them, witheringly. 'Life-haters. Just as well to keep them all locked up together – keeps the rest of the world nice and interesting for the rest of us!' At least, that's what she said when she was herself, at home.

Now, in the Corporacy Community Education Centre, her hair was flat and her head stuffed up and she didn't know what she thought about anything.

'Just think,' the voice was continuing. Magdalen tried

to think. She couldn't remember quite what thinking was. 'If you can give your loved ones the things they need, how happy they will be. If you can provide for them, feed them and give them the lifestyle they deserve – the security, and the prosperity. Aren't they worth it? Of course they are!'

One or two people at the seminar thought, at the dim backs of their minds, that surely *all* loved ones deserved comfort and security – and people who weren't loved deserved them too, maybe even more . . . But the idea slipped away.

'Aren't *you* worth it?' said the voice persuasively. 'Of course you are! You can have the things your parents were never lucky enough to be able to give you.' Sympathy dripped from the words. 'You can give those things to your children. You can make the choice about the life you want to lead! Embrace your aspirations! There's nothing to be ashamed of. Fulfil your dream! Be the self you always dreamed of being!'

Everyone was smiling now. That sounded good.

'Money is good, money is worth it, and it is great that you can get as much as you want! The harder we all work for the Corporacy, the more money we will all have! With the Corporacy, you can work hard and play hard and know that your efforts are doing the best for your family. You can be the best! Challenge yourself! Reach that target! Make those sales figures! Build that business! Grow your share! You can make good money and lead a stylish life.

There's no need to be afraid of embracing your aspirations!'

The voice went on.

Magdalen was frowning. A low voice deep in her heart was answering back: 'Those *aren't* my aspirations. I don't want lots of money and a stylish life made of fake things, cut off from the real world. I don't want the Corporacy to make money out of me while outside in the world children can't afford medicine . . . I want to be left alone . . . I want Charlie . . . I'm afraid . . . I'm afraid they're sucking my brain out . . .' But the voice was slow and weak.

Aneba thought: God, I'm tired. I'm tired. I want a drink.

Magdalen looked at him. He looks bored, she thought. Perhaps he doesn't love me any more.

Then the little voice in her shrieked out loud, and she fell forward clutching her head. 'Aneba!' she cried. 'Aneba – wake up, wake up! Darling, Aneba, they're killing us, they're killing us . . .' She shouted and wept.

Aneba stared at her.

She was disturbing the Profit Motive Seminar.

A manager from the Wellness Unit came and took her away. They gave her some medicine and then she was quiet. While she was quiet they gave her some more. 'You can visit her soon,' they told Aneba.

He stared.

*

After about ten minutes, Charlie listened at his bedroom door to check if Lavinia was still lurking about. Gently, he pulled the door open.

She was lying curled in a heap in the corridor, fast asleep. Charlie smiled and stepped quietly over her. Daft place to kip. He slipped down the cool-tiled corridor. His feet made a soft padding noise, and he was grateful for the fact that the flat smooth floors didn't creak.

He found his way easily enough down to the dining room on the first floor. Low voices were murmuring inside, talking Italian. It was Edward and Signora Battistuta, and another voice, a man's, deep and flowing. Out of curiosity, Charlie listened, but he couldn't make much sense of what was being said – except for one word: *Leoni*.

Why were they talking about the Lions? What were they saying?

Suddenly he heard chairs being pushed back, and the change of breathing that denotes people standing up and starting to move. He slipped into the shadows and waited.

Three figures emerged from the dining room, still talking softly. They crossed the big chamber and went out through an arched doorway to the stairs. Silent and quick like a millipede on a wall, without even knowing why he was doing it, Charlie followed them.

Downstairs, across the lily chamber, through another arch, down a vaulted corridor, and then they emerged into the purple light of night. Charlie hung back in the doorway.

The three stood on one side of a courtyard, a sort of cloister with arches on each side, and a fountain in the middle. It was lit up by moonlight, and the scent of roses and jasmine hung on the cool night air, reminding Charlie of his garden at home in London. The scent gave him a pang of pain.

From his safe spot in the dimness of the doorway, Charlie could see the Lions moonlit at the other end of the arcade. They were lying about, as they did, under the arcade, and the sight of them in their friendly pile filled him with affection. Only the Young Lion was prowling about at the back. Charlie could well understand why.

The Lions were behind a heavy metal grille. The moonlight reflected dully off its grey bars.

After all they had been through to win their freedom, they were back in a cage.

Charlie's fury jumped up within him, banging at his chest and rattling in his lungs. How dare Edward put them back behind bars? No one, thought Charlie, is going to keep me apart from these beasts. We're a gang now. We've been through a lot. And this is not how it is meant to be.

How he wished he knew Italian better! The low urgency with which the three were talking made it clear that what they were saying was important and secret. Edward seemed to be leading the conversation, with Signora Battistuta supporting him and the new man – a small, crumply figure with a rumbling voice, who was evidently quite alarmed by the presence of the Lions, even behind bars – asking questions. They were looking at the Lions, gesturing towards them. You would think, to watch them, that they were making plans.

Charlie stared and wondered. Obviously, the presence of the Lions here had to be kept completely secret. It was so obvious it hadn't even needed agreeing on.

So who was this bloke? Turning up in the middle of the night? Without Charlie knowing anything about it?

And why is Edward making plans with him? Involving the Lions?

And why are the Lions back in a cage!

How dare he? And – Charlie gulped as the thought hit him – did King Boris know about this? And which was worse? If he did – which meant he approved of it? Or if he didn't – which meant that Edward was doing a bad thing behind the King's back?

The crumply man had something in his hand and was getting quite excitable. Edward seemed to be trying to calm him and persuade him to do something. The man, gesturing energetically towards the Lions, was refusing, but in a 'I'm not doing this thing but I still want to be your friend' kind of way. Charlie couldn't work out what it was that he was refusing to do.

Looking down the arcade, Charlie saw a pair of yellow

eyes staring unblinking at him. He knew that, unlike most cats, lions can't see very well in the dark, but these eyes could clearly see him. Which of them was it?

Ah – it was Primo. A Smilodon *could* see in the dark, then. Charlie raised his hand, very gently, in a tiny wave.

The yellow eyes blinked slowly, to return the greeting.

Charlie felt reassured by this. He raised his hand again, made a patting gesture, meaning 'be patient', and slipped behind the door out of view.

A few minutes later, the three grown-ups came back through, passing within inches of Charlie, and went back into the building. In seconds, Charlie was out of the door, down the arcade and lying alongside the bars, as near as he could be to his friends.

The Lionesses turned their faces away from him. He could see just from the elegant, offended angles of their heads how deeply insulted they were. The Oldest Lion gazed at Charlie sorrowfully. Primo lay in silence. Elsina looked nervously from one to the other of her companions. It was the Young Lion who spoke out.

'What's going on?' he hissed in a stony, furious voice. 'Where've you been? We had to let them put us in here – we didn't want to start mauling anybody – but good grief, Charlie! What's happening?'

'I don't know!' exclaimed Charlie miserably. 'I wasn't allowed to see you so I sneaked out, but they're all talking

Italian and I don't know what they're saying. I don't know what's happening. I don't know and I don't like it!'

If the palazzo, their safe haven, was not safe, then they were really in trouble.

CHAPTER FIVE

'And so you shouldn't like it,' said the Yellowest Lioness.

'It is bad,' said the Silvery Lioness.

'Edward has a plan that none of us would want,' said the Bronze Lioness.

The Lionesses hardly ever spoke. Charlie looked to them eagerly.

'How do you know?' he asked.

'He was talking about it,' said the Yellowest Lioness.

'Do you understand Italian?' exclaimed Charlie.

'We've spent time in Abyssinia,' said the Silvery Lioness, as if that explained everything.

'So what is he saying?' asked Charlie.

The Lionesses looked a little embarrassed.

'He's talking about the Doge,' said the Bronze Lioness, 'and about wings, and how we're not to be allowed out, and you're not to see us, but not to be made suspicious either.'

Charlie's temper flared up again. Who did Edward think he was, putting them in a cage and saying Charlie couldn't see them? Charlie was pretty sure this could not be the King's idea.

'Don't worry,' said Charlie. 'I'll come and see you every moment I can, and I'll get you out of here. Could you understand anything else?'

'Just that it seems we're to be here for a while. They've given us all these cushions, look, and hangings for shade at midday. They're being very kind,' she said, her voice full of sarcasm.

Sure enough, within the iron bars there were large brocade cushions in gold and green lying about the Lions' quarters, along with big brass bowls of cool water and some good fresh meat. The shades were brocade too, heavy and old and decorated with swirling flowers and leaves, with gold and silver threads running through them, smelling slightly of metal. They looked dusty, and Charlie's nose twitched. Just the sight of them made him feel asthmatic.

The Oldest Lion said, 'We'll keep our ears open. They don't know we understand them. Come to us tomorrow, and perhaps we will all have found out more. Meanwhile you must concentrate on getting news of your parents.'

Charlie lay on the cool stone floor alongside the Lions' cage. He rubbed their ears through the iron bars and breathed in the deep sweet wild smell of them. Elsina tickled him a bit, teasing him. She was so young that her nose was still pink – later it would turn black, like the others'. It looked very sweet in the moonlight.

The Young Lion would not settle down. 'We must do something,' he said. 'We're Lions, for goodness' sake. We must fight, fighting is what we do. We should make a run for it . . .'

Even he didn't seem quite to believe what he was saying, but they all felt the strength of his feelings. Charlie was full of love for his Lion Gang, and desperately sorry that he hadn't managed to keep them free.

He couldn't stay long though. He didn't want to be caught down there. Looking up, he could see the windows of the upper storeys of the palazzo. Anybody could be peering out. Even here, he'd have to hide.

The next morning, Edward had an early phone call. He heard that a crazy English boy was being held at the secure hospital in Paris with serious injuries that he was claiming had been inflicted by a Lion. To begin with everybody had assumed he was mad or on drugs; but, as it turned out, a troupe of Lions was missing from the famous Circus of Major Thibaudet, and the youth's story was now being reconsidered – though his allegation that the Lions had left Paris on the *Orient Express* was being put down to the fever that his injuries had induced.

Edward thought about this for some time. He took a sip of his small strong black coffee. Then he took up his newspaper.

Charlie came down late and helped himself to sweet

cakes with a sort of delicious cream in them, and cherries, apricots and small dark figs.

'Charlie,' said Edward, putting down his newspaper and leaning forward, 'we must have a chat.'

'All right,' said Charlie, who had learned that the more you could seem to be agreeing with people, the less suspicious they would be of you.

'There's a problem,' he said. 'I didn't tell you – I didn't want to worry you – but the fact of your Lions escaping has been in the news. I hoped it would die down but it hasn't. In fact everybody knows about them, all across Europe. It's – well, look.'

He handed Charlie the newspaper: an Empire paper, published in English all over the world. On the front page was a small headline: 'MISSING LIONS STILL NOT FOUND, see page 7'. And on page 7 it read as follows:

MISSING LIONS: REWARD OFFERED

ALPINE SIGHTING UNCONFIRMED

Major Maurice Thibaudet of Thibaudet's Royal Floating Circus and Equestrian Philharmonic Academy (better known as Tib's Gallimaufry) has announced a reward of 15,000 dirhams for information leading to the recovery of the six lions that went missing from the Circus the night of their debut performance. Major Thibaudet himself made the announcement in Paris, where the show has been wowing the cognoscenti, despite the absence of the popular lion act.

'The lions are very valuable, highly trained and extremely vulnerable creatures,' said Major Thibaudet in a statement. 'They need their medicine. They need to eat properly. They must be somewhere, and it is vital that they are returned to those who know how to care for them as soon as possible.' Monsieur Maccomo, the lions' trainer, has not been seen in public since their disappearance, and sources close to the Circus say that he is suffering considerably from stress and is too upset to speak. His assistant, Charlie Ashanti, went missing the same evening. It is not known if the two developments are connected.

The lions' place in the Circus performance has been filled by Miss Mabel Stark, performing with her troupe of tigers. Miss Stark has previously been romantically linked with Monsieur Maccomo.

Reports that creatures which may have been the lions were spotted during last week's Alpine blizzard, in which the *Orient Express* was stranded for several days with the King of Bulgaria aboard, have been dismissed by the Alpine Transport Police.

Charlie slowly put the paper down. He wasn't surprised.

'His Majesty won't be very happy about this,' said Edward. 'He doesn't like his name appearing in the news. And it's curious that they seem to think there are only six – newspapers always get things wrong.' He said this with the air of satisfaction of someone who is certain that he is always right. 'But,' he continued, 'none of that is the point. The point is, things will take a little longer than we might have hoped. They can stay here for the time being, as planned, until we find a safe way of shipping them back to Africa. It will be fine, but it means you'd better stay in as well, to be on the safe side. With a reward offered, it's only sensible.'

Charlie was about to dispute this. It were as if a net was falling over him and one by one his intentions and plans and needs and desires were being trapped in it. But Edward leaned back again and changed the subject.

'And we have another problem. I have received information on your parents' whereabouts.'

Charlie's hands seemed cold suddenly.

'I'm afraid they're not here. Your information was wrong.'

Very cold.

'They have not been in Venice,' continued Edward. 'I'm making inquiries and hope to be able to locate them in due course. But you will not find them here.'

Charlie stared at Edward and the words rang in his head.

'My view is that you should remain here, quietly, until further information comes through,' said Edward. 'All ears are open. We'll hear something else soon.'

This was not Charlie's view at all. His view was that he should immediately go to . . . somewhere . . . and . . . do something.

Edward smiled at Charlie encouragingly. Charlie felt as if his stomach had dropped sixteen floors in a lift without him. He was still staring at Edward. A large and frightening question was forming in his mind.

Was Edward lying? And if he was lying, was all he was saying lies? Or was some of it the truth?

The newspaper was true – he could see it with his own eyes.

Why weren't they here? Sergei had told the Lions Venice!

Sergei couldn't have lied – he wouldn't have. Surely he wouldn't have.

So, was it a mistake?

Bother this game of Chinese whispers!

What did Edward want anyway? What was he up to?

Rats rats rats rats rats. And he didn't want Edward to see how upset he was.

He took a couple of breaths. Then: 'Edward,' said Charlie politely.

'Yes?' said Edward, just as politely.

'Why am I not allowed to see the Lions?'

'Not allowed?' said Edward. 'Dear boy, of course you're allowed. Who's stopping you?'

'Yesterday I was prevented from visiting them,' said Charlie.

'Well, what nonsense,' said Edward. 'In fact I want you to go and see them now. Been thinking about ways of getting the animals out, you know, need to know their size and weight. Need you to measure them.'

Charlie was stopped in his tracks. Measure the Lions? Why?

It must have shown on his face.

'For transportation,' said Edward. 'So they don't sink the boat. Come on, there's a good boy.'

Good boy. Suddenly Charlie thought of Rafi back in London saying, 'Be a good boy.' He thought of how he and his mum had used 'be a good boy' as code in the letters the cats had carried between them. He felt sick with anger. He hadn't asked to be helped, and now look: they were all locked up in a palace, the Lions were caged, King Boris was miles away, the paper was full of stories about them, and Edward was telling him to be a good boy. Sink the boat indeed. They hadn't sunk the gondola, had they?

Edward was lying to him.

Well, he wasn't going to be lazy and unfocused any more, and he wasn't going to rely on anybody else for help. For a start, if he were to measure the Lions he could be with them for a bit and perhaps talk to them . . .

'OK.' He shrugged. He'd play the trick he played on Rafi: let Edward think he was stupid, to put him off his guard.

Edward immediately whipped out a measuring tape from his pocket. Charlie recognized it. It was what the crumply man last night had been showing to Edward, and waving about.

So the crumply man was connected with the measuring. How interesting.

'There's one thing,' said Edward, on their way down to the *cortile*. 'For their own protection, the Lions have been given a security screen – we don't want anything to look unusual, you know, or to alarm the servants. Much better to have everything look normal . . .'

A security screen for their own protection, thought Charlie. Edward, you are a very sneaky sneak. He wondered again if King Boris had any idea how sneaky Edward really was. Could he get in touch with King Boris? He was pretty sure that he wouldn't approve of what was going on.

It was lucky Charlie had seen the bars before, because otherwise Edward would certainly have noticed his anger. As it was, Charlie was calm while Edward opened the gate in the bars and locked it again once Charlie was inside. Standing at a safe distance, Edward instructed Charlie in which bits to measure, and wrote down the results. He seemed to have forgotten about the weighing. What Edward wanted to know was the Lions' chest measurements, heights and the lengths of their backs. Charlie chatted quietly with the Lions as he worked.

'No news yet,' he murmured. 'I don't know what this is about, do you?'

'I think the measuring is what Edward wanted that man last night to do, but he was too scared,' said the Young Lion.

'But what for?' asked Elsina.

None of them knew.

They couldn't talk much. They didn't want Edward finding out, like Maccomo had.

In the Wellness Unit, Magdalen lay sleeping on a fake-wood bed under fake-cotton sheets. A blind with a computerized picture of a garden on it covered the window, which did not open. Air-conditioning pumped slightly sweet, too-cold air through the Unit. At the door of Magdalen's room a nurse sat on a fake-wood chair.

Outside in the grounds of the Community – well, in the air-conditioned fake garden that counted as the grounds – Aneba was walking about, breathing what passed for fresh air. He had long ago forgotten that this air was not fresh, that something was pumped through all the air in this building, something calming and stupid-making – or rather, something that stole independence and free thinking. A lot of the people here were very clever – like Magdalen and Aneba. And their cleverness was valuable. It was their independence that had to go.

Aneba walked as far as he could. After half an hour, he came to a high concrete wall. He didn't think about how odd that was. He just turned round and walked back. After an hour, another high concrete wall. He did this every day. 'Exercise is good!' crooned the voice – was it in his head now? Or was it coming from a loudspeaker somewhere in among the top-quality, almost realistic plastic trees? 'It's good to look after your body! Pamper yourself! Love yourself! You deserve it! The Corporacy wants you healthy and well!'

Sometimes the voice addressed him by name: congratulated him on looking after his body. Once, after he'd bought three chocolate bars at the Treats Unit, the voice had asked him if he was all right, and warned him against the dangers of too much sugar, and later that day the Dental Section of the Wellness Unit had called him in for a check-up. (No one seemed to notice the contradiction between the Social Club wanting them to drink booze and eat crisps, and the Wellness Unit bossing them about their health – the reason for this was that most people paid for everything they used, and as long as they kept paying – for wine, for healthcare, for use of the gym – then the Corporacy was happy. They liked to get back all the money they paid their workers, and they didn't really mind how. As soon as Aneba and Magdalen were 'well' enough to work, they would be paying too.)

Aneba turned and walked back. He was just going to walk to and fro across this huge fake garden until he dropped dead. He couldn't think of anything else to do. Except that the voice would talk to him, telling him to go to the next class or workshop or therapy group or social club night. And they'd taken Magdalen away again. A tiny part of him knew that he had to fight, but he couldn't remember how to fight, or what he was fighting . . .

He reached a high wall again.

For a change, he walked along beside it.

Walk walk walk.

He stared in a blank way at his feet.

Walk walk walk.

Suddenly, something scratchy and furry and chaotic landed on his smooth shaven head.

Ow! He jerked up, staring wildly around.

The thing slid off: it was in front of him, staring at him, furious, wild and making a horrible noise.

It was a cat – a mangy, scrawny black cat with half an ear missing, and what looked like some kind of skin-disease round his rear end. It was glaring at him with eyes like dull-blue fire, hackles raised, legs stiff.

The cat hissed. Aneba held still, watching.

The cat spat. Aneba felt rooted to the ground.

The cat jumped on to a fake-rock, then leapt at Aneba's face and scratched him, hard, cleanly, down his cheek.

Aneba cried out, and his hand on his face was bloodied. The pain was excruciating. It cut through the fog of confusion that had held him in its thrall since he had arrived at this place. It cut through the cotton wool that had been wrapped round his brain, and the sludge which had bogged down his heart. It cut through the doubts and clouds and uncertainties.

The cat stared at him, challenge sparking out of his eyes. Then he turned and sauntered away, looking back over his shoulder as he went. At a safe distance, about ten metres, he turned and sat and stared calmly at Aneba. He yawned. The inside of his mouth was extremely pink. His teeth were tiny sharp yellow points.

Aneba, still gasping at the shock and the pain, looked at his blood on his hand, and looked at the cat.

'Mraaoow,' said the cat, gently, in a slightly ironic North of England fashion.

All clouds were gone from Aneba. He shook himself. He remembered everything. Delicately, he licked at his hand. The taste of his blood was sharp and salty and strong. That's me, he thought. Sharp and strong – me. For god's sake, man – they stole you for your brain – use the thing!

The cat seemed to smile at him.

Aneba thought about his son, Charlie. About how, during their journey here, a cat had brought them a letter from him, and taken a reply back. He smiled back. If Charlie had been there, he would have flung his arms round the cat in delight, crying, 'You're back! You're back! Have you brought a letter?' But Charlie was not there, and Aneba had no idea who this cat was.

Even so, when Sergei beckoned with his long scrawny tail, Aneba knew to follow him.

After talking to the Lions that day, Charlie went up to his room and wrote to the King.

'Dear Your Majesty,' he started. It looked wrong, so

he started again. 'Your Dear Majesty.' No. Umm . . . Your Majesty Dear . . . No, that made it sound as if Charlie were the King's grandma . . .

In the end he wrote 'Dear King Boris.' After that it got even harder. How to explain that he felt he was being betrayed by the King's head of security? It was a serious accusation. How to phrase it? He wasn't accusing the King himself – he was certain that King Boris was on the straight . . . Charlie chewed his pen and fretted.

In the end, he wrote the letter almost in the same style as he had written to his parents: trusting to the intelligence and honesty of the person reading it to get the message.

Dear King Boris

Well here we are in your house which is really nice. Edward says what I came here for is not here after all. Also he is having my friends measured – I don't know why. What do you think? He says it will be a while before we can move on because the Circus and the police in Paris are angry but I just want to get on and leave and find what I am looking for or at least get my friends on their way. I am getting lots to eat which is good but I am not allowed out much and there is no one to play with. In fact I am just feeling a bit stuck here. This doesn't mean I am not grateful. I am very grateful especially for the food.

I hope you are well and that you will come here soon.

Yours

Charlie

He read it over. It looked OK. He hoped King Boris would pick up its real meaning: Edward is trapping us here, come and save us! He hoped that just in *case* Edward got hold of it, it would look like an innocent note from a kid who has no idea what's really going on.

At the same time, Charlie knew that leaving the palazzo now would be extremely dangerous. French police? Maccomo? Rafi? Major Tib? That reward? No, thank you.

He had a horrible feeling that he was safer being kept prisoner. So, was this feeling more or less horrible than the feeling that the longer he stayed here, the tighter the net would close on him?

No. That was a useless question about which he could do nothing. The important question was, how was he going to get the letter out? He certainly wasn't going to give it to Edward to post.

Over the next couple of days Charlie carried the letter in his pocket, and thought intently about how to take control of his situation.

He acquainted himself fully with the building. He went into every room, climbed every staircase, opened every door, looked out of every window, went through every archway. On all four sides the palazzo was bordered by canals. Across the canal at the back a narrow (and gated) bridge led to a small but handsome piazza. The doors in and out of the palazzo were huge, old, locked and bolted. All the windows on the ground floor were barred.

Charlie remembered King Boris's fear of assassins, and his big beefy bodyguards, and he sighed. He went up on the roof: there was a wooden terrace built over the slopes of the red tiles, but although the view was enchanting (as long as you didn't look to the Giudecca or San Giorgio Maggiore) and the roofs very climbable, they just didn't lead anywhere else. There was no cellar.

So he needed an ally. Signora Battistuta was out of the question. He considered making friends with Lavinia, and getting some information out of her. In the end he decided against it. She was just too peculiar. She wasn't like a child at all and he didn't know how to trust her or even understand her. He had a feeling that even if he spoke perfect Italian, or if she spoke perfect English, they would still somehow not understand each other.

For long hours he would stare out the back of the palazzo, across the small canal to the piazza on the other side. There were people there – could he call to them? What would he say?

And there were cats. He called and called to them, the first time. But he didn't dare call too loud, and anyway the window was high, and there was the canal, and the wind was in the wrong direction. Either they didn't hear or they didn't understand. Whatever the reason, they didn't respond.

Charlie stared out at them, willing them to turn, to hear, to come over to him. They didn't. They weren't very nice cats – they seemed to spend a lot of time ganging up on each other. And if Edward was telling the truth, and his parents weren't here, then why would the cats know anything anyway?

Whether or not they knew, they weren't answering him. He watched and stared in vain.

But he had to speak to somebody. His parents always said, 'If you don't know what to do, find out more.' He had to get some information, because otherwise he was just stuck here for as long as Edward chose, in Edward's power, and it was driving him mad.

'I think it best that you don't go to see the Lions for a while,' Edward had said earnestly. 'It looks peculiar, and we must avoid attracting attention. We don't want the servants gossiping. It's hard enough to keep them loyal, with that reward being offered.'

Seeing that the servants were Signora Battistuta, who seemed to know all Edward's secrets and anyway had the air of a woman who did exactly what she liked, and little Lavinia, who was about as threatening as a very old J-cloth, Charlie didn't fall for this. But he didn't want Edward to know that he mistrusted him, so he carried on pretending to fall for Edward's tricks. It wasn't fun.

Mostly, during those days, Charlie just ate (prawns, fish, fennel, ice cream) and gazed out of the windows, at the canal to the front and the piazza cats to the rear, and schemed. They could ambush a boat, and leap out the window . . . could they swim? Perhaps they *could* get away over the roof, the Lions were good leapers . . . But after Charlie's first visit, the roof terrace had been locked.

Edward was a cunning man, a man with spies and power. No half-baked plan would do.

At night Charlie went secretly to the *cortile* and lay about with the Lions; in the morning he stared out at the piazza cats; and at noon he laid his telephone on the window ledge in the Chinese room, with his mother's that he brought with him from home all those weeks ago, and watched them as they charged up under the sun. The phones never rang. There were no messages. He played Snake. On one occasion, angry with frustration, he tried to call Rafi to have a fight, but a computer voice came on, telling him he had no credit. Of course: he had been away too long; he had no vouchers left.

Quite often he saw the lean shape of Claudio, sunburnt and strong, his back bent over his pole, gliding by almost without a splash, and they would wave to each other. The boatman seemed amused that Charlie would be at a different window each time. Often he was singing, and he would sing to Charlie, larking about. There was one particular tune that he sang which Charlie liked, and would listen out for. Claudio noticed, and made a point of singing it as he approached.

'*Quando vado in gondola sogno sempre sempre di Elena*,' he carrolled.

Claudio's Gondola Song

R. LOCKHART

'What do the words mean?' Charlie called one morning.

'It means when I go in my gondola I dream always always of Elena!'

Charlie took to humming the tune, but instead of Elena he found himself singing 'Aneba', which fitted very well.

So Claudio and Charlie started looking out for each other. It became a sort of game they played together.

'How the Lions?' the boatman would call, and Charlie would make a face, as if to say, 'Well, so-so.'

'I like Lions,' the boatman would say, warningly, as if to say, 'Take care of them,' and his gondola glided on by, going about his business.

One time, Charlie said, 'Claudio, could you do something for me?'

'Sure,' said Claudio.

Charlie, fluttering with nerves, asked him to post the letter for him. 'Everyone's gone out,' he explained, with a 'silly-me' shrug. 'I forgot to give it to Signora Battistuta.'

'Why don't you post it yourself?' asked Claudio, a little puzzled.

'I'm not allowed out,' whispered Charlie, between the bars of the window.

Claudio's gondola rocked on the wake of a passing *motoscafo*.

'Why not?' he said carefully.

Charlie grinned nervously. He hadn't a clue what to say.

'Please post it!' he said, and tucked the letter through

the bars. Claudio manoeuvred the boat closer and, balancing easily, leaned in to take the letter.

'Of course,' he said, giving Charlie a curious look. Then he said, 'The Lions, are they happy inside there?' and Charlie replied directly, 'No, they're not.'

'Tell me,' said Claudio, in such a straight and friendly way that Charlie was very tempted to. But he didn't. A letter was one thing – a risk worth taking. But Claudio worked for Edward, and Charlie wasn't about to forget that.

Rafi was definitely feeling better. He was well enough to sit up and read newspapers.

'Hi,' he said to the nurse.

'Hmph,' she replied.

'Sorry I've been such a pig,' he said, giving her a really very beautiful smile.

The nurse was quite young. Now her bolshy patient had rediscovered his manners, she was quite taken aback by how . . . attractive he was. Before long she'd brought him all the newspaper reports of the Lions' disappearance, Maccomo's disappearance, Charlie's disappearance, the terrible weather in the Alps and the fact that the train got stuck in it.

Now why would Charlie have got on that particular train? Rafi wondered to himself. Was it just the first train they came to?

Rafi didn't think that anybody, not even a kid like Charlie, would just try to take six Lions on the first train he came across. He must have thought about it.

He was struck by the fact that the train went via Venice. Venice sounds very like Vence, he thought – knowing perfectly well that Vence was the nearest town to the Corporacy Community where Magdalen and Aneba had been taken.

But how could Charlie have known anything about that?

He read on. 'Reports that creatures which may have been the Lions were spotted during last week's Alpine blizzard, in which the *Orient Express* was stranded for several days with the King of Bulgaria aboard, have been dismissed by the Alpine Transport Police.'

But the Lions could not be anywhere else other than with Charlie.

And he had *seen* Charlie on that train!

And – he had seen which carriage Charlie was in. The second one after the fuelwagon.

Ha! Dingbat! All he had to do was find out who or what was in that carriage on that journey! See if they were powerful enough – and mad enough – to prevent it from being searched! That person would be protecting Charlie and the Lions.

Rafi was really feeling a lot better.

Then: 'Hang on,' he said to himself. 'Hang on a minute.' Rafi, when visiting the doctor, was not above looking at the celebrity and royalty gossip magazines. He longed to be rich and famous and, when no one was looking, he liked to scrutinize photographs of swimming pools and luxury villas, and fantasize.

'The King of Bulgaria?' he said. 'The famous eccentric reclusive King Boris of Bulgaria – who – hang *on* – has his own private carriage on the *Orient Express* and sometime *drives* the dang thing? And – now I think I'm right – owns a traditional Italian-style palace on Venice's world-famous Grand Canal, into which no celebrity magazine has ever been invited . . . Of course! Of *course*!'

Rafi felt absolutely fit as a fiddle. He would bet his recovering right arm that King Boris was his man. All he had to do was get a phone number, maybe an address, and he could track the Lions – and Charlie – down.

Venice, eh.

He laughed so loud and long that the nurse came back to check on him.

'Hi there,' he said. 'What's your name again?'

Late one afternoon, Charlie was staring out at the piazza. There were an awful lot of cats. Most of them were pretty skinny. It was the fatter skinny ones, he noticed, who ganged up on the skinnier skinny ones.

There was a group of young children playing with one of the fatter skinny ones, trailing what looked like a feather on a stiff long plastic cord, which made the feather twitch and jump. The fat skinny cat – not much more than a kitten really – jumped and leapt after it, hunting it down, then pretended to ignore it, then sneaked up on it from the side, pouncing and leaping. It made Charlie smile. He'd like to have played with the cat like that. One of the children, a small yellow-haired girl in a grubby dress, pounced on the cat and carried it with one arm round its chest to the fountain in the middle of the piazza. She was rubbing her nose on its head and hugging it while it struggled, mewling, its back legs flopping, its forelegs waving in outrage, its clean white furry tummy displayed for all to see. Charlie laughed out loud.

Charlie had a loud laugh, like his dad.

When he laughed, one of the older cats looked round suddenly.

Charlie saw the movement. He turned swiftly and caught the cat's eye. Laughed again – a fake laugh, but a loud laugh – a loud, fake Cat laugh.

The older cat stared at him and twitched his ear. Charlie stared back. 'Come to me come to me come to me come to me,' he urged silently. Could he risk shouting out?

He did.

'Come and talk to me!' he shrieked, from his high window, at the top of his voice, in Cat. To any listening human, it would have sounded as if a cat had been trodden on.

Did the sound carry over the little canal? Did it carry

through the late-afternoon sounds of children and cats and life on the piazza?

Did the cat hear him?

It might have.

Did it respond?

If a flicked ear and a sudden intense look were a response, then yes it did.

Did it come over and talk to him?

It did not.

The next day Charlie was loping around on the first floor, in the great chamber, the *portego*, which stretched the length of the building. It had high, deep, mullioned windows looking out over the Grand Canal, and a flat stone balcony, with arches and decorations that he had admired from the outside. He had gone out on to the balcony, and settled himself on the broad, high ledge, leaning against the carved stone wall and staring with dry, angry eyes not at Venice, but at the curls of stone and metalwork that decorated the outside of the palazzo. It was strange to be seeing it from inside out, close up, from the wrong direction. It was like sitting on the rim of someone's eye, looking up at gigantic eyelashes.

What was Edward up to?

Charlie didn't like the view from this balcony – when he looked beyond the close-up-from-inside carved ice cream he could see the weird floodsite with all its paraphernalia and debris, looking smaller under the high midday sun. He was just deciding to go and find another place to sit and either think about what on earth they were going to do, or, as was happening more and more lately, feel miserable about the fact that he had been so close to his parents in Paris and now he had lost them. God only knew how they were, where they were, if he would be able to make contact with them again . . . Or he could fret about his letter to King Boris – had Claudio posted it? Had King Boris received it? When would he hear anything?

But then a small commotion at the front door below attracted his attention.

A smallish *motoscafo* had pulled up, making a creamy wake to her stern. The curly old bloke driving it was instructing a younger man to unload some very big, odd-shaped packages on to the steps of the palazzo, and someone at the door was telling him not to. There was a bit of shouting, and then the *motoscafo* drew off, taking its big packages with it. But it didn't go away; it drew round the corner into the damp little sun-dappled canal that ran along the side of the palazzo.

Maybe it's going to a back entrance, thought Charlie.

He was curious.

Jumping lightly down from the window ledge (the Young Lion had given him some landing lessons, showing him how to spread the bones of his feet so as to be light and silent like – well, like a cat. Sigi Lucidi would have loved it), Charlie slipped across to one of the rooms overlooking the side canal.

Sure enough, he heard voices. Signora Battistuta was giving someone a ticking-off in the back hall, but at the same time there was the huff and puff and creak and scuff of things being unloaded. Charlie hung out of the window as best he could to see the boat, and the figures popping in and out.

As soon as it was all done, and Signora Battistuta had bustled off to find somebody else to boss around, Charlie sneaked downstairs into the back hall to look at the packages: one fat bundle, and two the same peculiar shape – about six feet long and flat, but curved. Charlie was intrigued.

Behind him came a soft fall of footsteps. He slipped behind the big coat cupboard (thank goodness Venetian furniture was so huge) as Lavinia and the young man from the *motoscafo* came into the room, and started squabbling quietly about how best to manoeuvre the long, stiff packages out of the room. One at each end, they tried to edge the first of them through the doorway. The young man must have hit his hand on something, for he suddenly swore and dropped his end of the package.

The paper caught on the door's heavy latch, and ripped open, a long revealing wound.

Inside the brown paper was white soft paper, and inside the white paper all was feathers – creamy-white feathers tipped with crimson, lying smooth and plump like the most inviting bed, or a swan's breast. And in among the feathers were eyes: golden eyes.

Eyes!

Charlie couldn't see how they were made – embroidered, perhaps, with gold wiry thread? Or were they printed on the feathered base?

Eyes. Feathers.

It reminded him of something. Something recently . . .

When the packages had all been carried away, Charlie went back up to the Chinese room and lay on his bed, thinking about feathers and eyes.

Feathers and eyes.

When he woke up half an hour later, he knew what was in the packages, and he had a pretty good idea why.

CHAPTER SIX

After lunch, everybody would go for a siesta and the palazzo was quiet. Charlie, though he had snoozed that morning, would have happily snoozed some more, as his late-night visits to the Lions were taking it out of him, but instead he went to the window at the back and stared out over the sun-drenched piazza. That cat yesterday had nearly responded to him. Perhaps he would be there again now, looking for a place in the shade to rest during the afternoon heat. Charlie leaned against the cool stone of the window frame and sniffed the damp canal smell rising up. He scanned the piazza as well as he could from this distance. There was a gang of the fatter cats, lying about in piles, stretching out their legs and arching their backs a little as they settled in for a good laze. There was the fatter skinny cat with the white tummy, the one the blonde kid had been teasing the other day, and one of the skinny skinny cats, on his own. He couldn't see the cat who had almost noticed him. Rats.

Oh, look – there was the blonde kid! She was alone

today. She was too little to be out on her own, in Charlie's opinion. She couldn't have been more than four or five. Maybe her brothers were round the corner, out of Charlie's view.

A couple of the fatter cats were making comments about the skinny cat. Charlie could tell just from the way they were lying about that they were being insolent. The skinny cat avoided them, stalking instead down towards the canalside, in Charlie's full view. He didn't look very well, to tell the truth.

Suddenly, the little blonde girl spied the white-tummied cat – 'her' cat, the one she had had such fun with before. She jumped on it but it ran away. Annoyed, she pounced instead on the skinny cat, and much to her own – and the cat's – amazement, she caught it. She was delighted. (The cat was not.)

With the cat scratching and kicking in her arms, she sat down and hugged it to her. She kissed it, she talked to it, she ruffled up its fur with her free hand, and then quickly clamped down again when the cat seemed likely to wriggle out of her grasp. Charlie watched, with mild interest. He was a bit sorry for the cat, actually, but really he was still looking out for the older one, the one he hoped to speak to. His attention wandered from the blonde child and her poor furry victim.

He only noticed what was happening gradually. There was a noise: from the piazza, so distant, but unmistakable nonetheless. Had it been going on for long? It was a noise Charlie had hoped never to hear again: harsh, small, rasping, punctuated with coughs. It was like breathing, but too short, too high, too hard, too painful and uncomfortable, with a nasty hollow cough on the in-breath. It was the sound of a small child having a sudden, severe asthma attack.

Charlie looked back at the girl. Her shoulders were high, swamping her neck, and her face was pale. Her chest was sunken, rising and falling swiftly. Her eyes looked small in her face. He knew that look; he knew that feeling.

Charlie shouted.

Were there any grown-ups over there? Who was with her? She needed her medicine and she needed it now.

Even as Charlie shouted, he noticed the fatter cats leaping up from their reverie. As a gang, they turned on the cat the girl had been holding and ran at him. But it was as if he had expected it – he was already away and running down a narrow street off the piazza, terrified. The others chased after him, vicious, hunting, caterwauling.

Charlie was shocked. He was used to cats fighting. He'd seen enough of them in the Ruins at home, but he had never seen cats gang up like this. What was it about?

Two women had appeared beside the little girl. Charlie leaned right out of the window, craning to hear what was being said. He could hear something about *soldi* and *medicina* and *non posso* and *sporco gatto* – he knew that meant filthy cat – but he couldn't understand. He could see that the girl was not being given any medicine. It seemed that neither woman had any.

Maybe it's her first attack, he thought. If they didn't know she was asthmatic, they wouldn't know that she should take her medicine with her everywhere.

Then he remembered what King Boris had said about people not being able to afford medicine.

Without a second thought, Charlie pulled his puffer from his pocket (he had spare ones in his bag). He knew that you shouldn't lend or borrow medicine, but this was an emergency. He yelled out to the women.

'*Signora!*' he shouted – he knew that meant 'Mrs'. '*Signora!* Here!' And he threw the puffer as hard as he could, out of the window, across the canal. Don't let it fall in, he prayed.

It didn't. It landed near the little group, and one of the women picked it up. Clearly she did know the child was asthmatic, because they both knew exactly how to use the puffer. As the child breathed in the medicine and the mother – so Charlie supposed her to be – hugged her and helped her, the other, older woman fussed around them.

The child took a puff, breathed for ten breaths, took another. Charlie knew the routine. It was hard to tell from so far away, but it seemed she was calming down. Another puff. They'd just have to keep at it till they could get her either breathing properly again or to hospital.

The older woman, reassured now that the child was improving, had turned to face over the water to Charlie. She was craning to see him, holding her arms out.

'*Grazie, bambino!*' she called out. '*Sei un angelo venuto dal Cielo! Grazie a Dio eri qui con la medicina, senza di te non so che cosa sarebbe successo, sei gentillissimo, vieni qui, vieni fuori, vogliamo ringraziati, vieni, per favore, vieni . . .*'

She was beckoning to him. She was getting rather enthusiastic. It seemed she wanted him to come out and be thanked. Charlie smiled at her, and withdrew from the window. He couldn't go out. He wouldn't understand what they had to say anyway. He didn't want to attract any more attention, and have Edward or Signora Battistuta come and shout at him. He was sorry to have to withdraw, because he was glad to have helped, but what else could he do?

Ten minutes later, he risked looking out again. The girl and her mother were gone, but the older woman was still there. Perhaps she was the granny.

The moment she spotted Charlie she started up her chorus again. '*Vieni, angelo salvatore della figliola, vieni . . .*'

Charlie ducked away again. Oh dear. Was she going to stay for long?

Ten minutes later she was still there. Five minutes after that she was gone, and Charlie settled back to his vigil, watching for the Cat Who Had Responded.

The Cat Who Had Responded, it turned out, was watching for him too. He was sitting on the window ledge, licking his paws. When Charlie, safe in the absence of the granny, looked out the window, the cat mewed right in his ear.

'Aggh!' cried Charlie. 'Don't surprise me like that!'

At that the cat fell in the canal. Clearly he was more surprised than Charlie.

It took a lot of chat and reassurance to convince him that Charlie was not a ghost, a spook, a goblin, a werewolf, a phantasm, a zombie, a leprechaun, a sprite, a boy witch, a vampire or any other kind of bad creature – merely a young boy who could speak Cat. Even then, after the cat had dragged himself out of the canal, he preferred to sit on the next window ledge along, partly because there was sun there for him to dry off in, but mostly, Charlie suspected, because he felt safer out of reach.

Charlie was actually quite pleased not to be greeted yet again as '*That* boy' by a cat who seemed to know more about him than he did about himself.

'So tell me,' said Charlie, once they had settled down, and once it was apparent that this cat hadn't a clue who he was and didn't know anything about his parents. 'What was that this afternoon? What happened?'

'Again a pigging asthma attack,' said the cat, whose name was Enzo.

'But I don't understand,' said Charlie. 'Last time that girl was playing with the cats she was fine. Why should she have an attack now?'

Enzo looked at him sideways. 'You notice that, eh?'

'Yes, and I also noticed the way that gang of cats, the healthy-looking ones who hang out by the fountain, were after him. And how they'd been ganging up on all the skinnier cats. I don't understand.'

'Humans usually they don't notice these things,' said Enzo after a pause.

'Humans usually don't speak Cat,' said Charlie, not unreasonably.

Enzo licked a paw, rubbed his ear, and stared at the canal.

'Humans don't even like cats now,' he said quietly and bitterly.

'Yes, we do!' cried Charlie. 'What do you mean? That's a horrible thing to say. Why do you say that?'

Enzo turned to him and narrowed his eyes. 'Humans don't want to keep cats now. They can't know who is Allergenie and who is not, and the medicine is too expensive and they can't afford. So we are all out on our ears.'

Ah.

Now they were getting somewhere.

This time, Charlie was not going to blow it. He was going to get to the bottom of this Allergenie thing.

'So,' he said slowly, 'do you suppose that girl used to have medicine, but stopped taking it because her parents couldn't afford it?'

'Yes, I suppose,' said Enzo firmly.

'And . . .' Charlie was taking a big risk with what he said next. But he had heard enough, and thought enough about it, and he had to know. 'Do you suppose,' he said, 'that cat is an Allergenie?'

'Of course,' said Enzo. 'Even without immediate and very strong asthma attack of the small girl, which show he is much more allergenic than a normal cat even if the normal cat is normally allergenic, you can know because he – well, the thinness, and the thinness of fur. General bad health.'

Allergenic. Charlie was not familiar with the word but it was pretty obvious what it meant. Being allergenic meant you made allergic people have attacks. He knew that some cats were more allergenic than others because he'd seen it with his friends and the Ruins cats. And now he knew that Allergenies were specially highly allergenic.

And humans couldn't tell which cats were Allergenies, and so treated all cats as if they were, and they couldn't afford the asthma medicine for their children so lots of cats were getting chucked out of their homes . . . It all fell into place.

No wonder the cats were so desperate for Mum and Dad to find their asthma cure. If the children could just stop being allergic, then it wouldn't matter how allergenic the cats were . . .

And meanwhile the cats were ganging up on the Allergenies because they blamed them for the trouble.

Poor Allergenies. Poor cats as well! What a terrible situation.

'But Enzo,' said Charlie. 'Where do the Allergenies come from? Were there always Allergenies?'

Enzo was silent a moment before speaking. Then: 'No one really knows,' he said. 'Some of them just arrive, newcomers. One day they weren't there, the next day they were. But . . . there is a story. Five years ago, there was a strange thing happened. Lots of girl cats disappear. Not just here in Venice. We hear about it from all over. They disappear, then a few days later they come back. Later, they have kittens. No one knows who is the papa. A lot of the kittens they look the same – not so healthy little black and white guys. Skinny. Some people say these girl cats had Allergenie babies put in them, someone want Allergenies put all over the world. I say, why? Who need to do this? It's not a easy thing to do – Oh, I'll just make lots of Allergenic babies now before I have my lunch. You know Latin?'

Charlie did know some Latin.

'*Cui bono?*' said Enzo.

'Who benefits?' translated Charlie. 'Who is it good for?'

He had a little think.

No one benefited. Not cats, not Allergenies, not humans . . .

As he was thinking he looked up. Oh. There was Granny, hobbling back into the piazza. She was carrying a bunch of flowers and a cardboard sign and what looked very like a deckchair.

'Uh-oh,' said Charlie. 'Gotta go. Come back later, would you? I'd like to talk to you some more.'

'Of course,' said Enzo civilly. '*Ciao.*'

The lady was unfolding her chair right by the canalside opposite Charlie's window. She set up her cardboard sign against a mooring post, and laid her bunch of flowers on the stone canal kerb.

Oh dear.

Now she was fishing in her pocket and getting something out.

Ah. A candle – one of those little low ones you see in churches, or in coloured glasses on café tables. She put it by the flowers and, after a bit of fumbling, lit it. She looked up at the window and smiled and waved. Then she settled herself into her chair and took out her knitting.

Charlie hid.

Edward received a telephone call. A voice introduced itself.

'Ah,' said Edward. 'Yes, I know who you are, Mr Sadler. I thought you were indisposed.'

'Well, I was,' said Rafi, miles away, leaning against the window in the public ward of the hospital. 'But now I'm better.' So much better, in fact, that he'd been on to the Railway Gentleman, the police and the doctor and pointed out that there was really no reason to keep him in hospital any more. He was no longer sick, he'd committed no crime, he was terribly sorry for having made such a fuss while he was in his fever, but they'd arrested no one whose crimes he had witnessed, so if it was all the same to them . . .

They'd scratched their heads, and tried to think of a reason to keep him, as he was obviously up to no good. In the end, the policeguy said, 'Well, if we need you as a witness to anything you'll have to come back,' and Rafi had said, 'Oh, of course, sir, of course', sniggering the moment the policeguy turned away.

'Yeah, I'm much better now,' said Rafi.

'Should I care?' asked Edward.

'Yeah, you should,' said Rafi. 'And so should those Lions you're hiding. You know, they're pretty visible from here.' There was a small brown cat snoozing on the window ledge. Rafi scratched behind its ears.

Edward said nothing.

'And if they're visible from here, they're likely visible from all over.'

Edward said nothing.

'And there's some people, you can imagine, you wouldn't want seeing them.'

Edward wondered.

'Their owner, for example. Not the Circus – you don't worry about them, they're straight decent people. I mean the other guy,' said Rafi.

At this, Edward wondered a bit more. He considered

that he knew most things – but he didn't necessarily know this.

'That weird psycho African who's disappeared,' said Rafi. 'You don't want him turning up on your doorstep, do you?'

Ah. The trainer, Maccomo. Yes, that would be a bore. Edward had plans for the Lions, and they didn't involve any turning up on any doorsteps, especially not his.

Edward thought for a second. Rafi, smiling, left him to think.

'So what do you want, boy?' asked Edward.

Rafi smiled. 'Nothing,' he said, and hung up. He had what he wanted – confirmation that the Lions and Charlie were at King Boris's palace in Venice.

'Off we go, then!' said Rafi cheerfully, shrugging his leather coat on carefully over his delicate shoulder, and picking up the big box of painkillers he'd scrounged off the nurse. 'Venice here I come!'

It was only at that point that Rafi remembered he had a dog. Even as he said, 'Off we go, then,' he realized who it was he was addressing – Troy, his slavering hound. Troy, who wasn't there.

For a moment, a tiny pang went through his heart. Where was Troy? Then: 'Well, he's scarpered, hasn't he?' Rafi decided. 'No such thing as loyalty in this wicked world. He's just dumped me while I was down. Typical. Still, who cares about a stupid dog, anyway . . .'

And with that he left. By the back, while the devoted Troy dozed in the shade under the bushes by the front door, where he had been ever since his master had entered the building, waiting for him to come out again.

The moment Rafi had left the room, the small brown cat shot off the window ledge, all snooziness gone, and headed to the station, where her uncle was a traincat. If she made it there before the five-thirty left, the message would get south tonight.

In the corridor outside Magdalen's room in the Wellness Unit, Aneba, holding a bunch of too-bright, too-pretty flowers that had no scent and had certainly not grown in any earth, approached the nurse with a too-bright, too-cheerful smile. Like the Motivational Manager's, Aneba's smile was all mouth. His eyes looked cool and not very clever.

'Hello,' he said. 'I've come to see my poor old wife.'

'Of course, Dr Ashanti,' said the nurse, giving him a matching fake smile. 'Lovely flowers. From the Floral Retail Unit? Come on in. I think she's asleep still, but it'll be wonderful for her to see you. Ooh, what have you done to your face? That looks nasty!'

Aneba pushed his fake smile a little wider still. It was getting uncomfortable (which was nothing to do with the scratch) and he didn't know how long he could hold it, but it seemed to be the badge of having given in, and so he wore it. He didn't want anyone to think he was still having independent thoughts, and drag him off for another round of therapy and medicine. No, he wanted to look as if he completely agreed with everything everybody said.

'Oh, it's nothing,' he said. 'Just a scratch.'

The nurse showed him into Magdalen's room.

'Do you think she might be ready for a gentle stroll in the garden?' Aneba asked cheerfully.

'Well,' said the nurse doubtfully.

'Such a lovely day,' said Aneba with a grin. His cheeks were aching.

'True,' said the nurse.

'She could lean on my arm,' he purred, with a loving, husbandly look at his wife.

The nurse liked to see couples together. So many families nowadays all fallen apart, divorces and whatnot. It was good to see a husband so devoted.

She smiled him a smile that was almost genuine (for the nurse was, underneath, a decent woman, and it wasn't her fault that she had been seduced by the Corporacy). 'Oh, go on, then,' she said. 'Bit of fresh air. Do her good.'

Aneba flashed her a smile that was absolutely genuine. The nurse was momentarily dazzled. Any genuine emotion would have dazzled her, because she had not seen any for years, but Aneba's smile was legendary even among genuine smiles. And this was one of his best. Reeling from the strength of it, the nurse left the room.

Aneba worked quickly. First, he pulled out the drip

that was feeding medicine into Magdalen's vein. Then he splashed cold water on her face. Then he rubbed her feet, then he kissed her. Like Sleeping Beauty, she opened her eyes. Even as they opened, his were there to meet them, to send a message of strength and awakeness.

She looked shocked and scared.

'Wake up,' he said. 'Really wake up. Fight it. Fight harder. Fight harder than you ever fought.'

She blinked.

He broke off some petals from one of the flowers. 'Even this artificial version has some power,' he murmured. 'It's not as strong as the wild flowers from the forest, but it can only help.' He had recognized the flowers as one of the main ingredients in Magdalen's Improve-Everything Lotion.

He squeezed the petals so they were bruised and damp, and laid them on her tongue.

'Suck them,' he said.

He wiped his hand on the still-bleeding scratch across his cheek.

'Lick,' he said. 'Take strength from my blood.'

She licked. She blinked again.

'Water,' she said.

'Not *their* water,' he replied. 'Everything here is full of their power to stop us thinking. Their food, their medicine, their water, their air. It isn't clean. Come.'

'Not strong enough,' she murmured.

Aneba laughed. 'Don't give me that,' he said. 'You are the strongest woman I ever met.'

She smiled at his laugh. She tasted his blood still on her lips. She felt stronger.

'There's a cat,' he whispered. 'He knows a way.'

She felt stronger still.

'And?' she whispered.

'And we're going for a nice walk in the garden,' he said.

Later that afternoon, Edward went out.

Forty-five seconds later he came in again.

'Charlie,' he said.

'Yes?' said Charlie.

'Why is there an old lady outside with candles and flowers and a sign saying, "In this palazzo lives an Angel of the Lord, he saved the life of my granddaughter Donatella, join with me in thanks for the miracle of the Young Brown Angel, pray for the Lord's Mercy in these hard times"?

Charlie gulped.

Oh no.

He was really embarrassed.

'To what Young Brown Angel might she be referring, Charlie?' Edward said.

Charlie felt his mouth opening and shutting but he really couldn't think what to say.

'You know we are not meant to be attracting attention, Charlie, don't you? In what way, exactly, does a woman with flowers and candles and talk of angels and miracles not attract attention to His Majesty's household? Why is she here?'

So Charlie told him. Just that a child had been having an asthma attack, and he'd thrown his medicine to her. Anyone would, he said. You don't just sit there and watch a child . . .

No, even Edward had to agree that you don't just sit there.

'Well,' he said. 'Let's hope nobody takes any notice of her.'

By six o'clock there were three more women with the granny. One of them was on her knees, praying constantly. It seemed her daughter was asthmatic too. Another had a sign reading, 'Doge of Venice, Hear your People! Banish the Cats from the City! Too Many Children are Falling Sick!'

They had all brought flowers. And candles.

Just before dinner, a young man rang the bell at the gate by the bridge.

'I am from the *Venezia Sera* newspaper,' he said to Signora Battistuta. 'I wish to know about the miracle of the Brown Angel of the Children with Asthma. Do you believe in miracles? Do you think the Doge is doing enough to solve the problems of sick children?'

Signora Battistuta said, 'Go away.' Looking out across the little bridge, she saw ten women, six children, three babies, fourteen bunches of flowers, twenty-two candles in a row along the canalside, four crucifixes, seven cards bearing pictures of the Sacred Heart of Jesus, some old asthma puffers tied with pink ribbons to the gate, and a teddy bear. In the early dusk, with the candles reflecting in the canal, it made a very pretty sight.

'Oh, for goodness' sake,' said Charlie. 'I only threw them some medicine.'

Later, some young people arrived with placards reading, 'Doge, Oppressor of Venice, Stop Ignoring Us!' They were selling magazines recommending getting rid of the Doge and finding a new government, and soon the Doge Guards arrived with truncheons and handcuffs, and took them away. The grannies booed and hissed at this, and one of the Doge Guards waved his truncheon at them too.

Charlie, watching this covertly from his window, realized that the Venetians *really* didn't like the Doge.

After dinner, Charlie yawned loudly and said he was very tired and would retire to bed. Edward stopped him, saying, 'Charlie, I've made a decision.'

'Oh yes?' said Charlie. He kept his face blank and friendly.

'It isn't really safe, Charlie, for the Lions to stay here. We might have been able to keep things quiet but – well. There is no chance now. There is too much attention on this house. The word may get out. The newspapers mentioned you, there's the offer of the reward, and now all this miracle nonsense. If someone puts two and two together – the Brown Angel and the brown boy from the Circus – well, our best hope is to get some protection for them elsewhere. And the person who can protect them is the Doge.'

Charlie could see his point about protection, though he thought the comment about him being brown was unnecessary. Loads of people are brown.

Edward had a suspiciously innocent look on his face.

'If we take the Lions to the Doge, and present them as his guests, he will look after them,' Edward was saying. 'He will adopt them, if you like, as his friends and friends of Venice, and then nobody will dare try to get them back for the Circus. Your circus friends need to perform in many places, including Venice, and if the Doge tells his friends to bar them, they could do it. No Circus would take on the might of Venice. The Lions would be safe.

'So we will visit the Doge. He is expecting us – I have not said who I am bringing, but he is expecting something.

You must come too. Of course. Lionboy. Claudio will be your translator. It will all be for the best.'

Edward's air of behaving as if everything was already arranged made it hard for Charlie to argue with him. But Charlie was worried. They didn't need to be protected in Venice – they needed to *leave* Venice. But then visiting the Doge would mean leaving Palazzo Bulgaria, and that could only be good. Except that he'd lose contact with Enzo, and he hadn't had a chance yet to ask Enzo to ask around about his parents.

A thought suddenly flew into Charlie's mind, clear as a bird.

Cui bono? Who benefits?

It was true that the asthma medicine companies weren't benefiting.

But did they know that?

Could they have known at the beginning what would happen?

They might have thought it would benefit them a lot. They might have thought that with cars banned there weren't enough sick children to need their drugs, and that making the children sick with specially allergenic cats would be really good for business. They couldn't have known that the parents would start getting rid of the cats instead of paying out for more medicine. They couldn't have known that it wouldn't benefit them. They might have thought it would.

The medicine companies could have something to do with the sudden appearance of the Allergenies. In which case . . .

Edward interrupted his thoughts.

'Well, goodnight, Charlie,' he said. 'There's a good boy. We'll be going out soon, in the next few days, to the Doge.'

The next few days! He'd have to make sure to speak to Enzo tomorrow.

Charlie smiled nicely. 'OK, then,' he said politely. 'Goodnight.'

He lay in bed for an hour, trembling with frustration, before he deemed it quiet enough for him to sneak down to the Lions.

When Aneba led Magdalen down to the high wall, Sergei was waiting for them. He was sitting like an Egyptian god with his ears – well, the complete one – tipped high. At his feet was an envelope.

Sergei had it all worked out. He had thought and thought about how to communicate with these precious humans. He'd shocked the dad into consciousness; given him an adrenaline rush that had cleared his head long enough for him to realize he had to keep it clear. (Interesting that he'd immediately gone sniffing around the plants. Sergei did a similar thing when he felt sick – ate grass.) And he'd ripped out a newspaper story for them, that was no problem. They'd have some background information on what Charlie had been up to. But how to get them to go to Venice? He *could* go to the library in the town and rip out a page with Venice on it. But the town was too far away and he was in too much of a hurry. And anyway, cats – specially scrawny bald-bottomed cats with half an ear missing – were not exactly welcome in libraries. Especially not when they started tearing pages out of books. Not that that kind of thing worried him. He could achieve almost any sneaky thing he chose, but – he didn't have the time. No, the newspaper story would have to do. Then he could lead them through the service tunnels and down to the station and get them on the train to Venice.

Sergei flicked the envelope to Aneba with his paw.

Aneba picked up the envelope and opened it.

Under an artificial bush, he and Magdalen read the newspaper story. (It wasn't the one that Charlie had seen, but another one, from a French paper. It gave pretty much the same information, though it didn't mention Mabel.)

They sighed. They smiled. They looked at each other. They remembered what their son was like.

'He's liberating Lions!' cried Aneba. 'Single-handed! Attaboy!'

'Shh,' shushed Magdalen.

Sergei gave a sharp mraow, and beckoned them.

The three of them slunk down alongside the high

concrete wall, with Sergei leading. After a while, a rather nasty smell replaced the cool, sweet air to which they had become accustomed. Actually, a very nasty smell. A smell of old food and steamed chips and fish skin and – *eeww*. Magdalen and Aneba wrinkled their noses. It grew stronger.

Soon it was explained. They came to an area, a sort of yard, with ranks of enormous dustbins lined up. The bins were moving, like slow soldiers in formation. Row by row, they slid forward towards – Magdalen and Aneba couldn't quite make it out – a sort of rack, where long mechanical arms came out, and grabbed the bins, and tipped their contents on to a conveyor belt with sides to stop the rubbish falling off. The conveyor belt led into a tunnel.

'Oh no,' said Magdalen.

Sergei went right up close to the conveyor belt, just as it entered the tunnel in the huge wall. Paper and plastic and rotten food and dustballs and coffee grounds and old wet rags and dead hair from hairbrushes and plastic bags and meat bones and the sludge from cleaning out the fishbowl and brown apple cores and used tissues and broken glass . . .

'Oh well,' said Aneba.

It was quite clear what they were going to have to do.

'But it's nice here,' said Magdalen. 'I don't see why we . . . we've been doing really well and it's all so pleasant . . .'

'Magdalen!' cried Aneba.

She looked at him blankly.

'I don't want to go in with all that filthy rubbish,' she said. 'I don't see why I should.'

'We make all that filthy rubbish,' said Aneba drily. 'You needn't be so proud.'

'I'm tired,' said Magdalen. 'I want to go back to my room. I'm not well.'

She began to cry. Rather loudly.

Aneba wondered if he should slap her. That's one thing to do with hysterical people.

He kissed her instead.

'Oh,' she said, blinking her eyes. 'Sorry. Sorry – I'll try . . .'

'It'll be OK as soon as we're out of their air,' said Aneba.

They looked at Sergei. Sergei looked at them. They all looked at the rubbish. It was only slightly less unattractive to Sergei than it was to the humans.

They all looked at each other. Two of them held their noses. They jumped on.

Squidge.

Yuck.

Ugh.

CHAPTER SEVEN

When Charlie came down to the Lions that night they were restless, prowling about in the cool night air. They hadn't finished their meat, and they were growing impatient. The Silver and Yellow Lionesses were lying in the moonlight looking for all the world like stone statues of St Mark's Lion. The scent of jasmine still hung on the air.

'So?' said the Young Lion, bounding to Charlie's side. 'What's going on? Any news about your parents?'

'The news is,' said Charlie, 'that I've made contact with a cat outside, Enzo, and he's a good bloke. The other news is – er – we're going to go and live with the Doge in a day or two, so that he will be our friend, and we will be safer.'

'What?' said the Young Lion, to whom this made no sense at all.

'I know,' said Charlie. 'It made no sense to me either, but there're these people setting up camp outside who think I'm an angel and then a newspaper guy turned up, and Major Tib's offered a reward for you, so we kind of ought to move. And at least we'll be out of this building . . .'

'*What?*' said the Oldest Lion, even more confused.

Charlie didn't mean to confuse them at all, and was sorry to do so. He explained the various developments.

The Lions were perplexed.

'But we only want to leave!' said the Young Lion. 'Why has it all got so complicated? King Boris was going to help us. All we need is a boat and we can be off . . .'

Charlie sighed.

'I think Edward has other plans,' he said. 'You know when I had to measure you . . . ?'

The Oldest Lion was just about to say, Yes, he remembered, when a loud and unexpected creak split the silence of the night.

Charlie quickly exchanged looks with the Lions.

A door was opening on the far side of the *cortile*.

Charlie made a dash through the shadowy arcade for the door he had come in by. He made it. Behind him, he could hear nothing but the silence that has a person in it, where previously there had been no person.

From his familiar vantage point behind the door, Charlie peered out into the night. The moonlit *cortile* looked like a stage set. The fountain splashed. Somewhere a lone bird let out a long low note. It was very still.

The person was Edward. With him was the crumply man. Behind them were the two men from the *motoscafo*.

In their arms were piles of creamy feathers, spattered with golden eyes.

Charlie slowed his breathing right down.

The men set down the feathers, and Edward eyed the Lions. Then he turned and said suddenly, loudly, shattering the silence – 'Come on out, Charlie, we need you.'

If Charlie ever swore, he would have sworn now. As it was, he emerged from the doorway and went over. There was not much else he could do.

'Naughty boy,' said Edward, but he didn't seem too interested in that really. He had other things on his mind.

'Here,' he said. 'Take these, and put them on the wounded one.' And he gestured to the men to pass Charlie the great pile of feathers.

Charlie knew just what was wanted of him.

'OK,' he said, and, taking hold of the bundle of feathers, he stood them upright to see, finally, if they really were what he thought they were. And he was right!

The piles of feathers revealed themselves to be wings. Long, beautiful wings, plump and sleek and rich like archangels' wings, or swans' wings. Like the wings Claudio had described from the Bible. Like the wings on the stone lion outside St Mark's.

As Edward prepared to unlock the gate, Charlie held the wings up and showed them to Primo. Primo blinked lazily from within his turban, and flicked his ears to, and fro, and to again.

Charlie was murmuring under his breath as he lugged the wings into the cage. The men stood well back, scared of the Lions.

'Charlie, what's going on?' exclaimed the Young Lion. 'What's with the wings?'

'Primo?' Charlie murmured. The men mustn't notice that he was whispering. 'You understand, don't you?'

Primo gazed calmly.

'It's like that lion on the column,' said the Young Lion.

'Yes,' said Charlie, giving his friend a smile. 'They want Primo to be the ancient lion, the one we saw. The one that's the patron of Venice. I think Edward is trying to fake a miracle – to please the Doge. What do you think, Primo? Can you do it? It's the only way we're going to get out of this fortress . . . What do you think?'

Primo smiled beneath his cloth.

'And what about my, er, wound?' he said quietly. 'Will my wound please the Doge?'

Charlie smiled too. He knew Primo was talking about his teeth.

'I think your wound will fill the Doge with fear and wonder,' he said. 'May I put these on you?'

Primo bent his head a little. His sad eyes said, 'Yes.'

'My, oh my,' murmured the Young Lion.

The Oldest Lion smiled grimly.

The crumply man tried to offer advice from beyond the bars, but Charlie ignored him and worked out for himself how the wings should be attached. They were beautifully made. Long, strong, unblemished white feathers had been sewn firmly on to narrow leather strips, and the strips nailed on to a wooden and metal frame that fanned out and folded down, and was attached to another frame the shape of Primo's back. This one had been padded inside with soft thick velvet (the colour of Primo's fur), so as not to rub and hurt him. It sat high on his back like a saddle, and was fastened beneath with leather straps as a saddle would be. The men gasped when Primo lay down to make the job easier, and again when he stood up for Charlie to reach under and fasten the straps. Once the big frame was positioned on Primo's back, the wings lay smooth and curved along it.

'Wow,' said the Young Lion.

The Lionesses breathed softly. They were all used to being magnificent, but even they were impressed.

Charlie stood back. Silvered by moonlight in the old, old courtyard, Primo looked fabulous, like a mythical beast, a great ancient statue. His cloth-wrapped head gave an air of deep and peculiar mystery – evil, archaic mystery. He looked like an Egyptian death-god with the body of a lion, the wings of a swan and the head of a mummy. The men behind Charlie gasped – even Edward.

'*Magnifico*,' murmured the crumply man.

The young man crossed himself.

The crumply man was trying to tell Charlie something.

He gestured to a short leather strap that hung at Primo's breastbone, and to a small wire antenna that hung from it. Glancing at Edward first, he handed Charlie a tiny remote control.

Charlie peered at it in the dim light.

'What does it do?' he asked.

The man smiled and said something in Italian. Charlie didn't understand it all, but got the drift.

Murmuring to Primo, Charlie pointed the remote and pressed the left-hand button.

Silently, gently, the Smilodon's wings spread and rose in the moonlight, until they stood full and proud and rampant for all the world, as if Primo were about to take off in flight. He raised his paw, and growled softly. When he rippled the muscles of his great shoulders, the wings rippled too, like water under a breeze, or a swan shaking out his feathers. It was completely convincing.

'*Fantastico*,' murmured the crumply man.

'*Ostrega!*' said the young man.

The curly man was dumbstruck.

Edward smiled softly.

'Way to go, Primo,' the Young Lion murmured.

The right-hand button lowered the wings. The middle button caused them to flap gently. Primo looked exactly like a giant, living, winged lion.

'Take off the bandages,' ordered Edward. 'I need to see the full effect.'

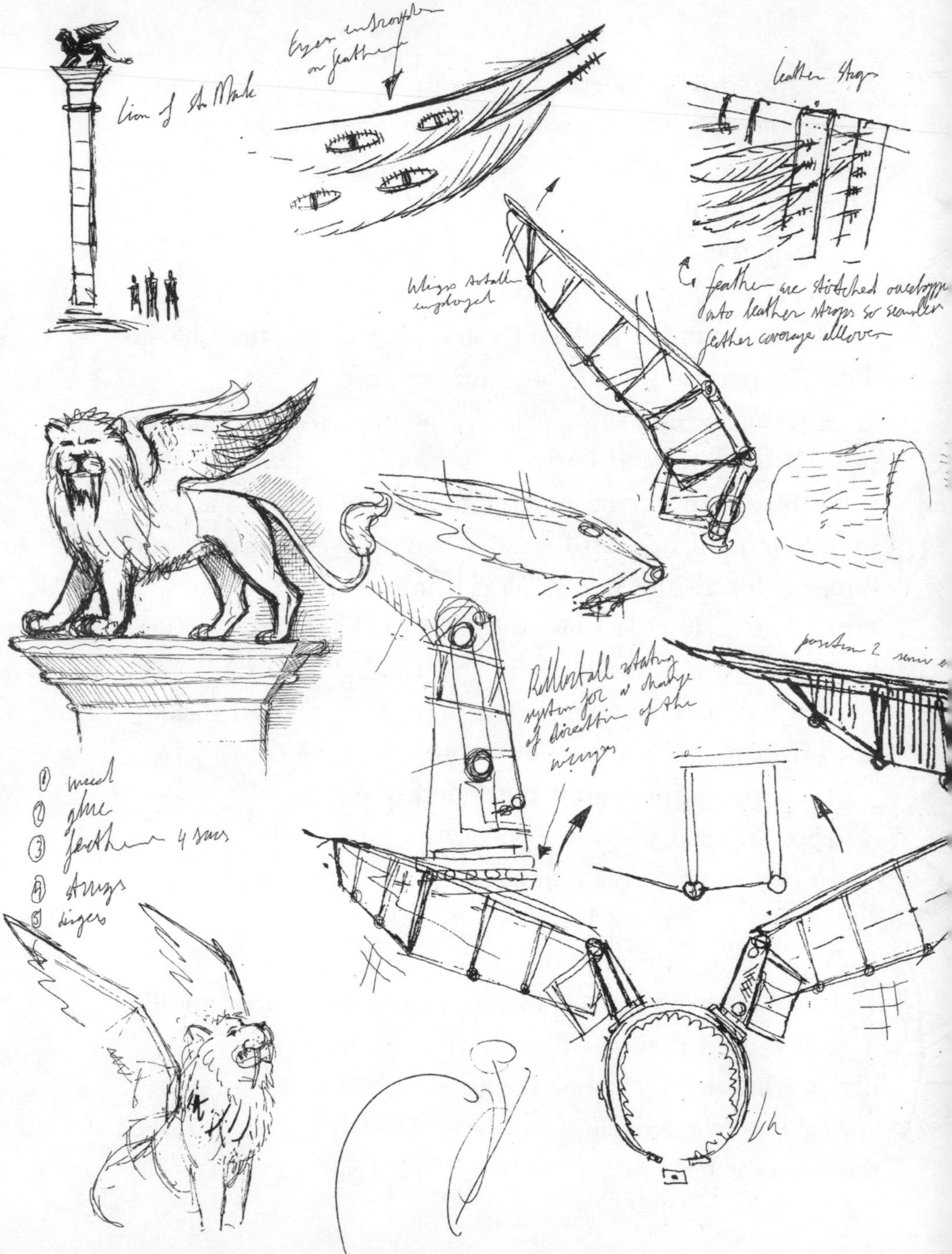
Lion of St Mark
leather straps
feather are stitched overlapping onto leather straps so smaller feather coverage allover
metal
glue

Rollerball hinge system for smooth operation while in use
fur will hide the edge of the saddle
Remote control with multifunction button control for wings positions
reinforced wooden framework on which the rods will be attached with rip stop strings
clip belt easy access
Radio receiver which is attached to the straps of the saddle

'Not yet,' said Charlie. 'His jaw is not strong enough yet.'

Edward gave Charlie a considering look.

'Really,' said Charlie. 'I'm good with ailments. Trust me.' He gave Edward a big smile.

Edward thought, and then nodded. 'OK,' he said.

Charlie knew Edward was thinking about his mother, the scientist. Did he know about her talents as a healer? How much, in fact, did Edward know about what?

At that moment a cold fear trickled into his heart and everything fell into place.

It started with a simple thought: Edward knows that my mum and dad have maybe got a cure for asthma – not just a cure for an attack, but a cure to make it go away, all over the world, forever. This was followed by: Edward is not honest. Edward is double-crossing King Boris. Edward is chumming up with the Doge by taking him this great offering of the Winged Lion . . .

And then the thoughts raced in, joining together and adding up.

What if, thought Charlie, the asthma drug companies *did* somehow make the Allergenies? What if *they* were the ones who took my mum and dad? What if they want to use them to make new things, if they want to use their skills and talents to make new illnesses that they will then be able to make new drugs for?

What if Edward is chumming up with them too? What plans might he have for *me*? He's been keeping me prisoner as much as the Lions . . . maybe he's planning to hand me over to someone for my own protection – i.e. for his own advantage. Everybody thinks I'm missing or drowned. The people who took Mum and Dad might try to use me to make Mum and Dad do things they don't want to do . . .'

All these thoughts tore through his mind and joined up to spell out one simple word: danger.

I've go to move fast, thought Charlie. The web is closing around us. I've got to get these Lions to safety and I've got to find my parents.

He was still smiling nicely at Edward. He felt sick.

'Give me the remote control,' said Edward.

Charlie looked at him, and looked at Primo.

Primo kind of winked.

Charlie handed Edward the little instrument. And the moment he did so, Primo turned to Edward, flared his yellow eyes, and began a low but unmistakable growl.

Edward flinched.

Primo growled a little louder.

Edward handed the remote control back to Charlie.

Primo smiled beneath his bindings.

Edward was relieved, but annoyed – embarrassed.

The Young Lion and Elsina stifled their smiles.

'The bandages must come off tomorrow,' Edward said, trying to reclaim his authority. 'How can we present to the Doge a bandaged-up Lion?'

*

The tunnel, the conveyor belt, the rubbish – it was all filthy and disgusting and smelt worse than anything either of the two humans had ever smelt before. Sergei, of course, was more used to it. Bliddy human softies, he thought, nibbling on a bit of fishbone.

It went on a long time too.

Magdalen threw up. It didn't really make anything more revolting because it was all so revolting anyway. Aneba said it was good because it would get some of the drugs out of her body. Magdalen said thanks very much and fell asleep. She had eggshells in her hair.

After a while, they were spewed out into the late dusk and the pale light of an early moon.

The conveyor belt was up in the air. Way beneath them was a vehicle park and recharging point lit by a low lamp. Ahead of them was the hugest pile of rubbish Aneba had ever seen. It was like a swamp of rubbish, or a moor, stretching for miles, with slopes and valleys of rough, scrappy, sludgy garbage: plastic bags flapping on top, unspeakable filth lurking below. Animals – they couldn't see what – scavenged about on the surface, lifting their feet delicately, sniffing and snuffling.

It went on as far as the horizon. The conveyor belt continued above it like a boring, stinky fairground ride. Boring, that is, until about 500 metres in, when the belt began to flex and flip like a great snake, chucking its rubbishy load off on to the vast dark pile. The smell was a hundred times worse, as the filth and detritus flew through the air, trash juice spattering about and lumps and scraps flying through the air.

It was clear where they had to jump: on the softness of the rubbish (Oh, yuck, thought Aneba) but right at the edge, before they got carried over on to the interminable plain and were chucked into revolting oblivion by the belt's bucking rodeo . . .

They roused themselves – carefully. They didn't want to fall on to the hard ground way below. The great filthy pile was approaching beneath them . . . the smell was outrageous . . . uughhh – NOW!

They leapt: man, woman and cat.

They rolled. It's better not to think about that bit.

They came to a halt at the edge. So far, so good.

Lying low, Aneba looked about. There was an old wet tea bag stuck to his ear.

Sergei peered about, then went for an innocent-looking stroll; sniffing around, checking that there was no one near.

Aneba clocked the vehicles. There was a petrol car – one of the old-fashioned ones. They were much faster than the solar vannettes and cycles. Plus they didn't get stopped by policeguys, because only important people had them.

There was no one around.

It was almost impossible to get fuel, but if there was a bit of fuel in it . . .

Many years ago, Aneba had learned to drive, and learned

how those engines worked. And how to hot-wire one when you didn't have the key.

He grabbed Magdalen's hand.

'Come on,' he said.

Two minutes later, they were on the road to Paris.

Ten minutes later, Magdalen cried out, 'Aneba! What about the cat?'

Nine minutes earlier, Sergei had stared in disbelief at the back end of the car as it disappeared without him. What were they thinking! They were meant to be super-intelligent, for crike sake! What were they doing just heading off like that, crike knows where? He was meant to be taking them to Venice! What the crike were they up to now?

'We can't go back,' said Aneba in the car. 'It's too risky.'

They'll be going to Paris, thought Sergei at the dump. Dingbats! They're just following the newspaper story, not me. He sat down on a pile of rotting banana skins and felt stupid.

He'd have to go after them and try to steer them to Venice. What a bliddy waste of time.

But then a fat whiskery brown cat rushed up to him out of the dim evening, brimming with important news, and Sergei's plans were changed again.

'The boy!' puffed the cat. 'The human boy who the Lionesses pushed in the water who was in the hospital.

He's left – he's going to get the Lionboy, the Catspeaker. Left this afternoon, going to Venice, thought you should know – my niece, anyway, in Paris thought you'd want to know, want to warn the Lionboy!'

'Dang blammit!' howled Sergei. 'Anyone'd think I didn't have a life of my own to lead!'

But as his own life consisted largely of eating, getting into arguments and wondering why things weren't more exciting, he was pretty happy really to send the brown cat back to Paris ('Follow those humans! Don't lose them!') and set off himself to Venice to tell Charlie that Rafi was out.

He only wished he were taking Aneba and Magdalen with him.

CHAPTER EIGHT

When the wings had been put away, and the men had left, and even Edward had gone to bed, Charlie sat at the window overlooking the piazza and pondered his situation.

They would have to go to the Doge. There was no way out. He had been searching this building for days, and there was no escape route. Plus the Lions were locked up and Edward was extremely careful with the key. He knew that Charlie and the Lions had already escaped from the Circus and he was taking no chances. Plus now there were all these people outside. He glanced over at them. Even in the middle of the night, there were a few holding vigil with their candles. Charlie was really annoyed. How could he get to talk to Enzo again if he couldn't wait in the window and let Enzo see that he was there?

He held his face in the shadow, glad that he wasn't white. White faces catch moonlight and reflect back. He and his dark face could hide while he thought and watched out for Enzo.

Security at the Doge's was likely to be just as tight, if not tighter. So, could they escape on the way to the Doge's?

The moon shone palely down on the piazza, and Charlie began to make a list in his mind, a rough list of questions and ideas.

1) How to get away without being seen?
2) A boat to get to Africa.
3) Or overland? No, too complicated, too many people. They'd have to go via Italy, but the Circus was going to be in Italy, and then they'd have to get a boat anyway at the other end of the contrary . . . If they took a boat all the way they could just hide.
4) They could hire a boat! With crew, paid to keep quiet.
5) Where would they get the money?
6) Why hadn't King Boris written back?
7) Food, preparations, all those things – navigation, sailing.
8) Boat, boat, boat.

Oh, but all of that was pointless. All of that was for the Lions, not for him.

He didn't know where his parents were, therefore he didn't know where he needed to go.

He thought about this all night, and all of the next day. He thought about it when he snuck down to see the Lions, but he didn't want to talk about it with them. He could talk about plans in general, of course, but even with the Young Lion it seemed disloyal somehow to bring up his longing for his parents.

Until the Young Lion himself brought it up.

'Charlie,' he murmured, 'don't you miss them terribly?'

Charlie knew at once who he was talking about. 'Yes,' he said.

'But you are planning all the time to carry on helping us, rather than to go after them . . . You are very loyal to us.'

Charlie smiled. 'We have an agreement,' he said. 'We'll help each other.'

'You're doing all the helping,' said the Young Lion. 'Don't think I haven't noticed.'

'You helped get rid of Rafi, you helped get me to the train on time . . . Anyway, it's not like that . . .' Charlie was a bit embarrassed to talk about it directly.

'Hmm,' said the Young Lion. 'Personally, I think we owe you a lot. And I think we need to think about your parents too.'

Charlie thought about them in bed that night, wishing that Julius was asleep on a bunk above him. Julius knew so much, he would have been able to help. But he had never been able to tell the truth to Julius, because he was a circus-boy and would not have understood about how the Lions had to escape. That didn't stop Charlie from missing him, though. He wondered if he would ever see Julius again.

He thought about it when he heard Claudio singing, and when he leaned out of the window to wave to him, and Claudio waved back.

Most of all he thought about it by the back window, because that was where Enzo would come. But it was hard: one morning a television crew had appeared, planning to await the next manifestation of the Brown Angel. 'Medicine falls from the sky like manna from heaven!' a small child told them. They stood around with their cameras and their long furry arm for talking into. They wore sunglasses and smoked cigarettes, and made comments about the girls who passed by. They laughed a lot. They were having a lovely time. They didn't go away.

Then finally at lunchtime, when the sun was at its highest and the heat began to beat down, the TV guys went off to find a cool café where they could eat. Charlie's fans moved their deckchairs into the shade and settled down for their midday snoozes. Silence spread over the piazza like melting butter.

Charlie sat in the shade of his window, and waited. And after a while, he snoozed too.

He was woken by a kerfuffle. The fatter cats, the lazy slobs who lay around all day, were all in a circle, hissing, arching their backs like a ring of outraged semicircles. Charlie could hear their vicious little noises, and see them striking out with sharp cat claws. They had someone in the middle, and they were ganging up again.

Charlie was surprised. In recent days there had been hardly any Allergenies about. It was as if they had learned that they weren't welcome here, and had decided to stay away. Charlie hadn't liked that.

Charlie knew his history. He knew about times and places where black people had been turned away from cafés and restaurants, schools and buses, hotels and hospitals, jobs and churches, because they were black. He knew that not so long ago there were places where he and his own mother wouldn't have been allowed to go together, because they had different-coloured skin. He knew that black people had been beaten up and punished by bullies, just for trying to go to work, or to college – for trying to lead their lives. It really really hurt him to think about those things.

That same pain in his heart told him that these cats had no right to bully the Allergenies, no right to try to keep whoever was in the middle of that circle out of the piazza.

There was a cry of cat pain from the middle of the circle.

Without thinking about it, without even remembering that he was meant to be hiding, Charlie lost his temper. He jumped up on to the window ledge and roared across the canal. He roared in Cat, but his accent was Lion. He roared threat and danger and warning to the bully cats. He roared that he had seen enough, that he would take no more, that they were to leave, NOW, and if they returned they would have him to deal with. In the silence of the Venetian midday, his roar was shattering.

The bully cats turned, and froze, and then like water drops from a circling hose they scattered and disappeared, terrified out of their wits by this roaring human Lion.

The fans of the Brown Angel woke with a start from their siestas, just in time to see the Brown Angel making like a mad devil in his window. '*E' l'angelo!*' someone yelled. '*Guardate! L'angelo!*' Look, the angel!

But before they could gather their wits, he was gone again. At the sight of them all goggling up at him, he had remembered that roaring out of windows was really not a sensible and discreet way for a boy to behave if he doesn't want anyone to know where he is.

He squatted down under the window ledge, in the cool dark beside the wall, and cursed himself for being so wild.

After a moment, a mangy furry head poked through the old salty, rusty iron bars above him.

''Ello,' said a rustly feline voice with a strong Wigan accent. 'There you are. I've been lookin' for yer, and then you apparate just at the right moment. That was excessively useful timing – thanks, mate. Can yer sew?'

Charlie looked up. It was a scrawny, mouldy-looking black cat, with bald patches on its bottom and milky-looking blue eyes. It was the kind of cat you wouldn't want to stroke in case it had fleas, or worse. Charlie was so pleased to see him he nearly hugged him. He stopped himself just in time, realizing that a) Sergei might not like it and b) he didn't look that well.

'Sergei!' he squeaked. 'Sergei! How are you? Where've you been? What's the news? Tell me everything! What do you mean "sew"?'

Sergei made himself exceptionally long and thin, and squeezed through the iron bars.

'I mean, I've already lost most of one ear and I'd like to keep the majority of the other, if it's all the same to you, so if you can sew, you could just go and get yer sewing kit and embroider my poor little aural protuberance back into its right and proper location,' he said. 'It's on the ledge there. 'Ad to drop it so I could talk to yer.'

Charlie stood up and peered carefully out of the window on to the stone ledge. There lay a sad little flap of black fur, with tiny speckles of blood along the edge.

It didn't look nearly big or tough enough to sew back on. He knew, too, that when things were sewn back on, the blood vessels had to be matched up, so the blood could keep flowing. Without blood-flow, the flesh would just die.

This poor little ear didn't really . . .

He looked at Sergei.

Sergei looked at him. For such a mangy scruffy old cat, he looked very perky and hopeful.

Sergei, who'd brought the letter from his parents when

he hadn't had to, who'd taken Charlie's letter back to them even though it was in completely the wrong direction. Sergei, who was here again, who had looked for him and found him . . . He really wanted to help him.

Sergei, who had told him his parents were in Venice when, apparently, they were not!

'Sergei!' he said. 'Are my parents here or what? You said Venice – at least the Lions said you said Venice – but Edward says . . .'

Sergei's eyes were looking milkier than ever.

Charlie looked at the ear again. It looked bad.

'OK,' he said. 'Tell me everything when I've sorted this out. Wait here.' He ran upstairs, grateful once again for the silence of stone floors, and grabbed from his room a tiny bottle, and flew downstairs again.

Two drops of his mother's Improve Everything Lotion, one on the bloody edge of the limp little ear and one on poor Sergei's tattered stump. Hold them together carefully . . . there now . . .

Sergei was trying to peer round sideways to see the side of his own head.

'Keep still!' ordered Charlie. 'I need to hold it in place . . . Stop wriggling.'

'What are yer doing? What's that?' Sergei said doubtfully, his nose all wrinkled up. 'What's that muck yer applying on me? Is that lotion? Lotion's not going to help, yer need to sew it . . .'

But the lotion did help. Ten seconds later Sergei was wriggling his ear, and saying, 'I don't believe that. I mean, that's not physically possible. That can't happen, that. I don't know what you've done. I don't know what that lotion is. That's a crikin' marvel. Look! I can twitch it!' And he did. Which was when Charlie noticed that it was on a bit wonky . . . but he didn't mention it, because frankly Sergei was such a mess anyway that it didn't show up much.

'Anyway,' said Sergei. 'My *apologias* that I couldn't get here earlier. I was attempting to avoid those detrital graspoles in that square, swanning around like they own the place and not letting people pass,' said Sergei. 'Despicable. Yeah, well, hello. Now we're finally here. Right.'

He fixed Charlie with his blue eyes. 'Yer mum and dad aren't, after all, in the vicinity. I said they would be and they're not and I'm sorry for that. I was wrongly informed. What happened is this: from Paris, they were escorted to Vence in the south of France.'

'The south of France!' screeched Charlie.

'They're all right,' continued Sergei. 'Their resistance is strong and in a way they were safe there. But there was a degree of re-education going on, which tough though they are was . . . effects were being had . . . Well, they're not there now.'

'So where are they now?' Charlie asked.

'On the way to Paris in a stolen petrolcar.'

Charlie's jaw actually dropped. He felt it. Quickly he closed his mouth again.

Paris? Stolen car?

'Did they get my letter?'

'Yeah,' said Sergei. 'And I gave 'em a news story to read, and . . . em . . . I was about to accompany them down here and deliver them in person to their esteemed offspring. But they, em, took off for Paris . . .'

'So I should go back to Paris,' said Charlie.

'Don't you even think about it!' shrieked Sergei. 'Paris is full of those circus people and police and all kinds, and . . . you probably want to know – well, you probably don't, actually, but you need to – your detrital homeboy has removed himself from hospital and is proceeding in this direction, with the intention of causing a pest of himself again, as usual . . .'

This was all rather too much information for Charlie. He blinked a couple of times.

'But are they all right?' he said in a small voice.

'Your parents? Far as I know, they're getting better all the time. Well enough to nick a car.'

Charlie shook his head. Stealing!

He really really wanted to go to where they were. He could feel it tugging at him like a rope through his heart.

'What's the set-up here, then?' asked Sergei.

Charlie swiftly filled him in – and as he went over it he realized there was indeed no way he could leave and return to Paris now. He'd never even make it out of the house. And anyway – he couldn't desert the Lions.

Not even for his parents?

No. He wouldn't desert his parents for the Lions, and he wouldn't desert the Lions for his parents.

Sergei listened carefully, and then they sat in silence for a while, pondering.

'So what are you going to do?' asked Sergei.

'Tomorrow we're all being taken to the Doge in his palace. One good thing – be harder for Rafi to track us down there. Then, god knows. We'll have to escape.'

Escape. There was the thing. The Big Thing.

'Yer doing a great job with the Lions,' Sergei said. 'And it's great yer lookin' after the Smilodon. How is 'e? Is 'e all right?'

'He's fine,' said Charlie. 'Sad, but well.'

'Yeah. 'E 'ould be. Anyway, everyone's delighted you've hitched up because, well, yer know, they'd heard about what was going on and everyone was really disgusted and upset about it, but no one really thought he'd survive, so now he 'as, it's just as well for all of us that 'e's escaped and got together with *you* –'

'Hang on a minute,' said Charlie. 'What? About the Smilodon?'

'It's great 'e's with you and that 'e's, you know, all right,' said Sergei.

'Yes, but what was that about hearing what was going

on? What *was* going on? What are you saying about him surviving?'

Sergei gave Charlie a fairly serious look.

'Yer know who he is, don't yer?' the cat asked.

'Yes. He's a *Smilodon fatalis*. The Oldest Lion named him Primo,' said Charlie.

'But yer know where he came from?'

'Do you?' said Charlie, suddenly completely eager. 'Where did he come from? We found him in Paris, near the Natural History Museum, and he told us what he could remember but . . .' Charlie fell silent at the memory of the Smilodon's miserable story.

'He doesn't know?' said Sergei, shocked.

'No,' said Charlie.

Sergei looked at his feet for a moment, then began to wash his ears.

'Well?' said Charlie.

Sergei's tail flicked: left, right, left again.

Charlie just kept on looking at him with his inquiring look.

Sergei looked up.

'You ever see that old film,' Sergei began carefully, 'where they got bits of old dinosaur DNA and . . .' His voice ran to a halt.

'Where they re-created extinct creatures. Cloned them or something,' said Charlie.

'Yeah,' said Sergei.

Charlie sat in silence for a moment.

'Is that how Primo . . .' Charlie didn't know how to put it. How Primo was born? How he was made?

'Yeah,' said Sergei

'Oh,' said Charlie quietly. Suddenly the world seemed much bigger.

They were silent for a moment or two.

'It's despicable, that kind of cloning,' said Sergei, 'and it's forbidden, an' all. Some cleverclogs might manage to make something, but then it goes wrong, and the animals just suffer and die. But there was one graspole scientist at the Natural History Museum who took it upon 'imself, who decided 'e was God . . .'

'Why did he do it?' asked Charlie. He didn't have to ask why it was forbidden – that, to him, was obvious. It was too unnatural, and the results – like Primo – would be sick, and lonely, with no family, and no history. It was cruel to create creatures. Creatures needed to be born.

'He was curious,' said Sergei.

Poor, poor Primo. No wonder he felt that he didn't exist, or . . . oh, all those confusing things he had said. Poor beautiful Primo.

And tomorrow he was going to be dolled up in fake wings to be presented to the Doge.

'Does Edward know who he is? How he was . . . how he came to be?' Charlie asked suddenly.

'NO!' screeched Sergei. 'And it is entirely necessary

that he doesn't ever know, not him, not nobody! The cats are fully acquainted with the whole shadoodle but the humans know nothing. What Primo needs is a safe secret location that he can inhabit, protected by good tough cats. Otherways, the humans will just want to do experiments on him, all the time, forever! They can't leave things alone. It's not in their nature.'

Charlie took a deep breath.

Should he try to stop Primo from being sent to the Doge? Should they try to get away tonight?

But how could they? How could they possibly?

He sighed. What a mess.

One other thing was bothering him.

'Sergei,' said Charlie, 'who had my parents? I worked out it might be the asthma drug people. Was it?'

Sergei looked at him. How much should he tell him?

'Because I've been thinking – about the asthma drug people – how they might want my parents to make things and to work for them – I don't know if I'm right but I was thinking, if the asthma drug people made the Allergenies somehow, then . . .'

At that very moment Charlie had a realization. Of course! How come he hadn't realized long ago!

'Sergei!' he cried. 'You're an Allergenie, aren't you?'

Sergei stared. Stiffened. His milky eyes hardened and his wonky ear twitched back and forth.

'So what?' he spat.

Then: 'So what?' he cried again. 'What do you care? You of all people –'

Sergei glared: furious and hurt. And then suddenly he was gone – out of the window, down a gutter, over the wall, slinking under the bridge by the deep and dark canal.

'Sergei!' called Charlie, jumping up. 'Sergei! I didn't mean – Sergei, come back! Come back!'

But he was gone.

Charlie clutched the iron bars. He was dumbstruck. Then mortified. He hadn't meant to offend Sergei. He hadn't realized that Sergei would take it like that. Oh no . . .

'Sergei!' he howled again, down towards the canal.

Oh no, oh no, oh no.

To have this friendly face appear so unexpectedly, bringing information and the possibility of help, had been wonderful. To have it disappear again, even more unexpectedly and over so foolish a misunderstanding, was almost unbearable. Charlie lay awake much of the night thinking about it, and by early the next morning he had made a decision.

He and the Lions couldn't go on like this, waiting around for things to be done to them. They – he – had to act, before they were carted off and imprisoned in an even grander cage. They needed an ally. And that meant they had to take a risk.

If anybody had been watching, they might have seen Charlie waiting behind the iron grille over one of the ground-floor windows. They would have thought he was just hanging around, as he usually did, and they would have thought nothing of his greeting the unshaven young gondolier who passed that way, as he did most mornings, singing his mournful, beautiful gondolier song.

'Claudio,' Charlie called, 'hi there.'

Claudio looked over. He seemed to notice that Charlie's greeting today had a different air, and brought his boat a little closer in. 'How are you?' he called.

Charlie waited till he was quite close. Now or never. Did he trust him? He had to.

He bit his lip, and looked Claudio full in the face.

'Not good,' he called quietly.

'How not good?' Claudio responded, his voice low too.

Charlie made a quick gesture and the shining black gondola drew in close by the palazzo wall. Claudio came to the bow to be nearer Charlie, fiddling with a rope as he did so.

'Did you post my letter to King Boris?' Charlie hissed.

'Of course,' said Claudio quietly. 'Have you not had an answer? Posts are slow . . .'

'I can't wait!' blurted Charlie. 'King Boris said he would help me to get the Lions to Africa and now Edward is saying we must go and stay at the Doge's Palace, and –'

'The Doge's Palace!' exclaimed Claudio, then swiftly shushed himself. 'Why?'

'I don't know!' said Charlie. 'That's the problem . . . We just want to get on our way, but Edward has got these wings, and I think he's . . .'

'Wings!' said Claudio.

'For the Lions – for Primo. He's making him into the Lion of St Mark and taking him to the Doge . . . He's going to fake a miracle, like you told us about . . .'

Claudio looked aghast.

'He is giving the Lion of St Mark to that stupid, greedy, wicked . . .' Suddenly he remembered himself, and looked over his shoulder to make sure nobody was near. 'Charlie,' he said, 'this is terrible.'

'But Primo isn't the Lion of St Mark . . .' said Charlie.

'Doesn't matter,' said Claudio. 'Listen.' He dropped his voice very low and talked very fast. 'The Doge is a bad man – he is so grand and important he forgets to do his own job, which is to run the city well for the people. He takes no notice of the people. He spends all the money on himself, while the hospital is falling down. He changes the law without asking, and when people protest he sends his policeguys to take them away. He owns all the newspapers, all the television, and makes them say all the time he is brilliant. He even made a law against making rude gestures at his boat – because every time he went out everybody was making rude gestures at his boat. Because everybody hates him. Hates him. Just the other day, he –' Claudio stopped himself. His face was hard.

'Oh,' said Charlie. Now he *really* didn't want to go and be locked up in this guy's palace.

'If he gets these Lions,' murmured Claudio, shaking his head, 'it can't be for good. Not good for the Lions or for Venezia.'

'So will you help us?' Charlie asked.

Claudio tightened his lips, and thought. Finally he said, 'You will be helping us, Lionboy. I have an idea.' He took a deep breath, and Charlie felt that he too was making a big decision.

Claudio gave Charlie a stern look. 'Are you brave, Charlie?'

Charlie stood a little straighter. He knew by now that he was brave.

'Yeah,' he said coolly.

'Then we will talk later today,' said Claudio. 'The time has come. Good. Yes. We will speak.'

And he was off, with a twist of his oar and a swirl of water beneath his boat.

Wow, thought Charlie. Now what had he let them in for?

Far away, in a small town on the Barbary Coast of Morocco, somebody else was watching a boat. On the shady terrace of a café on a square overlooking a harbour, a man sat, wearing a burnoose, its hood down on his shoulders, as the day was pleasant. He looked a little like an off-duty monk, but his thoughts were far from godly. He was drinking a small cup of sweet, very good coffee, and alongside it a glass of water with something – some drops – added.

I believe they will come by boat, he was thinking.

His expression was a little sleepy.

They will come by boat, and then I will get them.

He had been sitting for days, just thinking this.

After an hour or so, the man was joined by another man, brown and wiry, with a country look to him, and a leather bag on his back containing some unpleasant implements: a long fork with two prongs, good for pinning something down by the neck; a small grey gun for shooting darts with; the darts themselves, long and nasty and containing drugs that, when they pierce the skin, send a creature to sleep; ropes, chains, a big whip.

The two men talked, smiling quietly and coming to an agreement. The sleepy man – yes, it was Maccomo – gave the countryman a little money.

Finally they shook hands, touching their fists each to the other's heart. They had made a deal.

Behind them, on a bowing branch of a small tree that adorned the terrace, a swivel-eyed chameleon watched the man who watched for the boat, and the man with the nasty bag. He was as green as the leaves among which he sat, as quiet as the branch he clutched with his four-toed feet, as secretive as the men he was observing. He swivelled his eyes, one east, one west.

His name was Ninu. He noticed everything, and nobody noticed him.

CHAPTER NINE

Claudio was right about the Doge being grand. Later, he told Charlie just how grand.

'Each year,' he said, 'for many centuries, the Doge of the time would go out in the *Bucintoro*, his big golden barge, and marry the sea. He'd throw it a golden ring, and so the sea would promise to Love, Honour and Obey the Doge and Venice. The Doge and Venice ruled the sea the way, in the old days, a husband ruled his wife. But now, you can see what the sea did to Venice: sucked out the roots, drowned it bit by bit. So the Doge is afraid as well. His wife has turned on him. He is nervous about the sea.'

What Claudio didn't know was that some years before Charlie was born, the *Anna Maria*, a ship belonging to King Boris, had sunk in the Gulf of Venice. Much to the Doge's annoyance, King Boris had not been able to have it removed immediately (his marine reclamationguy was getting married that week and King Boris hadn't wanted to disturb him). As a result, several Venetian ships bashed into the

Bulgarian shipwreck. The Doge said it was an outrage to leave this dangerous wreck lying about. King Boris said the Venetian ships should look where they were going. The Doge said King Boris was to have the wreck of the *Anna Maria* removed IMMEDIATELY. King Boris said it would take months, as the ship was laden with extremely delicate and precious crystal. The Doge said, *Really?* and announced the next day that as the ship was in Venetian waters it was now Venetian property. King Boris said the Doge was a thieving old pirate. The Doge said King Boris was to take that back, and sent his own reclamationguys to start working on the ship, diving down with cushioned baskets to bring the valuable crystal bowls and plates up in, one at a time to keep them safe. King Boris said the Doge was hated by his people anyway, and stealing a load of Bulgarian treasure wasn't going to make them love him. The Doge said that King Boris was speaking mighty freely for someone so scared of assassination. King Boris said it would take a better ruler than a thieving old Dogey-poo to assassinate *him*.

The night he said that, a great storm blew up, scattering the ships of the Venetian reclamationguys, drowning six of them and burying the *Anna Maria* and her cargo several metres deep in mud. King Boris said, 'Gosh, your wife's really angry with you, isn't she?'

(He was sorry later that he'd said that, especially because of the guys who had died. None of it was their fault.)

Anyway, the Doge and King Boris did not get along.

Edward felt it would be a good idea if they did. Arguments are so tiring. Bad feeling is so depressing. It is so much more useful for a country to have lots of friends and allies to support them, rather than enemies who will louse things up for them – as the Doge always did, at the slightest opportunity.

So when Edward, as the representative of King Boris, applied to visit the Doge, the Doge was curious. Particularly when Edward said he would like to bring something for the Doge. About time, thought the Doge. King Boris is going to apologize, and I'll get a present. It had better be good.

Thus it was that late that night Edward called Charlie once again to the *cortile* and required him to dress Primo in his artificial wings.

'And these,' said Edward. He handed him a pile of leather and chains.

Charlie's heart fluttered with anger when he saw what it was – collars and leashes. He'd got rid of the circus collars back on the train. Now this!

'It is necessary,' said Edward peaceably. 'His Grace would be frightened if we brought him Lions unleashed. Do not be insulted. I know your control over them is miraculous.' And he smiled.

Charlie smiled back – a little thin smile. The Lions flashed their eyes at him and he could read what they meant exactly. 'There'd better not be too much more of this!'

they were saying. 'We'll wear them for now but the point of this whole escapade is ESCAPE and FREEDOM!'

As Charlie put the leads – scarlet leather, with beautiful strong silver chains – around his friends' strong furry necks, he murmured words of apology and explanation in their ears.

'It's not for long,' he said. 'There's a plan. Don't worry. We'll be on our way soon.'

'There'd better be,' muttered the Young Lion.

The leads were stupid anyway: if the Lions had decided to run away, they could have broken them in seconds – bitten through them, ripped them, ignored them. But if the Lions ran away, where could they go? Major Tib had the police looking for them across Europe, Rafi was out and on the prowl, god only knew where Maccomo was – and everybody else would be looking too, because of the reward. They would be followed, chased, cornered, or worse . . . Charlie knew that only sheer cleverness could help them now.

'I don't think the bandages matter,' said Charlie conversationally, as he and Edward surveyed the Lions. 'They just show that the Lion has been wounded. Like Venice. As the Lion heals, so Venice will heal. It's a good omen. They'll love it.'

Edward looked at him sharply.

'Don't you think?' said Charlie. 'And really, the longer we leave it on, the better his jaw will be in the long run. We can take it off later.'

Edward, knowing perfectly well that no one but Charlie would be taking the bandages off anyway, decided to agree.

Charlie felt cold as he and the Lions were ushered out of the back door. He made sure to greet Claudio only briefly as the Lions poured into the depths of the gondola that was waiting on the small canal alongside the palazzo. It was dark and quiet down below on the canal, but way above ragged clouds scudded quickly across the sky, and the waning moon appeared and disappeared behind them. Charlie and the Lions immediately perked up. They were outside!

Scarcely a splash disturbed the night as Claudio rowed them quietly out on to the Grand Canal and turned to the east. Charlie admired the great white dome of the church called the Salute, held up by its big coiling snail twirls, but he looked away before the ruin of San Giorgio Maggiore slid into view behind it. Looking out over Venice, of which he had seen practically nothing that could not be seen from the windows of his prison palazzo, he wondered at it. The famous beautiful city gleamed in the intermittent moonlight, her domes and porticoes like ghosts under the pale, flickering light. The gondola moved on silently, and the cold, dark smell of the canal rose up out of the darkness. It was late, and few lights were on across the city. The great bell of St Mark's, the Marangona, rang out. It sounded peculiar in the night air. One o'clock.

Charlie shivered. The Lions eyed him from the bottom

of the boat. Only Edward seemed relaxed. He lit a small cigar, and the hardly perceptible hiss and crackle as he smoked it added to the tiny noises of the night. Alongside them slid black water and the pale palazzi of the Grand Canal.

When they drew up by the Doge's Palace, Charlie recognized the two tall columns, one of which had the bronze, agate-eyed statue of the Lion of St Mark on top. Claudio said nothing as he pulled in, but Charlie noticed him glance up at the Lion and down at Primo, and saw his eyes flicker with intelligence.

The black covered cart was waiting for them again, with the four men – Charlie assumed they worked for Edward – to pull it. The Lions slid in. The Young Lion flicked his tail quite hard against Charlie's legs as he went, as if to remind him that their patience was not infinite. Elsina gave Charlie one last, desperate look as she slid from view, and he felt once again the strong pang: they are depending on me. I promised them. The cart looked too much like something that might go to a funeral.

Charlie looked back at Claudio.

Almost invisibly, his fair hair gleaming in the moonlight, Claudio winked one of his sea-blue Venetian eyes. Charlie felt a little better.

Edward was striding ahead. A man in a suit, accompanied by four men in uniform, had come forward to meet him.

Behind them loomed the Doge's Palace, the great pink building layered with arcades and balconies, columns all in a row.

Edward greeted the man, ignored the soldiers, and moved swiftly round to the left, under the arcade, ushering the cart along with him. He didn't want to lose sight of it for a moment. Glancing up at the columns as he rounded the corner, Charlie saw that each one was carved with leaves or vines or animals or heads: lions' heads, mostly. Hurrying on, Charlie kept pace with the adults. As he caught up with them, Edward took him firmly by the arm and smiled down at him.

'Come along,' he said, as if he were an uncle taking Charlie to the fair.

Charlie tried to smile back.

To their left was the huge piazza that they had glimpsed on their way from the station. Near them at its edge sprang the enormous bell tower: way way up above them a spotlight picked out the Marangona, and beneath it a stone lion, winged, holding his book. They passed a massive wooden flagpole: a moonbeam caught it, lighting up a winged lion on its base. Ahead of them was the clock tower: a golden lion shone from its vivid blue frontage, wings and book standing proud. At its feet were two roaring lions carved from red marble. To their right was the great gateway through which Charlie and the Lions were to pass: above it, in pride of place, a great stone lion, with wings, holding the book.

As they approached the gateway, Charlie saw something that gave him a curious feeling deep inside. On the corner of the building ahead of them – a side wall of St Mark's Cathedral, covered with an inlaid pattern of marble – stood two men, hugging each other. They were statues, he realized almost immediately, very old, made of some dark, polished stone, set right back against the wall – but looking at them, he saw that they were not just dark in colour. They were black. The one on the right, specially: worn though his nose was, it was a broad nose – an African nose. His mouth too was full and curved like an African mouth. Yes, and the one to the left too – he was black.

Charlie smiled. These two black men, ancient warriors in their old carved stone armour, filled him with courage. It made him feel that he was a man, and his father was hugging him. It made him feel brave and proud, and it was with that feeling in his heart that he approached the huge gateway in front of him.

The gateway was studded with carved lions' heads – fifty, sixty of them, or more. Each had a subtly different expression. They were the same lion, but somehow not. Everywhere he looked, Charlie could see the figure of the winged lion. All that Claudio had told him about Venetians loving lions was reflected in this building. Well, Charlie just hoped they loved them enough and in the right way, because he and the Lions were never going to get out of this palace if they didn't.

The massive wooden door in the gateway creaked open for them and slid shut swiftly after they passed through. Looking back, Charlie saw the great metal bars and rivets that criss-crossed the back of the door, the massive bolts, the heavy black locks bigger than his father's hands.

Then he turned round to see where they were.

To his right was a huge, wide, pale arcaded courtyard, dimly lit by the transient moon and a few gas-lamps. The lampposts had lions carved on them. The walls were fantastically carved: figures on pinnacles against the dim blue night, lions' heads and more lions' heads, round windows with fancy tracery, rows and rows of pointed Gothic arches. Directly ahead was an enormous staircase. Two gigantic figures stood on either side of a doorway at the top: two great half-naked stone men, ten metres high, strong as gods and motionless in the moonlight. Above the doorway was a massive stone lion, with wings, holding the book.

Charlie breathed his special don't-get-asthma breath. He was frightened – he couldn't deny it, he was very frightened. This place stank of wealth and power, and bound up with it was this image of the lion.

It became apparent that they were to climb the enormous staircase. Edward was disputing: Charlie could tell he didn't want to let the Lions out of the cart yet, but the man in the suit was insisting. Charlie supposed that the Doge wasn't going to come out into this *cortile*, any more than he would come round to someone else's palazzo. No doubt he just sits on a throne, being honoured all day and all night . . . ridiculous, thought Charlie, and the thought made him feel braver.

Edward and the suited man had come to an agreement. The suited man spoke to the uniformed men, Edward handed each of them a dark scarf, and they proceeded to wrap the scarves round each other's heads as blindfolds.

'*Anche Lei*,' said Edward to the suited man. You too.

The man protested.

Edward lit another small cigar, and just looked at him.

It was a strange scene. The tip of the cigar glowed bright and orange as Edward sucked on it. Everything else was silvered and white. The high wind had blown the clouds away.

The courtyard was exceptionally beautiful.

The man in the suit swore. Edward offered him a dark scarf, and helped him to tie it, fixing it firmly. Then he took him by the arm.

'Let them out, Charlie,' said Edward.

Charlie looked to Claudio, and together they opened the side of the cart. The Lions slipped out, a stream of golden fur in the silvery moonlight, lean and long and so beautiful that even Charlie, who knew them so well, had to gasp. They roiled around him like a whirlpool of muscle and fur. The blindfolded men stood, nervous, unsure. One of them spoke, asking a question, but Edward, a look of fascinated terror on his face, swiftly shushed him.

Charlie was murmuring softly to the Lions as he took the leads, apologizing under his breath. But there were too many leads for Charlie to hold. The Lions would have tripped over each other. So Charlie offered the Lionesses and Elsina to Claudio, who, with an expression of stunned amazement and delight, took them, two in each hand. The Lionesses looked up at him. The Bronze Lioness kind of meowed, letting him know it was all right. The blindfolded men shifted uneasily when they heard the noise, and Claudio held the leads as if – well, as if they were made of silver, and had Lionesses at the other end.

Edward gave Claudio an amused look. 'Better get used to them,' he murmured.

'Of course, sir,' said Claudio. But when Edward turned his attention back to the stairs, Claudio turned to Charlie and winked. Elsina pulled a little on her lead and he looked at her. She flicked her ears at him. He gasped. Charlie could have sworn that Elsina smiled.

And so the strange party started to climb the huge wide staircase, under the gaze of the huge stone gods and the ever-present, never-moving lion. The Lions on their leashes lead the young brown boy and the long blond Venetian boatman; Edward, pale and wary, and the gang of blindfolded flunkeys, feeling their way, clutching the balustrade, tripping and flinching, desperately nervous about whatever it was that they were not allowed to see. Whatever it was – whatever *they were* – that breathed, and padded, and made mewling noises.

Even the steps were decorated: vines and leaves inlaid. Looking back, Charlie saw the domes of St Mark's rising against the night sky, like desert tents, or great fat beetles. The people on pinnacles seemed to be staring down at him as he followed Edward and the man in the suit through the doorway and right along the wide, arch-sided balcony overlooking the courtyard.

At the end of the balcony he could see where it met another balcony along the front of the palazzo. Beyond, through the dark silhouette made by those arches, across the pavement and across the water, he could just make out the floodlit ruins of San Giorgio Maggiore.

Gosh, he thought, it's really near. He wondered where the Doge had been when the great storm came and swept away his neighbouring island. Had he sat here, watching the sea swirl around the feet of his palace, wondering if he too was going to be swept away?

Suddenly he remembered the stilt-houses on the Thames, at home; how he had admired them as he came downriver on the policeguy's boat. It seemed a lifetime ago.

But then they turned left through a doorway, and up another staircase. The ceiling was iced in gold ('It's real gold,' hissed Claudio, when he saw Charlie staring), with paintings and statues fixed into it. And then they were led through enormous room after enormous magnificent room, dimly lit, their corners lost in shadow.

'These are the Doge's private apartments,' murmured Claudio.

'What are his public ones like, then?' squeaked Charlie, as they crossed a long chamber whose walls were all painted with maps. In the centre of the room were two massive globes, each considerably taller then Charlie; above them two enormous but delicate chandeliers, crispy and white like sugar.

The next room was lined with yellow silk, with a tall stone fireplace and on it a winged lion, and a baby angel riding a dolphin. The firelight flickered and gleamed on the walls. The next had a large dark painting of a black boy in turquoise and yellow tights offering something to a lot of old white men on red chairs, seated at a table. The fireplace, again, bore a lion.

More ornate corridors.

More fabulous chambers.

And then they came to the room in which the Doge was waiting for them. Edward, the man in the suit, and half the guards went in first. The man in the suit took off his blindfold as he went in, not caring now if Edward told him not to.

He didn't turn round, though. He's really afraid, Charlie thought. He's more afraid than he is curious.

Charlie peered through the gap between the door and the frame. Inside, just sitting there, he saw an old, tired-looking man in a deep-red robe and a small cap, on a throne of gold and red velvet, flanked by a couple of equally old-looking advisers, also in red. His face was wrinkly and his mouth was mean. So that was what a Doge looked like.

Edward was preparing him. 'We have for you, Your Grace, something quite extraordinary, quite magnificent and, if I may say so, extremely politically useful,' he was saying. 'We can give you something that can give Venice back to you. Your people – forgive my directness – do not love you. As you well know. This gift will make them love you. It will tell them that Venice is no longer cursed. All the bad luck will leave. And everybody will vote for you because you have lifted the curse. Anybody who speaks against you will be speaking against the great blessing you have brought them. You will be able to do anything you want.'

'What is it, then?' said the Doge impatiently, in a crackly papery voice. He sounded as if it would take quite a lot to impress him.

'Thus St Mark,' said Edward, 'symbolized in the Apocalypse by a lion, returned to the Lagoon, and forever.' It sounded like a quotation. The Doge seemed to recognize it.

'San Marco?' he said. 'What nonsense is this?'

'Powerful nonsense,' said Edward, his eyes gleaming. 'Charlie! Claudio! Enter!'

The Lions, almost laughing, looked at each other. Claudio and Charlie too. Without a word they all agreed – Claudio and Charlie slipped the scarlet leashes, and the Lions, free and beautiful, leapt into the Doge's chamber.

CHAPTER TEN

The little car was whizzing along.

'We were going south before, so if we go north till we see a sign we'll at least be going in the right direction,' said Aneba.

They were both feeling a bit shaky. Magdalen was glad to be in fresh air, filling her lungs with normal everyday pollution instead of the sweet, cool poisonous air of the Corporacy Community, or the fetid stink of the dump. Aneba was relieved to have her back, her mind intact. But over the past weeks both had been fed a lot of drugs, a lot of over-processed unnaturally delicious food full of strange sugars and peculiar fats, and most of all a lot of stupid ideas. Their bodies were confused and their minds were tired. It had been hard work fighting off the Motivational Management Officers, the Medical Officers and all the others. Now, for the first time in weeks, they had to think for themselves and make their own decisions. It wasn't that they'd forgotten how, more that they were out of the habit.

'I wish we could call Charlie,' said Magdalen. But Aneba's phone was at the bottom of the sea, and payphones were few and far between.

'Money,' said Aneba. 'We'll need money.'

When they came to a small town, they had to decide whether it was safe to use the cash window, or whether it was too dangerous to risk being seen.

'If only one of us goes we'll be less recognizable,' said Magdalen.

Aneba parked on a quiet street, away from the security cameras of the centre of town. Magdalen walked in, happy just to be walking down an ordinary street. She hadn't realized how much she loved the ordinary world. She found she was smiling.

There was, as she had expected, a cash window on the high street. She held up her hand for her prints to be read, and took out all the dirhams it would give her. 'You never know,' she murmured. Plus, the window would make a record of the fact that she'd been here, and if people were looking for them they might check those records . . . So the fewer times she had to visit a window the better.

She was reassured by the feel of the wodge of money in her pocket. Part of her had been afraid that the window wouldn't give her any.

'Petrol,' said Aneba.

That was harder. There were charging points for electros everywhere, even in the middle of nowhere, but you couldn't just buy petrol – you needed a licence, and a supplier. There were black-market petrolmen, but you had to know one – it was a risky enterprise, for the dealers and for the buyers.

'Not worth it?' said Magdalen.

They decided to dump the car. Then they changed their minds. How else would they travel? They'd be so visible – huge black man, red-haired white woman. If the Corporacy sent anyone after them – and why shouldn't they? They'd kidnapped them before – they would be instantly recognizable. And now they were villains anyway – they'd stolen the car. The police might stop them.

They changed their minds back. A stolen car might easily be spotted. Aneba wrote a note saying 'Sorry – had no choice', and left it on the front seat with some money. 'To show our good intentions,' he said.

They decided to take the train. Then they changed their minds: too visible. They decided to start walking. Then they changed their minds: pointless. Far too far, they'd never get there, they'd be even more noticeable.

Steal another car? Or a vannette, or a cycle? No! They both vetoed that.

Buy one perhaps . . .

Disguise themselves . . .

Which way was Paris anyway? Where were they?

They were beginning to feel hopeless.

'Dinner,' said Aneba.

They went to the charging point they'd passed coming into town. At the café they were able to clean themselves up a bit in the bathroom – get the tea leaves out of their hair, and wash the smelly smears off themselves. They wiped their clothes down as best they could. They looked and felt a bit better, but they weren't exactly fragrant.

Then they sat themselves down at a plastic-topped table and ate spicy red sausages and rice and salad. At the next table was a gang of North African truckerguys who had stopped for their dinner too. They all got chatting. Several of the truckerguys were heading to Paris. All of them were happy to give a lift to this well-mannered couple. One of them had a truck with a bunk behind the driver's seat.

'I sleep all day so I can drive at night,' he said. 'I like to drive at night – less traffic, and I am in love with the stars. You climb behind and sleep when you like.'

There were little curtains to pull across, bottles of water tucked behind the neat little pillow, and a Hand of Fatima to bring blessings on the lorry. There was also a mobile phone. 'You can use it,' the trucker said, and Magdalen's heart beat hard as she dialled Charlie's number – but there was nothing. Well. It would have been a miracle. She smiled bravely.

The bunk was snug and clean. Magdalen went straight to bed and slept, the remains of the drugs in her system giving her weird and lurid dreams. Aneba sat up for an hour or so, talking politics with the driver as they hurtled across France, heading towards Paris and news of their boy.

Rafi was following directly in Charlie's footsteps. The *Orient Express* was still the quickest way from Paris to Venice. During the journey Rafi sat up in the restaurant car buying drinks for one of the guards, who was very happy to tell him stories of mad old King Boris, including where exactly his place was in Venice, and also how he for one was quite convinced that those mythical Lions everyone had been going on about were *definitely* on the train during the big freeze, because the boy who cleaned the bathrooms had found some most peculiar tough golden hairs all over one of the King's bathtubs, plus he'd eaten about twelve times as much as he usually did, and most of it was steak . . .

(It was on this same guard that Troy's miraculous nose smelt Rafi's smell the following week. Rafi's scent had led Troy to the station and abandoned him there; the guard unwittingly led him to the right train, and the train brought him in the end to Venice, still doggedly and devotedly pursuing his mean master.)

Rafi was feeling very happy about his discoveries when he received a phone call.

'Chief Executive, Corporacy Community, here, Sadler,' said the voice.

Rafi stopped grinning.

'The materials you delivered have disappeared,' the voice continued. 'Of their own accord.'

Rafi had to think quickly. Disappeared! How?

'That's dreadful,' he said. 'And I took such trouble to deliver them to you as instructed in good condition. How terrible that you should have lost them now.' He was trying to make it clear that it was not his fault. Well, it wasn't! If they lost Aneba and Magdalen after he had delivered them, it was nothing to do with him.

'Yes, indeed,' said the Chief Executive smoothly. 'If, however, you had delivered the full consignment, we would now be in a better position to reclaim the missing materials. We're still waiting for the next batch, if you remember . . .'

Rafi remembered all right. He hadn't really thought that the Corporacymen would have forgotten either. No doubt they'd been happy not to worry about Charlie while they had his parents, but now that they'd disappeared – had they escaped? That was pretty clever of them! – of course Charlie could be used to blackmail them.

'So you just bring it straight along, all right?' the Chief Executive was saying.

No way could Rafi admit he had lost Charlie. They'd never employ him again. They'd paid him well for this job and what if they wanted their money back? Plus his name and reputation would be ruined. Everyone would think he was a fool, a stupid kid who couldn't hack it . . .

'Of course,' said Rafi. Quick, think of a way to buy time . . . 'I'm keeping the batch in a safe place, so it'll take a day or two to fetch it, but I'll be with you very soon. Thank you for letting me know the situation, I appreciate it. I'll see you soon and call you with the progress. Goodbye.' Yes, that was good. Efficient, authoritative, grown-up.

Now he just had to get that sniking boy.

From the Lions.

Rafi's heart sank. Ever since his arm had been half bitten off, he really didn't like the Lions.

The chamber was lined with red and gold silk; its ceiling was studded with gold and turquoise rosettes. Though small compared to the others Charlie and the Lions had passed through, it was still bigger than most rooms Charlie had ever seen before he came to Venice. But as they entered, Charlie and the Lions did not notice the chamber's grandeur. They hardly even noticed the Doge himself, papery pale and ancient on his throne. What they noticed was that on each wall of this room was an immense, gold-framed, vivid painting of a lion.

The lion.

In each picture he held his book, and his wings lifted elegantly from his shoulders. In each picture he faced to the left, so the effect was of a procession of him, circling the room. In each picture he had a halo, and his front paws were on the land, and his hind paws in the sea. He seemed to be standing on the end of the Giudecca, opposite San Giorgio Maggiore . . . i.e. on a place which was now under water. All the things that Charlie had seen so far in that palace seemed to be show-off things – about power, and how far the Venetians had travelled, and how great they were – but this suddenly brought them down to size. Their great lion was standing on a piece of land they had lost back to the sea. There was a rose bush beside him, which somehow made it even sadder.

And between these painted lions and the real Lions, who had gathered, breathing and twitching at Charlie's feet, sat the astounded Doge.

He stared at them. At all the Lions, then at each in turn. Then at Charlie and Claudio, then, particularly, at Primo, who lay in the middle, with the Lionesses at his left, and the others on his right, and his creamy wings folded gently along his massive back.

The Doge said nothing. Edward waited.

The Doge sighed.

And then Primo glanced at Charlie, and slowly, languorously, he stood up. He turned sideways to the Doge, and fixed him with a deep stare. As Primo lifted his paw, Charlie pressed the button on the little remote he had in his pocket. The beautiful wings rose up, the feathers shifting gently with the movement.

Primo was the fifth of the old lions painted on the walls. And he was alive.

The old man closed his eyes and sighed deeply.

'Ahhh,' he said. 'My god, my god.'

And then: 'What's the matter with his head?' he asked.

'A hurt jaw,' said Edward. 'It will soon be better.'

The Doge nodded.

'And what do you want in exchange, Edward?'

'We wish simply to be friends again,' said Edward. 'Please, be a friend to King Boris, to Bulgaria and to the Bulgarian Security Forces.'

The Doge grinned a nasty old grin.

'I understand,' he said.

'The young men will stay,' said Edward. 'They look after them.'

Charlie was pleased to be called a young man, even by a double-crossing weasel like Edward.

'I understand,' said the Doge again. 'Foscarini, how long to prepare a pageant?'

'A few days, sir,' said one of the advisers.

'Prepare,' said the Doge. 'We will introduce the Lion of San Marco back to his people of Venice. It will be a miracle. They will all be very grateful to me and stop complaining. Is his face as beautiful as the rest of him?'

'Yes, sir,' said Charlie, who was picking up Italian quite quickly.

Edward frowned at him.

'Will it be . . . visible, after tomorrow?'

'Oh yes,' said Charlie blandly. None of these people knew Primo's secret. Only he and the Lions knew.

They were put in a huge room on the first floor, with a thickly ornamented golden ceiling, more fancy icing on the cake. It was covered with pictures of gods bringing tribute to Venice: great hairy sea-gods with big forks and green beards; beautiful goddesses in delicate nighties and thin gold crowns. In each one, Venice was an even more beautiful lady, golden-haired and long-faced like Signora Battistuta, lying about half-dressed, with a great curly golden lion at her feet, or under her hand, or, sometimes, she was sitting on it.

This chamber lay alongside the arcaded balcony overlooking the piazza where the two columns were. (Claudio had told him never to walk between them, because in the old days that's where criminals were hung.) When Charlie went out he could see the white-eyed lion on top of his column quite clearly, grinning in at them in the moonlight. They were on about the same level now. He called the Lions to look, and they grinned back at their bronze brother.

Charlie was thinking: Sergei knows that I am here. He could come to this balcony without too much trouble. If I hang out on the balcony Enzo might come, and I can send a message to Sergei to say I'm sorry, I meant no offence . . . He stared out over the Piazza San Marco, sending silent messages to Sergei, begging him to come back. From way across the piazza came the lilting strains of a beautiful tune. Charlie recognized it: it was the song about Elena which Claudio sang as he punted, played by the small orchestra outside the grandest café in the piazza. It seemed to yearn and dance at the same time, and Charlie felt it in his bones.

Charlie had been thinking a lot about his responsibilities. And about what Sergei had said. He had come to the conclusion that if his parents were all right, and free, then they might track him to Venice, in which case perhaps going off to Morocco was not the best thing to do. Or at least, perhaps *now* was not the moment to go off to Morocco. Perhaps he . . . well, perhaps he should stay.

But what about the Lions? How could they get away without him?

Could he ask them? Would he be letting them down?

He had lost sleep over this.

When they went back indoors, Claudio took Charlie to one side. He was troubled. Normally so relaxed and confident and elegant, he was nervous now. He was picking at his fingers.

'What is it?' Claudio said finally.

'What is what?' answered Charlie with concern.

Claudio stared at him.

'My friend – how do you do it?' he burst out. 'Please – if I am to be here with these wild creatures, trusting they not so wild they eat me – how do you do it?'

Charlie considered this. It seemed to him reasonable

that Claudio should want to know. And at least he asked in a fair and straightforward way. And he was going to help them. He *was* helping them. Without him, they'd be stuck here forever. And splendid though it was here – especially after they were brought a little late snack of beef for the Lions and *gianduiotto* (it's like chocolate only better, and comes swimming in whipped cream) – Charlie and the Lions did not want to stay forever.

'Do you talk to them?' asked Claudio. 'Just say yes or no. I have seen you – I think you are talking. Just say. I never never never *never* tell nobody. Nobody. Never.'

Charlie couldn't lie. He couldn't even deceive.

'Yes,' he said.

Claudio's pale eyes doubled in size. Then he started dancing around the huge golden room, he was so pleased. He did a backflip worthy of Signor Lucidi. He hugged Charlie, hugged himself and almost – but not quite – hugged the Lions.

Then he knelt down in front of Elsina and said to her, very slowly, 'Hello, beautiful girl Lion, how are you? I like you very much.'

Charlie laughed out loud. The Lions twitched their ears and the Silvery Lioness started to cough. The Old Lion put his nose on his paws.

Elsina replied, equally slowly, 'I am very well thank you, handsome Gondolier. How are you?'

When Charlie translated this back to Claudio, Claudio

was so happy that you would think he was in love. In fact, perhaps he was.

The Young Lion snorted with laughter. For a moment Charlie, sitting with the Lions, felt as if he too were a Lion and Claudio were the only human.

Merriment filled the room.

Only Primo didn't join in.

The Young Lion noticed, and nudged Charlie.

Claudio noticed too.

'What is it, Primo?' Charlie asked.

'Tired,' said Primo. 'Just tired.'

They had been provided with beds for the humans (huge carved ones, with angels on the headboards and high mattresses with rough thick linen sheets), and rugs and bales of sweet-scented straw for the Lions. Claudio pulled the straw from one of the bales and laid it out so it was comfortable for Primo. When Primo went to lie on it, with a gracious inclination of his head, Claudio stood over him for a moment, watching him.

'Strange beautiful beast,' he murmured.

It was time for the Lions to sleep. For Charlie too, but first he and Claudio had to talk and plan.

How peculiar it was to sit on the Doge's own balcony, plotting his downfall. The moon gazed down, but Charlie felt that even the moon was on their side, and wouldn't tell on them.

'It's like this,' said Claudio softly and urgently. 'The Doge is bad. Many many people want to be rid of him. Many have planned, many wish only for a leader, an opportunity, someone to say NOW! Here, now, we have an opportunity. If we, the boatmen, the *gondolieri*, tell the people that the Lion has come and the Doge has locked him up, then the Venetians will follow the Lion and say, *Arrivederci*, Doge. We can do what the Doge is planning to do. We can grab the symbol of good luck.'

'That is very risky,' whispered Charlie.

'Venetians are good people! And we all know each other. We will put the word out and everybody will want this. And of course, Charlie, there is you too – the *famoso* Brown Angel of the Sick Children –'

'I don't want to be famous,' said Charlie.

'Help us,' whispered Claudio, 'and we will help you. We can prepare everything for your escape. You want to go to Africa? We can give you a boat, supplies – if you like I can come too!'

'What about Primo?'

'He goes with you! Once he has given Venice a big blessing and we have the Doge and his people all put away in prison, then he can go to Africa with you. No one will mind. A miracle doesn't have to go on forever.'

A boat, thought Charlie. Supplies. And a boatman! Now that's more like it.

CHAPTER ELEVEN

Before dawn, after the long discussion with Charlie, Claudio slipped out on to the balcony, down a column to the piazza, and off to a bar where the gondoliers met to drink little cups of strong coffee before starting the day's work. There, he spoke to his friends.

Within the hour, all the gondoliers and half the other boatmen of Venice and the surrounding islands knew that the stupid old Doge, who had let their city fall down and been no better than the fascists, had, in his palazzo, miraculously, the Lion of San Marco, and was keeping him prisoner (along with his Lion friends and the brown boy who looked after him). They knew that the Doge planned to impress the whole of Venice by producing the Lion in a pageant, but that the Lion wanted only to visit and bless the city on his way back to – well, Claudio hadn't quite worked that bit out. But the boatmen got the gist. The Lion had come on an honest and miraculous visit to his beloved Venice after all these years, with his brothers and sisters, to remove the curse and bless the city in her time of trouble, and the Doge had locked them all up.

'He *what?*' exclaimed Claudio's cousin Gabriele.

'What a snake!' cried Gabriele's girlfriend's brother Vittorio.

'We're not having that!' expostulated Vittorio's uncle Leon.

'Why should the Doge claim the Lion's glory for himself?' sputtered Leon's brother Franco.

'The Lion is for Venice, not for the Doge!' declared Franco's niece Carlotta (yes, there are female gondoliers). 'Our Lion must be free!'

'And while we're at it,' said Claudio, 'why isn't *Venice* free? Why are we always talking about how bad this Doge is and yet still putting up with him?'

'This *porco* of a Doge!' muttered Carlotta's brother Alessandro. 'Enough is enough!'

The others agreed.

Claudio hummed his tune as the word spread. Then: 'So here is the plan,' Claudio said. 'Listen . . .'

Alessandro, whose job was changing the light bulbs in the electric lights on the buoys all across the lagoon, had left his phone at home. His mother, knowing that he would be sad without it, unable to talk to his girlfriend as he sped about in his little boat, and knowing that he would be taking a coffee at the bar on his way to work, brought the phone to him. On the way she ran into her friend –

Gabriele's mother – who came too as they were both heading to the market afterwards.

Overhearing the talk, the boatmen's mothers were very interested. Particularly when Claudio mentioned the brown boy, and how the Lions had been at Palazzo Bulgaria.

'*L'angelo!*' they cried. 'The Brown Angel of the Children of the Asthma is the friend of the Lion of San Marco!' The boatmen's mothers were amazed and delighted.

The boatmen were not at all surprised to hear that the Lion's human companion was in fact an angel – what could be more likely? The Lion of San Marco had returned to Venice with a miracle-working angel to bring blessings on the long-suffering people of his city, and to get rid of the selfish, greedy, unimaginative, useless, corrupt, old Doge . . . of course!

It was all Claudio and Alessandro could do to stop the boatmen's mothers from going straight down to the Doge's Palace and setting up candles and flowers and deckchairs there.

'Not yet,' they said. 'Not yet. We have a plan.'

'Really?' said the boatmen's mothers.

When they heard what the plan was, the boatmen's mothers said, 'About time too!' Then they hared off to the Rialto, to the market, to church and to the piazza behind Palazzo Bulgaria to tell everybody all about it.

By the end of the day, all of Venice knew that at the Doge's big pageant they would finally have the chance to tell him what they thought of him. All of Venice knew that something big was about to go off.

Including a baldy-bottomed, milky-eyed, wonky-eared cat, foraging for fish-heads over at the fishmarket.

Really? he thought. And munched, and thought.

And also including a handsome, tired-looking young man with a bad arm, recently arrived on the *Orient Express*, who was taking his morning coffee in a café up by the station. An Empiregirl, leaving that afternoon to return to the Homelands, talking half in English half in Italian to her Venetian boyfriend, was saying that she really didn't want to leave with all this excitement about the Lions and everything. The boyfriend was trying to persuade her to stay. 'We make history now!' he said. 'With the Lions, and the Brown Angel – fate loves Venice now! We have a big chance now! Stay here! You can help Venice to be free with her Lions!'

'*Questi Leoni*,' said the waitress. '*E' l'angelo, credi sia possibile, che è vero, e che abbiamo ancora il nostro Santo qui a Venezia?*'

The rest of the café joined in. Lions, Brown Angel, Doge's Palace, grand pageant . . .

Rafi got the gist. Charlie and the Lions were incredibly famous, everybody knew about them and loved them, and they were imprisoned in the ruler's palace.

He was going to have to think of a very clever plan indeed to snitch this adored boy from under all these

Venetian noses. Force would not work. Sneaky cleverness was the only possible way.

But at least they would come out for the pageant.

Rafi finished his coffee and set off for the Doge's Palace. He would have a look at this luxurious prison, and he would find a way . . .

For a moment, as he started out, he looked round for Troy. For a moment, remembering that his dog had run away from him, he felt a tiny sadness. Then he sneered. 'He travels the fastest who travels alone,' he said to himself.

Magdalen and Aneba reached Paris soon after dawn. The truckerguy dropped them off near the Bastille.

'It's OK,' he said. 'My brother lives on the riverbank just here – I was coming this way anyway to deliver him some scrap. The Circus is down there.' He pointed over the edge of the bridge. 'See that big pink ship? That's the Circus of Monsieur Thibaudet. Good luck!'

Magdalen and Aneba stood on the bridge and stared down at the *Circe*, the amazing circus ship. The Big Top was up amidships, its crimson and white stripes glowing slightly in the early-morning mist. The big, beautiful figurehead was visible, with her golden-red hair and her elusive smile. A dim light shone from her eyes, from the strange-shaped little cabin within which the twins, Lara and Tara, were starting to get up. Its funnels stood proud, and there was movement in the rigging: Charlie could have told them that it was Signor Lucidi and his family practising their acrobatics, as they did every morning at dawn. Soon the whole ship would be full of activity, as everybody woke and washed, ate their breakfast and greeted their colleagues, cleaned their animals' cabins and started to practise their routines.

Aneba was all for going straight to the Circus, waking everybody up now and making a big fuss. Magdalen stopped him.

'Let's get a hotel room, bathe, have breakfast, go out and buy some clean clothes, and visit them at a decent hour looking thoroughly respectable,' she said.

Reluctantly, Aneba agreed. Turning up smelly and hungry at five a.m. probably wasn't the best approach. But now that they were out of the clutches of the Corporacy, he just wanted his boy. He wanted him very very badly.

'Me too,' said Magdalen. 'That's why we must go about this carefully. Remember, Charlie ran away with their Lions. They're probably not very pleased with him.'

Three hours later, Aneba and Magdalen approached the gangway of the *Circe*. Aneba was wearing a clean white shirt and an elegant black suit: they had had to go to five shops to find one big enough for him. He had shaved – chin and scalp. His gold tooth gleamed. He looked handsome, impressive and not to be messed with. Magdalen had bought a white shirt, a pair of jeans, and a beautiful pair of boots. They reached the deck. There was a chain across the entrance.

'The Box Office isn't open yet,' said a pretty woman with a curling black beard, in French. 'You need to come after midday for tickets.'

'We haven't come for tickets,' said Aneba nicely. 'We've come to see Major Thibaudet.'

The Bearded Lady looked at him. She looked at Magdalen.

'Are you English?' she inquired politely.

'Yes,' said Magdalen. It was easier than Aneba explaining no, he was Ghanaian but he lived in England.

The Bearded Lady looked thoughtful.

'Come,' she said, 'I'll take you to him.'

As she led them along the deck, a curly freckled boy ran up to them.

'Hi, Madame,' he said. 'Um . . .'

And he looked at Aneba and Magdalen with great interest, and aimed a sort of questioning look at the Bearded Lady.

This made Aneba and Magdalen aim questioning looks too. What was going on?

'Actually,' said the Bearded Lady, and then she grabbed Magdalen's arm and pulled her quickly into a gap between two cabins. Aneba, prodded by the freckly boy, followed swiftly.

The Bearded Lady stared fiercely at Magdalen and Aneba in turn.

'Are you who I think you are?' she hissed.

The freckly boy was watching them intently.

'Who *do* you think we are?' asked Aneba cautiously.

'We think you're Charlie's mum and dad!' said the freckly boy. 'The ones who'd disappeared and . . .'

The Bearded Lady shushed him with a look.

'Are you?' she hissed.

Magdalen looked at Aneba. It was pointless to deny it – but there was something about being grabbed and propelled down a dark gap that made them both cautious.

'Yes,' said Aneba. 'We are. Who are you?'

'I am Madame Barbue,' said the Bearded Lady. 'This is Julius. We are your son's friends. Well, we were. Before . . .'

They all knew what she meant. Before Charlie ran off with the Lions.

'And now?' said Magdalen. 'What are you now?' She was wondering if it was the running off with the Lions that had upset them, or the fact that he hadn't told them.

'We don't know,' said Madame Barbue. 'We hear nothing from him, we don't know what to think . . .'

'We *can't* hear anything from him!' exclaimed Julius. It sounded as if they had had this discussion many times before. 'He knows Maccomo and Major Tib are furious with him, there's the reward on his head, police and everybody looking for them – how could he risk getting in touch? It's the same reason he couldn't tell us what he was doing . . .'

'He could have told us,' said Madame Barbue sulkily.

'We would have sympathized. We understand about animals . . .'

'He couldn't have known,' said Julius. 'He couldn't take the risk. How could he have known we'd be loyal to him not to Major Tib?'

'Oh, I know, but he should have trusted us,' said Madame Barbue. She looked up suddenly at the parents. 'But this is an old argument. Why have you come here? Are you looking for him? He is not here, you know that . . .'

'We need to find where he is,' said Aneba. 'We thought Major Tib might . . .'

'You don't want to talk to *him*,' said Julius. 'Even mention Charlie's name and he goes purple and starts throwing brandy bottles about. He's furious, specially since Maccomo's disappeared too – it turns out that he had been drugging the Lions, and Major Tib's angry with him about that because it's against regulations and could get Major Tib into trouble. It's been really bad . . . So you don't know where Charlie is?'

'No,' said Magdalen and Aneba. 'Do you?'

'No,' said Madame Barbue.

'No,' said Julius.

They looked at one another unhappily.

'Any ideas?' said Aneba.

They stood around.

'Well,' said Julius.

They all looked up expectantly.

'I'm pretty sure,' he said, 'that the Lions would have wanted to go home.'

'Of course!' exclaimed Magdalen. 'So where do they come from?'

'I don't know,' said Julius unhappily. 'Maccomo would know, but . . .'

That was no use. Maccomo wasn't there.

'Mabel might know,' said Madame Barbue.

'Mabel?' said Aneba. 'Who's she?'

On the day of the pageant, the Lions, Charlie, Claudio and the Doge went in the Doge's gondola round the island to the Arsenale, the shipyard where the *Bucintoro* lived. Charlie had heard that the *Bucintoro* was a fabulous ship, but when he saw her, lying in the great smooth bay of the Arsenale dock, he gasped.

She was a long barge, covered over like a building – covered in gold. And not just simple gold – this was more of the grand icing of Venetian ceilings, carved and moulded into ranks of winged women along the sides, into vines and sphinxes. On the poop were two golden lions, and on the prow a figure of Justice, larger than life, with her scales and a golden umbrella. Of course there was a great golden throne for the Doge – and on the bowsprit, leading the ship, sticking right out the front, stood another beautiful shining golden lion.

The floors were polished wood. The seats were red

velvet, and so were the walls. It was forty-three metres long and eight and a half metres high, forty-four men would row it, four to an oar, and the oars had stripes of red along the edges of the long, shining wooden blades. Golden vases were built into the decoration, and they had been filled with lilies, whose scent washed the air. A massive cloak of crimson brocade spread out behind, hanging from the high, carved, gilded canopy of the stern, with great corks sewn into its edges to make sure it floated.

It was in this ship that the Doge had gone out each year to marry the sea; in this ship, now, he was going to present Primo the Smilodon as the Lion of St Mark.

The other boats, gondolas and fishing boats, water taxis and all who were to take part in the pageant, were waiting along the way to join, or assembling already in the Bacino – the basin – of San Marco (it means basin, but it also means little kiss). The Bacino, at the end of the Grand Canal by the Doge's Palace, was the Piccadilly Circus, the Times Square, the Piazza Navona of the Venetian boatways. The centre of town.

The *Bucintoro* moved slowly at first, its oars rising and falling, coming over to the quay where the Doge and the Lions waited to embark. A great drum kept the oarsmen in time; its slow boom, boom, boom was soothing, and the water trickled from the blades of the oars as they rested for a moment at the top of each stroke. When the boat was alongside, the Lions leapt on happily. The Doge hobbled aboard, assisted by several men in medieval livery whose ancestors had always had the job of helping the Doge on to the *Bucintoro*. He slowly made his way up to the bow and sat in his golden throne, breathing heavily.

Charlie, who had been togged out in velvet tights, one leg red and one leg gold, with a laced-up jerkin like the boy in the painting, had to sit at the Doge's feet. This was apparently a great honour, but Charlie was rather annoyed as he wanted to run all over the fantastic boat looking at it, and after that he wanted to climb on the gold lions, and after that he wanted to hang over the edge and yell things at the passers-by and throw things in the water. But none of that was on the agenda: he was to sit at the Doge's feet, like an angel in one of those paintings of how powerful Venice was, and the Lions were to lie about, again like a painting, with their scarlet collars and silver chains.

Only Primo was to stand up, on the little platform above Justice's umbrella, where everybody would be able to see him, and he was to hold in his paws a great book that the Doge had produced.

'And what page will it open on, I wonder?' said Claudio quietly. '"Freedom and Justice for all"? Or "Give me all your money and stop complaining"?'

Charlie remembered how Napoleon had changed the words on the book to change the minds of the people of Venice. What would he write, if his writing could change how people think?

Primo still had his bandages on.

'Take it off now,' the Doge had said.

'Later,' said Charlie.

The Doge looked cross, but he said only, 'Before we get to the Grand Canal.'

Charlie had smiled politely.

The oarsmen were all in their places in the under half of the great barge. They were shipbuilders from the Arsenale. Claudio knew most of them so he went down to visit them. They grinned at each other and clapped hands a lot. Charlie, wriggling around at the Doge's feet, could see down into the oarsmen's section. He was jealous. Then Claudio came up again, whistling his tune, and sat with him. The Doge would have preferred not to have this common gondolier at his feet, but Charlie insisted, and the Doge had quickly recognized that if he wanted the Lions to behave (which he rather did) then Charlie was the one he had to be nice to. Also the Doge had noticed how flimsy the leads were, and didn't mind having a strong young man in place, in case. There was, of course, a row of elegantly dressed and heavily armed Doge Guards just behind him, but frankly none of them looked as if they would have a clue what to do with a Lion on the rampage . . . He had thought of putting the Lions in a cage . . . but then the effect of the Lion of San Marco in a cage was not quite the effect of the Lion of San Marco strong, beautiful and standing freely of his own will on the top of the *Bucintoro*, not eating the Doge. No, he would just have to be nice to this brown boy and his blond friend.

The *Bucintoro* was circling the whole main island of Venice. The lagoon, with its distant islands of Murano and Burano, spread off to the right. Charlie was happy to be able to see so far, having been locked up for so long. The water slapped against the flanks of the boat, the oars lifted and fell in rhythmic motion, and the *Bucintoro* slid gracefully along, golden against the grey-green waters. Charlie found himself humming the beautiful gondolier tune: today it sounded just sprightly and dancing and the sadness had gone from it.

When Rafi reached the Piazza San Marco it was still early, but people were already gathering for the pageant. He moved carefully through the crowds, heading for the Doge's Palace. Even if there had been time for him to try to raid the palace, one look at it told him that he would never succeed: the great doors, the high gateways, the rows of guards.

He moved on to the front alongside the Bacino, walking, as he passed, between the two columns where Claudio had told Charlie never to walk. He stared out at the ruins of San Giorgio Maggiore. He climbed to the top of the bridge there, and turned back to see the Bridge of Sighs, which led from the palace to the prisons on the far side of a small canal.

Looking down, he noticed moored on the canal a sleek and beautiful solar-powered boat, in which two young guys were stowing some stuff. They were talking in low, earnest voices.

Rafi was naturally a nosy person. He moved further down the steps and inclined his head. '*Leoni*', he heard, and also '*Charlie*'. He stopped. Most of the Venetians were talking about the 'Brown Angel'. So who were these people who knew Charlie by name?

He stood with his back to the parapet and leaned backwards, for all the world as if he were admiring the view. Their words rose up: too much Italian. Rafi couldn't make sense of it. He turned and leaned forward, for all the world as if he were admiring the Bridge of Sighs. Beneath his sunglasses, he dropped his eyes.

One of the young men was putting a leather bag into a locker: '*Sta più sicuro qui*,' he was saying.

Rafi didn't care what he was saying. He recognized the bag. It was the bag Charlie had brought with him from his parents' house all those weeks ago.

His mind ticked quickly.

He wanted the bag. Whatever was in it, Charlie would value. Rafi wanted the bag.

How to . . .

He had no time to think or plan.

But then it took no time to stagger, as if he had been

pushed, shout out in defensive annoyance and simultaneously shove the small girl standing next to him into the canal just in front of the sleek boat. It took no time at all to produce a scene of small local chaos, in which the girl was yelling and splashing, the people with her were crying out in alarm and rushing forward, one of the two boatguys was racing to the bow of their boat and throwing her a life-ring, and the other was jumping in, noisily and splashily, to save her. It was easy for Rafi to give the impression that he was trying to help, and stumbling, when in fact he was just taking the opportunity to throw himself on top of Charlie's bag. He'd been going for the handle, so he could pull the whole bag under his leather coat and then make off with it, but what he'd thought was the handle turned out to be the neck of the bag, and now his hand was inside instead.

He closed his hand on – what? A cool, smooth hard thing, and something papery. And then, proceeding with the masquerade of concern for the girl, he slipped the items into his big pocket, while shouting out, 'Is she all right? For crike sake, who pushed me?'

Then, swiftly, before calm reappeared and anyone asked him what on earth he was doing, he legged it.

Gazing off over the lagoon, resting his eyes, Charlie saw a low pile of rubble and a whirlpool effect, rising slightly above the water level. Beside it was moored a floating pontoon with an enormous crucifix standing on it, all alone in the middle of the flat waters of the lagoon, washing to and fro sadly on the tide.

Claudio saw Charlie looking at it, and crossed himself.

'What is it?' asked Charlie.

'San Michele,' said Claudio.

'And?' said Charlie.

'Beautiful church, beautiful *convento* . . .'

Ah, thought Charlie.

'And . . .' Claudio looked a bit sick. 'It was the island of our cemetery.'

Charlie looked at the tumbling waters, eddying above the ruins below. The water was darker there. The bright early-morning sunlight seemed not to touch it.

'Oh,' said Charlie softly. He thought a bit about drowned skeletons, and remembered a poem that his mother had told him, about a drowned sailor – 'Full fathom five thy father lies . . . Those are pearls that were his eyes' . . . something like that. But to be drowned after you are dead and buried . . .

Poor Venice. The tune in his head began to yearn again.

At that moment a little sparrow flew down and perched on a bit of gold icing just by Charlie. His scaly little feet gripped a golden nymph's ear, and he bobbed his brown head.

Spirits live on, thought Charlie, and he didn't know

where the thought came from. Bodies die, and buildings tumble, and Empires fall, but spirits live on.

The *Bucintoro* had now been joined by four smaller, outlying barges that came along after her, like very grand ducklings. Two of them carried musicians, who were playing as loudly as they could and keeping time with the *Bucintoro's* oarsmen's drum. Two more carried glass-blowers, who were making lovely little glass lions, which they threw to the children on the canalsides. And around them smaller boats were joining in their wake. They were scruffy, poor-looking things on the whole, but they had been decorated – all were decked out in red and gold, and were flying the Venetian flag of the lion, gold on red. Some had red cloaks floating behind them on the water in imitation of the *Bucintoro*; some had ribbons and garlands in their rigging and on their rowlocks.

As they rounded into the Cannaregio Canal, the boats that joined them seemed rather smarter, and when they turned into the Grand Canal, the standard went up again. Gliding past the palazzi that he had seen on his first day here, Charlie noticed that everybody was excited and happy. As they passed under the Rialto, rose petals fluttered around them. Balloons were unleashed from balconies along the way; people lined the quaysides and leaned from their windows, cheering and singing and, above all, gasping with amazement when they saw Primo. Amazement, as they realized that he was – real. He was Real.

Pageant

The Lion had returned to Venice! Venice was blessed again!

All alongside the Grand Canal, Charlie could make out more people in red and gold livery. They were handing out food and drinks from trays. Children were gnawing on what looked like . . . They slowed down and Charlie was able to look carefully. It was! It was little sugar lions, in pink and green and yellow and blue. Charlie laughed out loud. He wanted one.

As they reached the Doge's Palace, a twenty-one-gun salute went off. Several pieces of mosaic fell from the front of the cathedral. In the silence between the guns, you could hear them tinkle. ('Never mind,' murmured the Doge. 'It's worth it.')

The crowds in the piazza and round the Doge's Palace were enormous: monks and priests and nuns, the aristocrats and citizens of Venice, tourists and children, pianists and fishermen, footballers and teachers, beggars and drunks, journalists and charity workers, writers and administrators, dogs and cats, workers and layabouts, waiters and dancers and an English lad in a leather coat . . . Everybody in Venice who wasn't on a boat was there in the crowd. (Except for small quiet bands of gondoliers who were at the telephone exchange, the station, the Arsenale, the TV headquarters and the main bank – all of which were closed for the pageant. Swiftly and carefully, whistling between their teeth and throwing each other little smiles, the gondoliers were breaking in, changing the locks and hacking into the computers.)

One cat in particular was watching carefully and biding his time.

As the *Bucintoro* hove into sight, the Marangona began to ring, and the people began to shout. Flags were flapping bravely against the blue bright sky – red and gold, blue and gold – and the musicians in the duckling boats were joined by another orchestra on the Doge's balcony. They weren't quite in time but even so the sound was glorious, especially when all the bells of the churches of Venice joined in, from the Redentore and the Salute, Santa Maria dei Frari and dei Gigli, from the Gesuati and the Pietà. One old lady in the crowd said that even the drowned bells of the drowned churches of San Michele and San Giorgio Maggiore were joining in from under the water.

'They will rise again!' cried the Venetians.

'They will rise again!' cried the boatmen.

'They will rise again!' cried the children and the tourists and the priests and the drunks.

The Doge smiled.

The boats crowded round.

Some people fell into the Bacino, so crowded were the banks. Others hoicked them out again, and their dripping added to the chaos.

Primo looked at Charlie. 'Now,' he gestured.

Charlie leapt up on to the gilded platform where his friend stood, high and visible to the whole city of Venice, and swiftly unwrapped his huge and terrifying head.

Primo raised his head, and shook out his magnificent mane.

Charlie pressed the button on the remote control and the broad creamy wings rose up. Primo shivered his muscles, and the wings quivered as if they were alive. He wrinkled his great black lip in a proud grimace, and as he did so his long, strong, sharp teeth, curving from his pink gums over his furry golden jaw, shone in the sunlight.

People looked.

People gasped.

Venice, home through centuries of all that is rich and strange, had never seen anything like Primo.

And then Primo roared.

CHAPTER TWELVE

'Who's Mabel?' Aneba had just said.

'Mabel Stark,' said Julius. 'She's Maccomo's girlfriend. She's pretty cool.'

'Why do you just say, "She's Maccomo's girlfriend"?' asked Madame Barbue. 'She's also only the best tigertrainer of them all. That's more important than who is her boyfriend . . .'

'Sorry,' said Julius.

Magdalen had gone quiet.

'Is she here?' she asked.

'Yeah,' said Julius. 'Her tigers have replaced the Lions in the show.'

'Don't her tigers want to go back to *their* home?' asked Aneba.

'No – they're Circus-bred. They wouldn't know what to do in the wild. Maccomo's adult Lions were caught.' Julius looked a bit disgusted.

'So where is she?' said Magdalen. There was something urgent in her voice.

'Mabel? She'll be – I'll go and find her,' said Julius. 'You stay here out of sight.'

'I'll take them to my cabin,' said Madame Barbue. 'Major Tib is doing his exercises in the Ring. He won't see them. It'll be safe.'

So Aneba and Magdalen found themselves in Madame Barbue's neat little cabin, meeting Pirouette the Flying Trapeze artiste, and drinking lime-leaf tea while they waited for the tigertrainer to arrive.

And when she did, tough and beautiful in her scarlet leather practice suit, which was scarred with tiger scratches and tiger bite marks, with her flaming red hair held back in a tight plait and her whip and gloves in her pale, muscular hand, which was almost as scarred as her suit, the famous tigertrainer took one look at Magdalen and fainted.

When she came around she almost fainted again. 'You!' she cried. 'You! That boy – that thieving boy – is your son!'

'Yes, darling,' said Magdalen.

The others, as you can imagine, stared.

'Well, I'm not helping you,' said Mabel. 'I'm not helping him. He's ruined Maccomo. He's – I'm not helping even if I could. I don't care.'

'Mabel?' said Aneba.

Mabel looked at him.

'You are Mabel?' he said.

'Yes!' she almost shouted.

Julius, Madame Barbue and Pirouette were agog.

Aneba turned to them, but Magdalen cut in.

'She's my sister,' she said. 'She ran away from home to join the Circus. We – we haven't seen each other for a while.'

When Primo had roared before, the whole of Paris had shuddered in it boots. When he roared now, Venice stopped breathing.

The sad and haunting beautiful sound rolled across the waters, filling the ears and bellies and hearts of all who heard it – and they all heard it.

The Doge, who was close by, and could see the teeth clearly, passed out clean on the deck. The Dogepolice on either side tried to catch him, but they were too stunned by the roar to move fast enough.

The other Lions leapt to their feet and encircled their father, their brother, their cousin from long ago.

The people in boats stared and gasped. Some gripped the rails, some fell overboard.

The people at the back cried, 'What is it! What is it!'

The people at the front said, in small voices, 'The Lion! It's the Lion . . . !'

The oarsmen smiled brilliantly.

Edward, in his special guest-of-honour gilded gondola, turned white, and picked up his phone.

Rafi murmured, puzzled, 'I don't remember *that* Lion . . .'

Claudio jumped up beside Primo, pulled out a megaphone and, as the last of the roar rolled away across the waters of the lagoon, cried out, 'Citizens of Venice! The Lion has returned! The Lion of San Marco, our beautiful noble and sacred patron, has returned to us in our time of need to lift the curse and give Venice back to her people! See how the scurrilous Doge lies quivering on the Deck of History!' (The Doge was indeed quivering.) 'See how his treacherous soldiers quake in the Face of the Truth!' (The Dogepolice looked around. Did he mean them?) 'See how the Noble Lion shows his teeth in defence of Freedom, and raises his wondrous voice for Democracy and Justice! Doge! Present yourself before the Lion of the City of Venice! Prostrate yourself before the Will of the People!'

The Doge was standing now, white as a sheet. Dogepolice surrounded him, their guns drawn, and a group of boatmen – the rowers – were facing them.

'Never!' cried the Doge, in a shaky voice. 'Never! The Doge does not prostrate himself before dogs!'

'Citizens of Venice, your so-called leader calls you dogs!' cried Claudio.

One or two of the Dogepolice were looking nervous, fingering their triggers – and then the Young Lion stepped forward. He stood straight before the group of Dogepolice, staring at them with a deep and baleful glare. Swiftly, the other Lions followed him. They began to growl, softly. The Young Lion unsheathed his claws, and scratched them gently on the deck. The Doge's musicians had stopped playing. Their music faded away and the sound of the scratching claws carried.

One of the Dogepolice raised his gun and aimed it at the Young Lion. A horrified silence hung over the scene – and then just as the Young Lion prepared to leap, a child's voice rang out: 'DON'T YOU DARE!'

It was Lavinia, at the front of the crowd. 'Don't you dare hurt that Lion!' she shrieked, and behind her a thousand voices joined in: Signora Battistuta's, Alessandro's mother's, Donatella's, the grandmothers', the TV crew, the crumply guy – all the people of Venice.

The Dogepoliceman quickly lowered his rifle. He was only eighteen. He didn't at all want to kill the Lion and he thought the Doge a very rude old bloke anyway. Within moments the boatmen had surrounded the Doge's group, and the Dogepolice had melted away.

The crowd started to cheer.

Charlie watched all this in amazement.

And then Primo, still standing high and visible, lowered his head and called, 'Charlie! I am staying here!'

'But Primo –' Charlie said, and Primo looked down at him and said, 'Little boy, I am staying here.'

Charlie gulped. Who was he to say 'but' to a prehistoric sabre-toothed Lion?

'But Primo . . .' said the Young Lion. And by the look on Primo's face, he too said no more.

The Silvery Lioness turned sadly to him.

'Are you so sick?' she asked.

Primo looked down at her, and murmured, 'Yes, I am so sick. And they like me. This city, like me, is out of time. I will stay with them and sink with them. It will make them happy.'

Charlie realized there were big tears in his eyes. The Young Lion had wrapped his tail round Charlie's leg.

'Charlie,' hissed Claudio. 'What are they saying?'

'Primo wants to stay here!'

'*Favoloso!*' cried Claudio.

The crowd was getting louder, pushing and calling out.

Charlie just stared at Claudio blankly.

'Your boat is waiting,' Claudio said. 'Or are you staying too?'

'We're going,' said Charlie. 'We . . .'

He had been about to say, 'We go,' when he realized. He didn't want to go. He wanted to stay, to find his parents, to go home, to be safe.

But how could he tell the Lions?

Claudio would look after them on the journey, of course . . . but they'd come through so much together. He didn't want to let them down.

Elsina was kissing Primo. The Oldest Lion was talking to him in a low voice. The crowd was jubilating: '*LEONE! MARCIANO! LEONE! VENEZIA!*' They sounded like the biggest football crowd in the world.

Claudio jumped up beside Primo again, with his megaphone. It took another snatch of a roar from Primo to shut the crowd up.

Primo said, 'Charlie, have your translator translate.'

So as Primo spoke, Charlie translated it into English, and Claudio translated it into Venetian, and spoke to the citizens of Venice.

'I, Primo, the Lion of St Mark, have returned to Venice. I am staying here with you. You, the people of Venice, are my protectors. My brothers and sisters are leaving. My human friend is leaving. My teeth are at your service' – here Primo grinned, and many more people fainted.

The roar that went up from the crowds was louder even than Primo's, and it was full of love. Even the Doge realized it, as the boatmen gently wrapped him in his own red velvet robes and carried him down to the rowing deck. 'Come on, sir,' they murmured. 'Don't think you're wanted any more . . .'

Charlie was still thinking about the Lions. I'll take them some of the way, he thought. Then I can explain to them why I have to return, and they'll understand – I can't change the plan now, I –

'Primo,' Charlie called.

The great Lion turned to him.

'Goodbye,' Charlie said quietly.

Primo looked at him a moment.

'Thank you, Lionboy,' he said.

And so Charlie and the other Lions, bidding their swift

but heartfelt farewells, slipped quietly down the back of the *Bucintoro*, on to the deck of the big, solar-powered speedboat that Claudio and his friends had brought, laden with food and supplies and money for their escape. If all had gone according to plan, Charlie's bag would be there too.

'Claudio, come on!' hissed Charlie.

A small gaggle of boats – gondolas and motor taxis, *vaporetti* and motorboats and a dairyboat that usually brought milk from the mainland, and a highly decorated ice-cream delivery barge belonging to Claudio's brother-in-law – was hiding them from onlookers on the other side, bobbing about on the tide and the busy wakes from so many craft, circling and goggling. Even so they had to be quick.

'Charlie – I'm not coming,' Claudio hissed back, down from the deck of the *Bucintoro*. 'I can't now. Look at this! I have to stay. I'll look after him. He is so fine!'

Charlie and the Lions looked at each other.

'Well,' said the Oldest Lion.

'That's fair,' said the Yellow Lioness.

'But –' cried Charlie.

His dismay showed on his face. If Claudio stayed, how could he, Charlie, ever get away? The Lions weren't safe alone – they couldn't operate the boat! How could he desert the Lions and find his parents? By the time he had delivered the Lions to Morocco, his parents might be anywhere!

Tears sprang to his eyes, and he turned away to hide them. He didn't want to upset the Lions. He must be brave now. He blinked, then turned back and swiftly passed up Primo's remote control up to Claudio. 'Good luck!' he called, his voice wobbling.

The crowds were cheering for Primo. Claudio was calling out, fine noble words about freedom and redemption and the Glory of Venice.

'Charlie?' said a low voice. It was the Young Lion.

'Do you need to stay?' he asked gently. 'If you need to stay, just say so. You have done enough for us.' The others were behind him, tough and glorious, their Lion eyes full of understanding.

Charlie burst into tears. How could he desert such kind and generous animals?

'No, I – ' he said.

'We'll be all right, you know,' said the Oldest Lion.

One of the Lionesses offered her tail for him to wipe his tears on.

'But decide quickly,' said another, looking over her shoulder at the rippling, roiling crowd of boats around them.

'I – ' said Charlie.

'Yer goin',' said a low, rustly, scratchy voice. 'Yer parents'll locate yer. They've gone to the Circus and somebody'll tell 'em yer going to Morocco. Me, if need be. Go on – 'oppit. Go with yer mates. Yer can't stay here, there's a price on yer 'ead, remember?'

'Sergei!' yelled Charlie. 'Sergei! I'm so sorry . . .'

'Shut it,' said Sergei. 'I'm down off my *haut cheval* now. Forget it. Yer've to get a move on!'

'Are you coming too?' cried Charlie.

'Yeah,' said Sergei. 'At least till you deign to send me back to bliddy Paris with some missive for your esteemed mum and dad.'

Charlie grinned and grinned.

'Give me one good reason why I should tell you where they're going,' said Mabel.

'Because he's my son and your nephew,' said Magdalen.

'He's a thief and a troublemaker,' said Mabel. 'Give me one good reason why I shouldn't just head off myself and get the Lions back.'

'Because they want to be free,' said Aneba.

Mabel stared at him.

'How very sentimental,' she said, with a brilliant smile. 'OK, here's what we'll do. We'll all go after them. I think I deserve a head start, don't you? I'll let you know – *later* – where you're going.'

And she left.

'Why – why does she hate you so much?' asked Julius quietly.

'It's a long story,' said Magdalen.

Charlie didn't know how to drive a speedboat, but it scarcely mattered.

By the time they had crossed the great greeny-grey lagoon, past the Lido, the last island of Venice, and into the Adriatic Sea, he had the hang of steering perfectly. Soon after that he discovered the onboard computer, with its navigation system and movable screen for using either in the cabin or in the cockpit. 'Essaouira non-stop,' he tapped in, and smiled as the screen responded: 'Heading south Adriatic Barbary Coast Essaouira non-stop as per instructions.'

'Great,' he said, and now that his hands were free he started to pull off those ridiculous tights. But the jerkin he quite liked. Unlaced, with his old canvas trousers, it looked rather cool. His trousers though, he realized, were somewhat shorter on him than they had been. 'Oh, well,' he said, and rolled them up. He felt like a pirate.

Sergei lay at his feet, complaining.

Behind them, as they headed south towards Africa, Charlie and the Lions could still hear the bells ringing out, and if they had looked back later that evening they would have seen the sky above Venice alight with fireworks. But they didn't look back. They were off. They were free.

CHAPTER THIRTEEN

On the marble pavement in front of the Doge's Palace, Rafi was fighting his way through the jubilating crowds along the canalside, heading west towards the open lagoon. He'd fought his way to the front and seen that weird giant Lion with the teeth. He'd seen Charlie up there with the weird Lion and that gondolier making the speech. He'd seen the other Lions. And he'd seen, suddenly, that they were no longer there.

The Venetians were too busy overthrowing the Doge to care, but Rafi had only one interest here, and what interested him seemed to have dissolved off the face of the earth. Now Rafi knew that this could not actually happen. He also knew that it is often easier to disappear in a crowd than in an empty place.

First your prey are on a boat before your very eyes, then they are gone. Their boat, however, is surrounded by other boats.

So they slipped on to another boat. Fair enough.

Aha. Rafi remembered the boat from this morning, with Charlie's bag aboard. So they had a plan. They were slipping on to a boat and scarpering.

But where were they scarpering to?

They'd be heading out to sea, or to some place down the coast, or perhaps back on the mainland to the north, or to one of the islands of the lagoon, or over to the Yugoslav lands. The fact they were on a boat meant nothing – you could hardly leave Venice without being on a boat, unless you took the one road or the one railwaytrack. Boats led to a great many more places.

All around him the people were jumping about, happy and excited, hugging each other and shouting and singing, in love with lions and deliriously glad to see the back of the Doge. On that glorious sunny day, Rafi was the only angry thing in Venice: a resentful, snapping packet of dark, burning anger.

Actually that's not quite true. Edward was angry too. But not in the way you might think. Edward was angry with himself.

Edward, in the face of all the hoo-ha, had quickly, and with a certain amount of success, presented himself as being entirely on the Lions' side. 'Long live the Lion of San Marco!' he had cried.

Claudio had given him a funny look.

'It's marvellous, isn't it?' cried Edward, fairly convincingly.

'What?' replied Claudio.

'His Majesty's Lions!' cried Edward. 'Bringing such joy to the people of Venice! His Majesty will be so pleased! He loves the people of Venice! Marvellous! Marvellous! *Meraviglioso!*' he cried in Italian, just for good measure, so the Venetians would know he was on their side, not the dreadful old Doge's.

Claudio looked quite disgusted, and just before being hauled off to the cathedral with Primo by the adoring crowd, he hissed to Edward, 'If His Majesty knew what you have been doing with his Lion friends and his young friend Charlie, he would be VERY VERY ANGRY!'

It was the word 'friend' that made Edward stop and think.

He hurried back to the palazzo, out of the way of this crazy crowd, shouting '*Viva il Leone!*' (Long live the Lion!) whenever he thought anyone was looking at him.

The King would be angry!

Would he?

But Edward had done all of this for the King's sake! To bring the King and the Doge to friendship again! Admittedly the timing turned out to be bad, with the Doge losing power, but even Edward couldn't have known that was going to happen . . . All Edward wanted was for the King to be happy. Edward was devoted to the King. He would never do anything to upset him. He'd only not told him because he'd wanted to surprise him with the Doge being his friend again.

Would the King be angry with him?

For locking up his friends and tricking them and trying to give them away as if they were things, not living, thinking beings let alone friends of King Boris . . .

Well, when you put it that way . . . Friends . . .

Oh, lord.

King Boris would be furious.

Edward was a sensible person. He didn't try to blame anybody else. As soon as he got in he put a call through to King Boris.

'I'm glad you called,' said the King, who had just half an hour earlier received Charlie's letter, and was deep in thought about the situation. 'I was about to ring you. Now what on earth is going on?'

'The Doge has been overthrown!' said Edward.

'Oh, good,' said King Boris. 'Dreadful man. Never liked him. Will they have a republic now? I do hope so. I was thinking of getting one here . . . only if I can be president . . . But that's not what I was talking about. What's going on with Charlie and those wonderful beasts? Have they left yet? Did you find them a boat? What did you do about food? I was very worried about meat storage for the Lions, because they wouldn't want to be going ashore the whole time for supplies . . . What route are they taking? I'd hate there to be any delay . . .'

Edward gulped, blushed, and thanked his lucky stars that he could say, in all honesty, that the Lions and Charlie were on their way.

'Excellent,' said the King. 'Well done.'

'Thank you, Your Majesty,' said Edward palely.

'Credit where it's due, eh?' said King Boris.

There was a small pause, before Edward sort of coughed and said, 'Er, yes, Your Majesty.' Even he couldn't barefacedly claim the credit for something he had tried so hard to sabotage.

'And not where it's not,' said the King, a slight sternness in his voice.

'Er, no, Your Majesty,' said Edward.

The King remained silent long enough for Edward to realize that *he* had to speak.

'Sorry, Your Majesty,' he said. 'I thought . . . I thought I had thought of a better plan . . . I thought I knew better . . .'

'Yes, well, you don't want to go thinking that, Edward. Not while you're working for me.'

'No, sir,' said Edward.

And you will realize, from this, that the King preferred to solve the problem without having to accuse Edward or be angry with him. This is called diplomacy, and it's a very good way of getting exactly what you want.

'Good,' said King Boris.

*

The Lions were happy: completely happy to be in the open air, to be going home, to be free. The Oldest Lion stood at the prow of the boat, much like the golden lion on the prow of the *Bucintoro*, gazing south towards Africa, with a poetical look on his face and the salt spray foaming up beneath him. The Lionesses, much to Charlie's amazement, made a circle by taking each other's tails in their mouths, and did a stately dance, round and round, on the foredeck. The Young Lion stretched and rolled and somersaulted, and then ran up and down the deck, and up and down again, and up and down again. Elsina made herself into a ball and rolled all over the place, tripping the others up.

Sergei positioned himself in a safe place in the cockpit, and shook his head. He considered them all completely mad.

Charlie smiled. The sun was shining and they were heading south, his parents were free, he was free, and this boat was a real gas – he could steer it and make it go faster and slower, but the whizzo computer navigation system meant that it wouldn't bump into anything. He'd keyed in 'Essaouira', and now it would take them there itself, avoiding all the pitfalls and recommending good restaurants along the way. Except unfortunately he couldn't key in 'avoiding any likelihood of bumping into other human beings'.

So they bounced along, fully charged up, laden with food and water, as cheerful as they could be.

'I propose a toast!' cried the Oldest Lion, turning from his vantage point in the bow. He looked unusually playful, and his mane was curling and flouncing in the wind. 'To us! To how magnificently we have achieved what we set out to achieve! To our bravery and patience, long may they stay with us, to our brothers and sisters, and to our true friend Charlie, without whom we could not have done this.'

Charlie blushed.

Sergei snorted.

'And to our new friend Sergei,' said the Oldest Lion, 'to whom I gather we also owe some thanks for the assistance he has rendered to the parents of Charlie.'

'Honoured,' said Sergei.

The Young Lion raised one eyebrow.

Charlie kicked Sergei gently.

Sergei stood up. 'The pleasure is entirely mine,' he said. 'Erm – yeah. Honoured.' And he sat down again.

'I miss Claudio,' said Elsina. 'He was so polite. I don't really miss Primo, though. He was nice but he was so . . . sad. I'm quite glad it's just us again. Our gang.'

The Yellow Lioness cuffed Elsina gently with her paw.

'I'm just really really glad we're on the move again,' said the Young Lion. 'Really really *really* glad.'

Charlie grinned at him, because he felt exactly the same.

'So tell us, Sergei,' said the Oldest Lion. 'What has been going on? Tell us all that we haven't heard while locked up in circuses and palaces.'

Sergei blinked at him and scratched his bottom.

'Not much,' he said. 'The world's been taken over by genetically modified felines who make kids sick with asthma, so that the Corporacy can make loads of money out of flogging medicine to their loving mamas and papas, and the two Profs have been kidnapped for daring to think up a cure, and were carted off to one of the Corporacy Communities to be brainwashed. But now they've escaped, largely thanks to Lionboy here and, of course, me, and we're all going to meet up back at your gaff, and, erm, live happily ever after. Well, not me, obviously, because I'm a miserable depressive genetically-modified aberrance, but the rest of you. That's about it.'

'What's happened to Rafi?' said the Silvery Lioness, with a little smile. His blood had been the first fresh living blood she'd tasted in a long long time, and it had been sweet.

'What, Mr Adolescent Fancypants? He's out of the 'ospital that I believe you, madam, put 'im in, and no doubt is pursuing us as fast as his little legs'll carry 'im, except that he'd probably not know where we're going. But, er, the Corporacy will want yer parents back, Charlie, and as Rafi was meant to send you to 'em as well, they – he – might decide that you'd be a bit easier to catch. A good bait, if you pursue my drift. To get yer parents to go back.'

'So Rafi *was* taking me to the same place?' Charlie said. 'All this time I've been chasing after my parents, and if

I'd stayed with Rafi I'd have ended up with them anyway.'

'Er – yeah,' said Sergei.

'Well, for –' said Charlie.

'Yeah, but,' said Sergei, 'yer'd've been drugged and brainwashed and a liability to 'em, if yer'd been in there with 'em. Whereas, being on the outside and running around all over everywhere being, you know, a boy hero, yer've been a challenge and an inspiration. It would've been harder for them to escape, with you there. And with you elsewhere, they *had* to escape.'

Charlie could see the logic in that.

'Listen,' said Sergei. 'The cats in Paris know you're going to Morocco. They'll find a way of getting it through to yer mum and dad. Yer mum and dad'll find yer – they'll track you down. Come on, they're scientific geniuses! They'll find yer!'

'Yes, and Rafi might too,' said Charlie.

'Don't you worry about him,' said Sergei. 'Look who yer mates are.'

'No, don't worry,' said the Silvery Lioness. She looked as if she might lick her lips.

The Oldest Lion gave a cautionary growl. Charlie knew what it implied. The Lions really weren't meant to eat humans. At least not on human territory.

Aneba was following Magdalen, who was following Mabel across a railway station towards the ticket office.

'Go away,' said Mabel over her shoulder.

'Make me,' said Magdalen.

'Sweetheart,' said Aneba. 'Is this really the best –'

'Yes,' said Magdalen. 'Unless you can think of anything better.'

'Well – your, er, sister –'

'I know,' said Magdalen. 'It's strange. But for now, we just have to find out where our son is or soon will be, and this bolshy redhead will lead us there whether she wants to or not.'

'Go *away*,' said Mabel.

'No,' said Magdalen.

Mabel, reaching the ticket office, made a big show of talking very quietly and hiding her business from her sister. Magdalen lurked over her shoulder quite shamelessly, then when Mabel had finished and got her ticket, Magdalen barged straight up behind her and said, 'Two more just like that one, please. Seats next to her,' with a gorgeous smile for the ticketguy.

Mabel was trying to race off to the platform, but Magdalen was right behind her, and Aneba was right behind Magdalen.

'*Go AWAY!*' shouted Mabel.

'I'm not your kid sister any more, Mabel,' Magdalen said. 'You can't just tell me to go away any more.'

Mabel turned and stared at her.

'*Go away*,' she hissed.

'Anyway, that's *your* speciality, isn't it?' said Magdalen. 'Going away? Just buzzing off and never telling anyone where you are, for *nineteen years*!'

For a moment Aneba thought Mabel was going to hit Magdalen. But she didn't. She took a breath, and looked down her haughty nose.

'I'm not going to dignify that with an answer,' she said.

'Oh, grow up,' sneered Magdalen.

'Girls, girls,' Aneba protested. He almost found himself telling them to play nicely or he would send them both to their rooms. 'Come on. We're travelling together.'

'You do what you like,' said Mabel. 'I'm travelling alone.'

Mabel was feeling very confused, and for a number of confusing reasons. There she was, quietly being a world-class tigertrainer, living in Paris, travelling around, happy enough. Then suddenly her old boyfriend appears, wanting to have dinner with her, but behaving actually quite oddly – affectionately, but more as if she had invited him. And then he'd produced this curious crony – boys that age always made her feel nervous, and this one had been no exception – and had to talk business with him in the middle of their date. Then that very night his Lions disappear – six Lions, into thin air, even though Maccomo was always fantastically careful with his Lions, as careful as she was with her beloved tigers. Then he disappears – without a word to her, despite all that he'd been saying during the evening about how he was happy to be with her again. And then . . . and then Magdalen turns up. Her kid sister Magdalen. Grown up, married, a professor, a mother. When Mabel had left, Magdalen had been thirteen, a plump little kid with her hair all over the place. Look at her now! And her kid was that Lionboy of Maccomo's!

Mabel hadn't been home since she was fifteen years old. Hadn't seen her mum, any of her friends, anyone. She had chopped her childhood off like a branch.

And now, her sister, her sister's kid . . . Mabel felt a pang in her belly.

Maccomo had said the boy had a good bond with the animals, but how can a child run away with six Lions?

And meanwhile, Major Tib had revealed to her that Maccomo had been drugging them. Traces had been found. Drugging them!

If Maccomo had been anywhere in reach Mabel would have taken her rhinoskin whip and belted him. You don't drug big cats. Even Lions, which of course aren't as fine and magnificent as tigers. You just don't. And Maccomo had been drugging them every day, for no one knew how long.

The child wouldn't necessarily know that. He would be off with a pride of Lions coming up from drugs: getting stronger and wilder and more independent by the day, and at the same time confused by the change in themselves, maybe panicking and needing the drug they'd become addicted to.

Those poor Lions.

And, yes, that poor boy.

So what was Maccomo up to?

Mabel had not been sleeping well. She'd been thinking a lot about where Maccomo would have gone. She'd worked out, late on those sleepless nights, that he could not be responsible for the Lions' disappearance. Therefore, he would want to get them back. Therefore, he would work out where they'd gone, and go there.

So where would they go?

Home, of course.

And where was home?

She'd laughed, lying in her bed, and pulled her phone to her. Mrs Chan in Hong Kong would know. Mrs Chan knew where all the big cats in captivity came from. She had sold most of them in the first place. She was the biggest big-cat merchant in the world. Mabel bought all her tigers from her.

Mrs Chan did not know.

But that didn't matter. There were very few independent big-cat suppliers. Maccomo would have acquired the Lions either through Don Quiroga in Cochabamba, Bolivia, or through Sidi Khalil in Casablanca. And those were not Latin Lions. They were African. So she rang Sidi Khalil, and he confirmed that Maccomo had bought his Lions from Majid, Lioncatcher of the Argan Forests of Essaouira.

Mabel did not like to leave her tigers. Not at all. If she had not had Major Tib to leave them with, and her own very reliable tigergirl, Sophie, she probably would not have gone. But she was very angry with Maccomo. She was still half in love with him, and she wasn't about to let a man she was half in love with either leave without saying goodbye or, more importantly, drug his Lions. She wanted an explanation, so she was going to get one, and if she had to go to Morocco to get it, then to Morocco she would go.

Magdalen, sitting opposite Mabel on the train heading south, knew none of this. She just saw her big sister who she had adored – grown up now, a tigertrainer, beautiful, wonderful, with this shocking temper and dreadful-sounding boyfriend and no concern whatsoever for her old family or her new nephew. Magdalen felt like a little girl inside. She was very angry with Mabel, but she still desperately wanted her to be nice.

Magdalen chewed her lip and felt about six.

Mabel just put on a haughty expression and closed her eyes.

Rafi was hustling through the crowd, trying to escape from it. He thrust his hands deep into his pockets, pulling his leather collar down hard against his shoulders until it almost hurt, and he jostled people, elbowing them in the ribs and treading on their feet on purpose. He wanted to kick them. He was in trouble and he needed a stroke of luck. Or a plan. Or an ally.

He cut down an alley and found himself in a quiet square, with a bench. He sat, feeling the sun on his face.

Now. What was it he had stolen from Charlie?

He pulled the parchment from his pocket.

'Ay, ay,' he murmured. 'What's this, then?'

He unfurled it on the stone bench beside him. It had been tightly rolled and kept trying to spring back again, so he fixed one end under his knee. It was upside down. He turned it round. It still looked upside down.

Funny-looking brown ink.

Rafi frowned.

Either way up, it looked like science.

He got to thinking.

He didn't know what it was. He didn't need to. Charlie was carrying it around in a very small bag with very few things in it: he valued it.

Rafi wondered how much he valued it. Enough to be tricked into trying to get it back? Enough for Rafi to blackmail and bribe him with it?

Science, eh?

Maybe Aneba and Magdalen would value it too. Maybe the Corporacy would value it.

He smiled.

'Hello, my stroke of luck, my plan, my ally,' he murmured.

A big grey cat with cobwebs in his whiskers gave him a distasteful look.

Rafi smiled to himself, and took out his telephone. He wasn't going to ring Charlie yet and torment him with the knowledge that he, Rafi, had the parchment. Not yet.

Then Rafi took out the other thing he had pinched. It was a small blue stone ball.

'Now what's this, then?' he wondered. 'Why's this so important that Charlie's taking it everywhere with him?'

He looked at it. Touched it. Stroked it. Peered closely at it. Sniffed it. Licked it even.

A stone ball, blue, with marbly markings in it.

'Dunno,' he said to himself. 'Dunno what that's about.'

Charlie could have told Rafi that it was just a ball of lapis lazuli that his mum had got on a trip somewhere, that she liked, and that he carried it for no other reason. His mum liked it. It reminded him of her.

Rafi wouldn't have understood that either.

Edward's telephone rang in his study at the Palazzo Bulgaria.

'No,' he said. 'Who? Oh, you, Mr Sadler. Well, no. What? Lions? You seem obsessed with them. Who? Charlie Ashanti? Never heard of him. Well, how could I know where they are, if I don't even know who they are?'

He was looking at his fingernails and listening very carefully to everything Rafi said.

'I think you're mistaking me, Mr Sadler,' Edward continued.

Rafi's voice on the line was casual but it had an undertone of urgency.

'His Majesty?' said Edward. 'Certainly not. We have no interest in this nonsense. Parchment? Thank you, we have our own paper suppliers in Venice. Mr Sadler – no, be quiet a moment – Mr Sadler, this is the only piece of information I am going to give you. Listen carefully. Here is your information.'

Rafi, sitting on his bench, listened, agog.

'I do not give out information. I receive it. Goodbye.'

Maccomo's telephone rang on the small low café table in front of him. Ninu's left eye swivelled towards it. His right eye stayed watching Maccomo. Their direction joined up again as Maccomo lifted the phone.

'Ah,' he said, reading the dial. 'My little friend.' Then: 'Hello, Rafi. What can I do for you?'

'I'm still in the market,' said Rafi. 'Just to let you know. The merchandise we were discussing in Paris. Nothing has changed for me.'

'Really,' said Maccomo. 'How interesting. For me, you know, there have been changes. For example, the price has gone up.'

'That needn't be a problem,' said Rafi. He wasn't intending to pay anything anyway. Now he had the parchment, he was intending to bully, bribe or blackmail Charlie into coming along of his own accord. He was only trying to find out if Maccomo knew where Charlie was, or where he was heading.

'But you understand,' said Maccomo. 'It is difficult merchandise to keep hold of.'

'Oh yes,' said Rafi politely. 'So – um – you have a hold of it at the moment?'

'Delivery is imminent,' said Maccomo.

Excellent! thought Rafi. Maccomo's expecting him!

'So when and where can we exchange?' he asked smoothly.

Maccomo smiled quietly to himself. He burned with a low, dangerous fury.

He still hadn't decided what to do with Charlie when he got hold of him. The Lionspeaking filled him with envy and desire – so would he keep Charlie, get his hands on the boy's knowledge, wring out of him the language of the Lions? Or would he punish him by selling him to Rafi, for whatever nefarious purpose he had in mind?

It was nothing to Maccomo if Rafi came for Charlie or not. However, Maccomo needed money. No longer living in the Circus, and no longer being paid Circus wages, he was going to be running short soon. Rafi would bring money.

Even if Maccomo decided not to sell Charlie, he could just steal the money Rafi would bring.

He chuckled. What a good idea!

'Come,' he said. 'Essaouira, on the Barbary Coast. I am here. Come.' And he flicked off the phone.

'Yes!' cried Rafi. That had been so easy! Now, where's the Barbary Coast?

'Hmmmm,' mused Maccomo. This would be so easy. Perhaps he would move to more comfortable lodgings.

Ninu flicked his eyes, left and right.

CHAPTER FOURTEEN

The happy days on the solarboat lasted almost long enough for Charlie to get bored of them. It was like when you're on a long summer holiday, and even though you spend all day at the beach playing and having fun, you still catch yourself wondering what the new term at school is going to be like. Charlie was so relaxed with the boat by now that he would draw it to a halt so that he and the Young Lion could dive off the front, splash wildly in the sea and then scrabble on board again, out of breath, giggling and shaking themselves, much to the annoyance of the Lionesses, who felt that cats should stay dry. There was some fishing kit on board, and Charlie learned to handle it quite well, pulling up tuna and swordfish, which the Lions happily tore to pieces – except Elsina, who wrinkled her pink nose and longed for proper fresh meat. The Young Lion was convinced that claws were better than hooks for fishing, and would trail his big paws over the edge trying to skewer fish single-handedly. He and Charlie developed a cheerful competition to see who could catch more. (Charlie

The French Weasel

won. Even after the Young Lion tried with a hook tied on to the end of his tail.)

To amuse them all, Charlie tried to teach the Lions to sing sea shanties. Their favourite went:

> 'One morning a weasel came swimming
> Over the water from France,
> And he taught all the weasels of England
> To play on the fiddle and dance.'

Elsina had a sweet squeaky voice and the Young Lion was very enthusiastic, so they made an appalling racket and

Sergei, who was rather musical, had to go and put his paws over his ears at the other end of the boat, muttering insults about tone-deaf, cloth-eared bliddy philistines. No one minded. After the long days and nights on the train, in the snow and stuck inside the damp Venetian palazzo, they were just happy to be in the sun, to fall asleep soaking up the warmth. Their skin and fur glowed under the sun's polishing, and Charlie's locks grew stiff with all the salt spray and the swimming.

One day, still encrusted with fine crystals of salt from a dip with Elsina, Charlie went to the water butt to refresh his sea-watery mouth, and noticed that the level was getting low. Not dangerously low, but low. They had passed round the heel of Italy, heading west for the second leg of their journey. It was good that the water had lasted so long, but now they would need to get more.

That evening, after Charlie's dinner of pasta, olive oil and chilli peppers (the Lions were not eating that day), he went to the solarboat's computer and asked it about going ashore. The information came up on the screen: they could put in at any number of little fishing towns and shipping ports along the coast.

Charlie frowned. They were a long way from Venice now, it was true, but he was reluctant to go to the mainland. For all he knew there might be 'wanted' posters up – policeguys lying in wait, fat rewards lying unclaimed, and hungry bounty hunters desperate to get their hands on the runaways. Plus most of the mainland down here, he knew, was a lawless area, run by vicious families who fought each other all the time: people who used to be farmers but whose lands had been ruined by chemicals and genetic modification; people with next to nothing, who stole from each other. He didn't want to have to go there, all alone, asking for water. They'd steal the boat.

Not that he'd blame them. He'd probably steal the boat too, if it were him.

The only alternative was the Islands. It was still risky, but one way or another they were going to have to take a risk, and Charlie felt that the Islands were safer, if only because their inhabitants were less hungry.

The Islands around the toe of Italy are exceptionally beautiful, so beautiful that Communitybuilders had snatched them up long before. Lots of rich people wanted to live there – they were warm and quiet and clean, and it hadn't even cost that much to bribe the shepherds and fishermen who had lived there to move away to Naples or Brindisi, clearing the way for the wealthy outsiders.

Charlie keyed the Islands' names into the computer. One after the other they came up and, yes, they were all new communities. One in particular caught his eye: Pantelleria, halfway between Sicily and Algeria, between Europe and Africa, a smallish island all alone.

It was on their course, it was big enough to have plenty of supplies, and far enough away from everywhere else not to have extra police nearby, or daily newspapers coming in. The information said it was beloved of pop stars, and listed some. Charlie had heard of them. They were the kind that did yoga and ate no meat. Charlie was pretty sure that such people would not deny a boy a butt of fresh water.

That's the one, he decided.

Later that night, the waves around their bow began to sparkle in the darkness. It was little scraps of glimmering green phosphorescence, thrown up like tiny diamonds in the pale ghostly lace of the sea spray, then disappearing, dissolving in the night.

The Lionesses gazed at it in awe. Elsina tried to catch it in her paws, until the Oldest Lion pulled her back by the tail. Even Sergei was rendered silent by the strange, otherworldly beauty of it.

'What is it?' breathed Charlie.

No one knew. It was just there. Everybody felt in their hearts the extraordinary, unnecessary beauty of the world.

But then suddenly, silently barging out of the magical darkness, breaking their quiet, wondering mood, there was a ship. It was big, but not enormous; it had no lights on. It had loomed up, completely invisible – there was no way they could have seen it coming. And it was almost on them.

Charlie yelled, and rushed to let off the solarboat's siren. The Young Lion was about to roar, but the Lionesses shushed him and the siren began to wail. The big boat changed course, drastically, and the solarboat bobbed helplessly in the waves it made.

'What are you doing?' yelled Charlie, into the darkness. 'You almost killed us, you stupid seahogs!'

From the ship, still so close, came the sound of groaning. Human groaning.

It rocked there, dark against the moonlight and the sparkling phosphorescence.

'Where are your lights!' shouted Charlie.

Of course no one could hear him.

'Charlie,' said Sergei cautiously.

'What!' said Charlie. He was really angry. How dare this stupid boat bear down on them in the middle of the sea with no lights on, making no noise – he had his lights on, didn't he? Port and starboard, bow and stern, just like Julius had taught him on board the *Circe* . . .

'Hush, Charlie,' said Sergei.

Something in his voice made Charlie do as he said.

For a moment, all was silent but for the low roarings of the sea moving over itself, and slapping at the sides of the two boats. And the groaning.

Then a figure appeared on the deck of the strange ship.

It called out, in no language that Charlie had ever heard, and he had heard most. It sounded sad beyond belief.

'What is it?' Charlie whispered.

Sergei was staring, his whiskers out rigid, his rounded head with its tattered ears motionless.

'Speed up, Charlie,' he said. 'We must get out of here.'

'Why?' said Charlie, always prepared to argue and discuss, but Sergei turned and hissed sharply at him, 'Get a move on! Now!'

Charlie was shocked at the sudden passion and anger in Sergei's voice. He swiftly scurried to do his bidding.

As the solarboat started away from the dark ship, the groanings seemed not to fade but to grow louder, a protesting chorus of sadness, a yearning, lonely sound. Looking back, Charlie could see more figures on deck, silhouettes joining the first one. Their arms were outstretched and their voices pathetic.

'Who are they, Sergei?' he whispered. 'What's the matter with them? Shouldn't we help them?'

Sergei was silent for a moment.

'It's a Ship of Fools, Charlie,' he said finally. 'Those are the Poor Fools.'

Charlie didn't understand.

'But who are they? Where do they come from?' he asked.

Sergei said, 'They're humans and they come from nowhere.'

'But nobody can come from nowhere,' Charlie began to say, puzzled.

Sergei interrupted him. 'They've nowhere to live,

because they left where they were, lookin' for somewhere better,' he said.

Charlie knew about that. That was refugees. Loads of people had been refugees at some stage or another: uprooted, thrown out, having to start over somewhere new . . . he knew about refugees. He always thanked his stars that London was somewhere refugees came, not somewhere whose people had to become refugees.

'So why aren't they in the place they were going to?' he asked. 'Or in a camp or something?'

'No place will have them,' said Sergei.

Charlie could understand that too. Places got filled up. 'Why don't they go back to their old place? Is it too dangerous for them?'

Sergei smiled, a bitter little smile. 'For most, yes, it's just that they'll be killed or put in prison. But for the Fools it's different.'

'How?' asked Charlie.

'Their old places don't exist any more,' he said.

'What?' said Charlie. 'I don't understand.'

'They don't exist,' said Sergei again. 'They've been abolished by law, or destroyed by war, or poisoned and blitzed and sunk into the sea. Those guys were calling out in Ukrainian. There has been no Ukraine for fifty years.'

Charlie stared.

'Shouldn't we help them?' he said in a very small voice.

'Cats don't help people,' said Sergei coldly.

'You help me,' said Charlie.

Sergei was silent.

'Humans fifty years ago should have helped them,' he said finally.

Charlie looked back to where the hulk of the Ship of Fools was disappearing into the darkness behind them. It wasn't fair. It wasn't right.

Charlie was very sad that night.

Rafi, however, was happy. He'd gone to the great electropark by the station in Venice and stolen a fantastic electrobike: a dark grey and silver Triumph with seismic suspension and a 12,000-volt chargesystem. It could go quicker than anything else on the road – and Rafi was making sure that it did. With his collar turned up, his shades on and his body leaning into the bend, he roared out of Verona heading west into the evening sun. He planned to cross the top of Italy, cut into southern France west of the Alps, and be in Spain within thirty-six hours and Morocco a day or two later.

Behind him at the electropark a great grey dog raised his head and howled. Once again his instincts had been frustrated. Once again the scent that he knew and craved had eluded him. After days of criss-crossing this smelly wet town, diverted by every whiff there was, he had found Rafi's scent again. And now it was gone – melted into the clean metallic smell of electrochargers. The merest wisp of it was on the wind . . . Troy couldn't help himself. His nose was stronger than his brain, than his legs, than any sense he might have had. He lowered his head and set off after that wisp.

Rafi wasn't planning to rest much, nor to eat. He was a man on a mission: strong black coffee and sheer anger would be his fuel. However, even a man on a mission, fuelled by strong black coffee and sheer anger, needs to pee every now and again. When he stopped in a lay-by outside Milan for just this purpose, his body juddering and his legs almost locked into place by gripping the bike at such high speeds, he noticed that his phone was beeping in his pocket. He had a message.

It was from the Chief Executive. At first Rafi wasn't even going to bother to listen to it. He knew what it would say. Then he did listen, because after all it might say something else.

It said what he expected. Things he didn't want to hear, such as: 'Where are you?' and 'Where's the boy?' and 'What's going on?' and 'Get a move on.' Oh, and 'We'd like to be able to continue to rely on your services, Rafi,' in a very insulting and patronizing tone of voice.

Rafi kicked a tree. He *hated* being patronized. Those sniking big boys at school, when he was a little kid . . . Yeah, but he wasn't a kid any more.

And his arm ached.

Angrily, he punched in Charlie's number.

Charlie, sitting on the deck of the solarboat with Elsina tickling his feet with her whiskers, picked up his phone.

'Hello, Charlieboy,' Rafi said. 'Hi there. How are you? Feeling pretty chipper? I bet you are. I bet you think you're doing just fine, don't you, running away with your little furry friends . . .'

As he recognized the voice, Charlie froze. Then he came swiftly back to life.

'Oh, shut it, Rafi,' he said. 'You're a bore. I've had it with you and these stupid phone calls . . . What's the matter, someone ticked you off again for being so stupid? Got to find a smaller kid to take it out on? Well, how small is that, you pinnock? Just proves how small *you* are, doesn't it –'

Rafi butted in. 'Bigger than you, Charlie! And cleverer.'

'Yeah yeah yeah,' said Charlie. 'Course you are, Rafi, which explains why I've escaped from you, and kept ahead of you, and know what you're up to. Come on, Rafi. Prove it. You're so big, prove it. Find me, for a start, and then let's see who –'

'Hey, *cleverboy*!' cooed Rafi, in a deeply irritating sing-song voice. 'Hey, *cleverboy*, I think you'll find I'm big enough to carry around something of *yours*, cleverboy . . . You take a look in your *handbag* and see what you're missing, why don't you. Go on! I won't keep you – I'll call you back later so we can talk about it.'

Rafi rang off. He felt a lot better now he had humiliated Charlie.

Charlie leapt up, flinging Elsina from him, and ran to his bag.

The parchment – his parents' formula, written in his mother's blood – wasn't there.

For the second time in his life, he swore.

CHAPTER FIFTEEN

Magdalen was reading a newspaper on the train. In the foreign news was a story about the recent miraculous events in Venice, where the Doge had been toppled from power by the appearance of the Lion of St Mark, who had led the gondoliers in a peaceful revolution, supported by an army of Lions and a small brown saint, who had provided heavenly medicine to the asthmatic children of the city . . .

Magdalen wondered.

Aneba was snoozing on her shoulder. She stroked his knee. When he awoke, she would show him the story.

Mabel was sleeping too. Magdalen looked across at her sister and wanted, more than almost anything, to be friends with her again. But she was so angry with her.

'There's Pantelleria now!' Charlie called. He had programmed the island's name into the solarboat's navigation system, and they were approaching the main harbour. It was low and rocky; hot and picturesque. Charlie looked forward to getting off the solarboat and running around a bit. He fancied a shower too. His coating of salt was getting just a bit too thick.

As they approached this beautiful island, something rather horrible happened.

A fence appeared out of the sea in front of them. Like the wall of the lock in Paris, it just rose up. But this was not a useful wall. It was a high metal fence with points to its bars – sharp points. It looked as if it were made out of spears, bound together with thick barbed wire. It was extremely unwelcoming.

The water rushed off it. It shone and sparkled. It blocked their way.

'Oh,' said Charlie.

The Lions growled. Sergei had a look on his face that suggested he wasn't at all surprised.

A voice came out of nowhere, over the water. A smooth female voice.

'Who are you?' it said, in English, French, Italian, Arabic, Greek and Spanish.

Charlie thought quickly – at least he tried to. Should he lie?

He couldn't bear to have to lie all the time. He hated it.

'Charlie Ashanti!' he cried, not sure how the voice could hear him.

'Do we know you?' the voice replied after a moment.

'No,' he said, 'but –'

'Then go away,' said the smooth voice.

'No, but –'

'Go away,' it repeated.

'We only want some water –'

'Go away.'

The fence rose another half-metre. The spears gathered a little closer together. Charlie might have been imagining it, but they seemed to be leaning slightly towards him.

'That's so unnecessary,' he said, but more quietly. 'We only want water . . .'

On either side, the fence reached around the island as far as he could see.

'That's so . . .'

The Lions, crouching down, aware and alert, growled softly.

'Please, we only want water!' Charlie shouted.

The fence lurched towards them, an army of spears about to march.

Charlie flung the tiller over and steered the solarboat full speed away from the island, his heart pounding.

'Now what?' he said to Sergei.

'Look behind,' said the cat.

The fence had sunk back below the waves.

For a moment, Charlie looked hopeful.

'Don't even think about it,' said Sergei.

'He's right,' said the Young Lion. 'Don't go back.'

'But what can we do?' said Charlie. 'We've hardly any water left, and –'

'We go on,' said the Oldest Lion. 'Quickly, and thirstily.'

Charlie squeezed the dry insides of his mouth with his teeth, biting at them to make saliva. He knew they were right.

'Only another few hundred kilometres to Tangier,' he said cheerfully. 'We can get water somewhere there. Or we could just go overland.' His lips were dry as he powered the boat up: full speed to the Straits of Gibraltar. His mind was hard and dry too – why were human beings so horrible?

Charlie woke early as they drew near to the Straits of Gibraltar. There was only enough water for breakfast, but he was happy. They had travelled swiftly and arrived well before dawn. They didn't want to land in daylight and risk the Lions being seen. They had an hour or so before sunrise during which to come ashore somewhere quiet and find water.

'Right,' said Charlie, raising his eyes from the computer screen, where he had been studying their course, and looking out at the great spaghetti junction/continental security system of the Straits of Gibraltar. Even at this hour many boats of all sizes were toing and froing in the narrow stretch of water, trying to move into the right lane on the right aqueduct level to get from Spain or Portugal to Morocco, or out into the Atlantic heading north into the Gulf of Cadiz, south or west, or back into the

Mediterranean going north or east. The overhead water-lanes were very crowded, and the little island of Gibraltar was gridlocked. This system was a nightmare to negotiate at the best of times.

Charlie tapped the keyboard, his tongue between his teeth as he concentrated. He was pretty sure it was all in place. The computer had read its maps and identified a location for them to land on the north coast of Morocco, near Tetouan, and it would just navigate them straight there, as soon as Charlie told it to.

He yawned. He hadn't slept much. Then he pressed the keys, instructing the navigation system. The Lions lay low around him, still snoozing.

The solarboat changed course a little, and sped up as the instructions went through.

It was ten minutes before Charlie realized that something was wrong. They weren't heading to the safe quiet landing place. They weren't even heading for the shore. They were heading swiftly and unstoppably up on to one of the overhead waterlanes, and they were going fast – too fast.

For a moment Charlie was about to panic – but he didn't. Furious, he turned to the computer screen. What had gone wrong? Trying to stay calm (and finding it pretty difficult as they flew up into the dark night), he asked the computer what the boat was doing.

Tap tap tap on the keyboard.

The answer came up on screen almost immediately:

'Heading south Atlantic Barbary Coast Essaouira non-stop as per instructions', it read. It had reverted to the very first thing Charlie had told it to do, back in the Gulf of Venice.

Charlie tried to gather his intelligence together. He glanced up at their surroundings. They were on a high one-way waterlane, being taken by the flow, surrounded by other boats.

Was it worth asking the boat to take them back to Tetouan or Tangier? He stared out over the tangle of waterlanes and shipping channels that lay all around them, at all the seacraft moving to and fro, many under the instructions of their computer systems. They were at the heart of a great constantly moving web.

Tetouan was already behind them. Tangier lay over to port. The stream of boat traffic going there was clearly visible many levels beneath the solarboat. God only knew how to get back and join that stream. Or how far they would have to go ahead before they would have a chance to turn back.

Charlie made his decision. They would go on. Then he laughed to himself, because it was foolish to imagine that it was a decision. They had no choice. They were heading out into the mighty Atlantic Ocean in a boat designed for the Venetian lagoon and the mellow Adriatic, aiming non-stop for Essaouira.

'What's goin' on?' said Sergei, his voice coming up from

the dim nightlit cabin. He sprang up to the deck, stretching. 'What's the matter?'

'Nothing,' said Charlie shortly. He was not in the mood for explaining and, in truth, he didn't know if he had made a dreadful mistake or if the computer had malfunctioned. And he wasn't about to find out, because the boat was going so fast he could hardly keep his balance, let alone work out what had happened.

Sergei glanced at him. He could see the situation all right. He curled himself back in a corner and started to lick his foot. None of his business.

The waterlane was dividing. Most of the traffic seemed to be going north, heading up the Gulf of Cadiz towards the coast of Portugal. The little solarboat was flinging itself into the portside lane, heading south. It veered and swerved and only just got into position as the lanes forked apart. Charlie stared at the screen. He had no choice but to trust that the boat knew what it was doing.

They were heading down now. The overhead waterlane began to glide back to sea level, and to the sea. Charlie looked up: there it was, spread out to starboard, silvery in the first shots of dawn light, huge, deep, stretching all the way to the Empire Homelands. The Atlantic. It didn't look in too good a mood.

Perhaps it was a wind rising with the sun. Perhaps it was an ocean tide. Perhaps it was a current surging forward. Perhaps it was a combination of all three. Anyway, the waves were big. That was straightforward enough. The wind was confusing – first this way, then that. The little boat, steering determinedly south – Essaouira non-stop! – was being buffeted. It was being carried faster than ever, in the right direction at least, but way too fast. The waves knocked it about. The sea was getting pretty rough.

Charlie checked the fastenings on his life jacket. He had no idea how the Lions could snooze through this. He was glad, though. He didn't want to have to say to them, 'Yes, we're in trouble.' But he knew that they were. He could feel it.

He wanted to ask the computer for a weathercheck. He wanted to ask it what it was doing, ask it to pull in now, at the next safe place. He wanted to kick it. He pushed the screen back into its cabin position, hunched himself over it and tapped at the keyboard.

No response. It was jammed.

Up on deck, a huge wave broke over the bow. To port, the sun started to rise out of Africa.

A huge valley of sloping water opened up in front of them.

There was nothing Charlie could do.

Sergei followed Charlie when he went down the companionway – another big wave threw the boat up, and Charlie lurched on the steps. He secured the hatch tight – he didn't think he would be going on deck again for a while. He sat himself on the edge of a bunk, first missing, then finding a gap between two of the Lionesses. Sea water was chucking itself over the portholes and the boat bucked and strained in its compulsion to make it south through these wild seas. On and on they surged, up each huge wave, and over. Up up up – pause – and over. Charlie was horribly aware of the deep dark cold water just below the boards under his feet, and of wishing it would stay there.

Sergei licked his paw and wiped his nose with it.

'Best leave the boat to do its job,' he said mildly. 'Either we'll get there in one piece or we'll not.'

Little as he liked it, Charlie had to agree. In a sailing boat they could perhaps have done something, but here they were powerless.

They surged terrifyingly for hours. The boat had gone mad and the sea was mad back. Charlie sat in his life jacket with his bag strapped to him, fantasizing about how to get life jackets on the Lions . . . At one stage he had unlocked the hatch again. Then locked it again. Then unlocked it again. Which was better? He left it closed but unlocked. He actually managed to sleep a bit – a tense, exhausted, buffeted sleep. He didn't notice when the Lions woke – perhaps they had been awake for hours. One of the Lionesses had been seasick, and every now and again Elsina howled very quietly.

'Charlie,' came the Young Lion's voice through the roar and the rush, 'it's not your fault.'

Other than that, nobody spoke. They just stayed in the cabin for hours, praying, holding on tight, straining till their muscles ached, trying not to be bashed and thrown about.

Elsina's howls became little mewing noises. Charlie could hear them, above the roar and crack of the sea.

CHAPTER SIXTEEN

Later, Charlie could never describe how it happened, or even really what happened.

Everything went crazy. The light went, the boat turned over, water filled the cabin. The Lions were just great presences around him in the water, everybody struggling, trying to breathe, the rush of bubbles, heavy bodies and slow flailing limbs. He pushed open the hatch, he remembered that. There was more water on the other side of it. He remembered coughing and spluttering, and that the light through the water reminded him of the frozen light through the windows of the *Orient Express*, and then he was in open water, big waves slooshing over him, punching him, trying to drown him. He remembered thinking, The sun can't still be rising, when for a moment he saw it hovering, yellow and burnt-looking, over the horizon, and realizing that no, it was setting, and so land would be behind him. He remembered looking for the Lions, and seeing nothing but water. He remembered kicking and kicking and kicking his legs, fighting towards where he hoped land would be, for hours – was it hours? He couldn't tell. He remembered mouthfuls of salt, and finally, miraculously, a feeling of rough sand under his face, warm against the cold sea still snatching at his legs. He remembered thinking, We've come so far and now, just as they are almost home, I have drowned them all. He remembered that his tears tasted sweeter than the sea.

It was Sergei who recovered his senses first, looked round, and didn't like what he saw. A long crescent of beach, wide and smooth, littered with bits of wood and ancient plastic, the sun setting and the surf pounding: that was all right. What was not all right were the four sodden piles of fur, and the figure of a young person way down the beach, carrying something, and approaching them.

Sergei sneezed, winced and shivered. The still-warm sun was shining on him. He stretched uncomfortably, then leapt up and ran to each of the sodden piles in turn.

Two Lionesses, the Oldest Lion and the Young Lion. They were all breathing. Where was Charlie? Where was the Silvery Lioness? And where was Elsina?

Sergei warmed up quickly in the last rays of the sun. Help was needed.

He raced down the beach towards the approaching figure.

There was a smaller pile between him and the person.

Sergei reached it swiftly. Yes!

He checked Charlie's breath. Yes! He licked his face.

Wake up, boy!

Giving a little snort, Sergei gave Charlie a swift, clean scratch. The shock of it worked.

'Wake up,' Sergei hissed. 'No time for a kip now. Yer got to hide! Four Lions down thataway. Hide 'em! There's someone coming!'

Charlie was so dazed he couldn't even pull himself up. So cold. He clutched at his bag and only half-heard what Sergei was saying.

'Oh, for sniking crike . . .' Sergei said. He hissed viciously at Charlie and turned on his heel. He needed local cats and he needed that bliddy sun to go down *now* so they'd be hidden by the darkness.

He raced on along the beach. There was a town at the end. He could see the tops of things – some old-fashioned towers. The figure was still approaching, walking slowly. He – it was a he – seemed to have a bucket. Probably collecting shellfish or something, Sergei thought.

Oh, well.

Sergei raced up to him, gave him a scratch across his bare leg, and raced on. The guy cried out in surprise and pain, and sat down with a bump.

'Sorry,' muttered Sergei as he ran on. 'Nothing personal.' But at least the man had stopped.

At that moment, Sergei got a whiff. Fish-stink!

He smiled in his whiskers. Where there's fish-stink, there's cats.

They were only a couple of hundred metres up the beach, at the base of an enormous wall that separated the town from the sea, scrabbling over a pile of fish-innards dumped, by the look of it, after the market had closed up for the evening.

Sergei sauntered into the circle.

They all looked up. There was a fair amount of food, but there was also a fair number of cats. Was this scrawny puss after their dinner? (They didn't know he was an Allergenie – this was the Poor World, and so few people could afford medicine that nobody had bothered to send Allergenies here.)

'There's four half-drowned Lions and a Catspeaker flung up on the beach,' Sergei announced. 'Two more Lions missing. They're cold and hungry and thirsty and on the run from the Circus. They're in danger.'

The cats looked at him. They looked at each other. They looked, in particular, at a big amber cat with pale-green eyes.

'Where?' said the amber cat.

'Follow me,' said Sergei.

Fifteen cats ran swiftly down the beach to find the Silvery Lioness and Elsina. Forty-five followed Sergei past the young man nursing his scratched leg (he took one look at the gang of cats and ran in alarm back towards the town) to where Charlie and the other Lions were. They breathed on them, stroked them, patted them, warmed them up. They woke them, talked to them, told them they were all right but must move immediately. As the last rays of the sun filtered out of the deep blue sky, the Lions and Charlie were coaxed to their feet and brought along the edge of the sea, back towards the town, to what looked like a tumble of rocks at the end of the great thick wall.

There was an entrance into the wall, an old doorway with rubble across it. Inside was a sort of room, damp, with whitewash peeling off the walls. Further in was another room, seemingly carved out of stone, with a high arched ceiling, stone benches built in round the walls and what looked like a broken fountain in the middle.

'It is an old hammam,' said the amber cat, whose name was Omar. 'Bath-house. Inside the ramparts of the town, against the sea. Very strong, very quiet. No humans come now.'

Charlie could hear the sea pounding against the outside wall. He had no desire to be anywhere near the sea. He wanted to be by a fire, drinking sweet fresh water, eating an enormous kebab. But he was glad to be there, in the damp, strong, quiet place. He sat on a stone bench, felt the cold come up through his body, and shivered. The Lions huddled close to him, their eyes wide with shock. He put his arms round the Young Lion's neck and buried his head in his fur. It was different. Salty, cold, damp. How could he have put his friends through this?

There was blood on the Young Lion's head – he must have been hit by something.

The other cats had left again – out looking.

'I am sorry no fire is possible,' said Omar. 'But water, yes.' He gestured to the fountain. 'Move stone and sweet water will come.'

Charlie moved the rock that blocked the end of the water-pipe. Clear clean water gushed out. They all bent their heads to drink from it, shivering with thirsty anticipation.

'Yuck!' yelled Charlie, spitting and retching.

The Lions were baffing at their mouths with their big paws, their lips curling back, their faces wrinkled with disgust.

The water was salt.

Omar was distraught. 'I do not know how sea water got in!' he cried. 'Apologies, apologies, my friends. I do not know . . . We must find you sweet water.'

Charlie, still spitting, opened his bag, and gave a drop of Improve Everything Lotion to each of his friends. It took the taste of the salt from their mouths, and they needed it anyway. Then he used the salt water to wash the Young Lion's wound. 'It's good to be inside and hidden,' he said. '*Shukran*. Thank you.'

Omar smiled. 'Catspeaker,' he said. 'A real Catspeaking boy. I am honoured. Welcome to Essaouira.'

Essaouira! Charlie's heart leapt and for a moment he forgot his thirst.

'We're in Essaouira, guys!' he cried out.

The Oldest Lion looked about him and sighed. 'Not quite how we intended to get here,' he murmured. 'But here we are. At least most of us . . .'

Charlie was incredibly happy to hear him speak. He rushed over and, before he could help himself, he had flung his arms round the Oldest Lion's neck, rubbing his damp mane with his hands, hugging him, and saying, 'I'm so sorry, sir, I'm so sorry, I nearly froze you on the train and I nearly drowned you now.'

The Oldest Lion looked at him in astonishment. 'On the contrary,' he said. 'You saved us from freezing on the train, and you have brought us to our homeland without drowning us. What on earth are you sorry about that for? And there is no time to be sorry – we must find our friends, and we must find water –'

'Cannot, sir,' said Omar. 'Sorry. Not safe. Cats will find, and cats will bring back to their family.'

For a moment the Oldest Lion looked as if he was going to object, magnificently, like a wounded king.

Sergei cut in. 'He's not wrong, yer know,' he murmured. 'Best stay here, all o' yer. For the duration.'

'Essaouira cats know where the storms throw things,' Omar said. 'Cats know which wind throws things where. Cats will find them.'

'And I'll get the water,' Charlie said. 'In a moment I'll go for it.'

The Oldest Lion knew they were right.

Omar smiled again.

Charlie was still shivering.

Omar watched him as he tried taking off some of his wet clothes and putting them on again, working out what would be warmest.

'Follow,' he said, and Charlie did. 'Also you,' the cat called to the others. They all went after him up a winding staircase at the side, moving slowly, all cold to their bones.

An arched doorway brought them out on to the flat roof. The sound of the surf was louder than ever. The sea was very near. A low wall surrounded the roof and Charlie, looking over it, could see the walled town spread out before him, the beach beyond, and the minarets and domes of the mosques.

'Stones still warm from the sun of the day,' Omar said courteously. 'Stays warm all night. Lie, like on heated floor. Feel better.'

Stiffly, the Lions lay down. Charlie too. Sergei curled in beside him, in a surprisingly affectionate way. The hot sun had pounded down all day on these stones, and now, in the evening, the heat was trapped there, ready for them. They all lay as flat as they could, shifting and rolling to get the warmth on to every part of their damp, battered, chilled bodies. The sky was huge above them, and a low moon was rising, lying on its back like a cradle. Charlie wanted to climb into it and sleep for a week. Instead he thought of Elsina, and the Silvery Lioness, and his thirst. He sat up again.

'Which way did the searching cats go, then?' he said to Omar, stretching out his stiff neck and being grateful for at least that short moment of relative comfort. 'Can you take me? I must be there to give the medicine. And I should bring some food and water.'

'Of course,' the cat replied.

'I'll come with yer,' said Sergei.

The Young Lion looked up. Charlie could see that he too desperately wanted to come, and to help.

'Stay,' Charlie said. 'You'd be seen. You're hurt.'

'I know,' said the Young Lion. 'But you're doing everything for us, Charlie. What are we doing for you?'

'You dealt with the Dogepolice, didn't you?' said Charlie. 'And with Rafi, when it *really* mattered.'

The Young Lion still minded. It wasn't that he was jealous of Sergei, just . . . but his head did really hurt.

Charlie and Sergei looked out over the town for a few moments before leaving. Omar pointed out the market (closed now), the medina (the old town), with its main street where the cafés were, the rocks down the beach where the cats had gone to look for Elsina and the Silvery Lioness.

'Onwards and upwards,' said Sergei. '*Per ardua ad astra. Illegitimi nil carborundum. Rien ne va plus.* Come on, lad.'

They went down the winding stairs, out through the rubbly doorway into the warm night, and on to the streets of Essaouira.

Outside one of the cafés that Charlie had seen from the roof of the hammam sat Maccomo. He'd just overheard the shoemaker say to the waiter that young Khaled had now completely lost his marbles: he'd been telling everyone that he had been attacked by an army of mad cats on the beach, and that there were shipwrecked lions that the cats were trying to hide . . . poor Khaled. Lost it completely.

Maccomo smiled, called the waiter over and ordered a couple of big bottles of water. When they came, he opened them. Then, carefully, without drawing attention to himself, he took a small flask from his pocket and poured a good dose of its contents into each water bottle.

A small boy was helping his uncle on a drinks stall across the way. Maccomo clicked his tongue at him, calling him over.

'There'll be a boy along soon,' he said. 'Tired-looking and grubby, not Moroccan. I'll point him out. Sell him this water and I'll give you five dirhams.' The kid shrugged, took the bottles, and sat down to wait for Maccomo's signal.

The cats were already bringing the Silvery Lioness and Elsina along the beach when Charlie and Sergei met up with them.

The two Lions looked terrible: cold, weak and shuddery. But they were alive. Charlie found that he was smiling. He only realized it now, but actually he had been horribly afraid for them. Funny how that happens – when the fear is there, you deny it, then when the crisis is over, it is safe to say, 'That was a crisis. Thank god we are OK.'

Charlie immediately gave them each some Improve Everything Lotion, and took Elsina into his arms to carry her. She was heavy and limp, her big paws flopping. Charlie kissed her and talked to her. 'Come on, girl,' he whispered as he carried her. 'You can make it. Come on. You're all right now. It's all all right now.' He thought he could feel her wanting to respond. The Lioness was a bit stronger, but she too had the cloudy eyes and absent look of utter exhaustion.

They slipped back into the hammam. It was hard work getting Elsina upstairs, but he managed it. He lay her out on the warm stones. The other Lions, warmed up a bit now, clustered round the two and cuddled close to them to give some of their warmth. The Young Lion lay down by Elsina and whispered to her. Omar was still there, watching over them.

They were all right. It was a miracle. They were all all right.

Water, Charlie thought.

*

As he approached the very first café on the main street, a small boy came over trying to sell him bottles of water. Charlie delightedly took the two big ones the boy held out to him. He tore the top off one and poured water down his throat – not too much. He had to take it to the Lions. But cool, sweet water. He shuddered in his skin, his body rippling with gratitude. It had been days since he had had enough to drink. He looked around for Sergei to offer him some, but the scraggy cat was already round the back of the café going through the bins, eating and drinking all sorts of stuff it's better not to know about.

In the café, a beautiful tune was playing on the radio, which immediately cheered Charlie up. He grinned and ordered twenty-five big kebabs, twenty-four of them raw, and sat down to a bowl of soup, hot bread and a big glass of orange juice while they were cooking. Thanks be for his mother's dirhams, which had survived the shipwreck, soggy in his pocket. Thanks be for food and drink. Relief flooded him.

Three doors down, Maccomo sat back in the shadows and watched. When Charlie collected all his meat and turned back towards the ramparts, Maccomo silently slid from his seat and followed. Invisibly, he slipped through the streets; patiently, he settled down in a dark shadowed corner in front of the hammam to wait for the medicine to take effect.

*

Further into the medina, a woman climbed out of a cab. Behind her, a man and a woman climbed out of another.

'You've just wasted fifty dirhams with your stubbornness,' called Magdalen. 'You're being really pigheaded. We could at least have shared the cab.'

Mabel ignored her, and strode ahead through a fairly nondescript stone archway, dragging her bag angrily after her.

Inside, even Mabel gave a little gasp. The archway led to a beautiful courtyard. Or was it a tall, open room? You couldn't tell if it was indoors or out, a chamber or a garden. The floor was stone, old and worn, but beautiful carpets were laid on it. The walls were high, and lined with wide balconies, each supported by rows of archways. Climbing roses and jasmine twined their narrow stone columns, and in the centre a fountain played, its basin strewn with rose petals, crimson and white. Low sofas and comfortable chairs sat in groups round small tables. Up above, the stars gleamed in the rich night sky.

Mabel, Aneba and Magdalen all went up to the reception desk. Mabel had booked her room, and she smiled as a porter took her bag and led her upstairs. Aneba started to arrange a room for himself and Magdalen (right next door if possible) while Magdalen stuck by her sister. She wasn't letting her out of her sight.

Which was just as well.

*

Maccomo's lodgings
Ramparts
Old hammam
Place Prince
Moulay El Hassan
Essaouira
HARBOUR
SCALE:
from here to here
= QUITE CLOSE

Riad el Amira
Gate to the dunes
TO THE FOREST
Ninu's café
TO THE BEACH AND THE DUMP

Maccomo was still in the shadows outside the hammam when the boy from the hotel found him. (Boys in small Moroccan towns always know where everybody is, even – especially – people who are trying to hide.)

'Madame at the Riad el Amira says please will you come,' said the boy politely.

Maccomo looked up, his eyes hooded in the darkness. He did not want to ask how the boy had located him – it suggested that he didn't already know, and he liked people to think that he knew everything.

'I know no madame,' he said coldly.

'Foreign madame,' said the boy. 'Very beautiful. Hair like fire.'

Maccomo's eyes flashed. Oh, really? And why was she here? How did she know where he would be?

He smiled.

Clever Mabel, lovely Mabel, had returned to him. It could mean only one thing. She was giving herself to him. This time he would marry her, she would help him, they would be together forever.

He must go to her now – immediately!

But did he have time?

The drugs would soon knock Charlie and the Lions out, but once out they would sleep for a while . . . and before then Maccomo would be back – with Mabel! And then, together, they could take Maccomo's revenge.

Maccomo went first to his lodgings, to wash and change

his clothes. He had to be beautifully presented to claim this woman as his wife. On the way from his room to the riad he didn't notice the mangy scrag-eared cat who had followed him from the hammam, and clocked where he lived, and was following him now as he swept into the Riad el Amira.

CHAPTER SEVENTEEN

Bathed and changed after her long journey, Mabel lay back on a low divan in a chamber off the courtyard. The chamber was divided with screens, exquisitely carved from dark aromatic wood, so that each set of divans, draped with ornate cloths, seemed to exist in its own little room. The night was growing cooler, and in the big stone fireplace on the far wall a wood fire was glowing and crackling. The smell of it was delicious. The sweet mint tea – emerald green leaves gleaming within the crimson and gold glasses on the low polished table in front of her – was delicious too. Tall white flowers in a dim corner emitted a faint, delicious scent.

Mabel stretched. How luxurious. If it weren't for the knot of anxiety in her chest, her slow-burning anger at Maccomo, her confusion about her sister, her nephew, and the fate of the Lions, oh, and the constant dull ache down her belly where a tiger called Rajah had ripped her open and taken a bite out of her many years before . . . If it weren't for all that, she would have felt marvellous.

She looked up. Maccomo was standing in the gap between the screens.

'Mabel,' said Maccomo. 'My love, you are here, you have come to me.' Before she could respond, Maccomo was at her side, taking her hand. 'My love,' he said. 'I know that I should address this to your father but as you have none, nor a brother nor an uncle, I will speak my heart direct to you. I wish to marry you, I wish you to honour me with your love. I am as you know me – a travelling man with little to offer but his skills and his heart. But before you refuse me because I am poor, listen: I have an opportunity. Some of this you know, but let me explain.'

Mabel was shocked. Marry him! She had been married four times already . . . She was not planning to do it again. But explanation – yes, that was what she wanted.

'My Lions were stolen from me,' he was saying. 'You must have heard about this. But I don't care so much about that. I will capture them again, label them bad and have them sold to some cheap zoo, where they will be punished every day for their folly in running away from me – they will live in small cages, their meat will be old, their water will be scant and dusty, and small children will tease and annoy them daily. But no – you remember my Lionboy. Charlie.'

Mabel remembered him, yes.

'My love . . .' Maccomo's eyes burned into hers and he

took hold of her elbow. 'My love. Have you heard tell of Catspeakers?'

Of course she had. It was an old legend among circusguys and zoopeople. A load of old nonsense.

'Charlie is a Catspeaker.'

Mabel stared at him, and in that instant knew that it was not a load of old nonsense.

Maccomo was holding on to her elbow so hard it hurt.

'Just so!' he said. 'He is the only one, for sure – probably the first for years. Think what he is worth!'

Mabel blinked.

She was thinking – he could talk to my tigers. He could tell me what they are thinking. He could – so where is he? Take me to him NOW!!! Mabel had never heard anything so wonderful in her life. Her own nephew! Everything else fell away.

'So my friend – Rafi Sadler. You met him,' Maccomo was continuing. 'He trades in . . . well, many things. Including, you might say, skills. People with skills. The people who would like to employ them pay him, and he takes them to . . . where their skills are most valued. So he has offered to take this Catspeaking Lionboy. He has a very good client interested – very rich powerful people. They are interested to know how the Catspeaking works, why he can do it, and so on. They will pay a lot for this boy – perhaps you know them. The Corporacy. Very powerful people . . .'

Behind one of the dark wood screens, at the next set of divans, Aneba jumped up, his face furious and his fist raised. Magdalen jumped up too and grabbed his face in both her hands. 'Shhhhhhhhhhhh,' she whispered, her face contorted with pain and the effort of keeping quiet. 'Shhhhhhhhh.'

Aneba took a huge, long breath, and silently, hugely, he let it out. He spread out his clenched fist and lowered his hands, gently, flat, in a calming gesture. 'I am angry but I control my anger,' he said to himself silently. And again. And again.

The firelight was flickering on the high, pale stone walls.

Mabel stared at Maccomo and forced herself to smile at him, but behind the smile her mind was in turmoil. 'Trades'? 'People'? 'Pay for this boy'?

Maccomo was intending to *sell* her nephew? To sell a boy?

That's slavery!

And to the *Corporacy*?

Mabel knew about the Corporacy all right. She hated the Corporacy, and all that 'you have to conform to survive' stuff; the new Communities with their rules and restrictions. That's why she ran away to join the Circus in the first place – to be wild and free.

As she stared at Maccomo, her smile in place, Mabel thought swiftly. She thought: I don't really know this man. She thought: I could never be in love with someone so wicked. She thought: I must pretend to be, and use his trust in me.

And so her smile broadened, and she cried, 'Darling, how wonderful!' and she snuggled up to Maccomo, and his heart swelled with delight.

Her heart, meanwhile, was fomenting deceit. She would talk to Magdalen. They would make up! Together they would rescue Charlie!

But Magdalen, behind the screen, heard only the words her sister spoke, not the plan that was in her heart. And she was filled with horror, and this time Aneba had to restrain *her*.

Charlie felt terrible. His head was heavy. It kept sort of falling off to one side. His eyelids had grown; they were too big for his eyes. His mouth was dry and his skin had shrunk. He felt very sick. He'd better lie down. Oh – look. All the Lions are lying down. I'll lie on them. *Lion* them. Ha ha.

He stumbled over the Oldest Lion's huge paw, and fell on top of the Yellow Lioness. She didn't stir. The Oldest Lion didn't stir. Their breathing was heavy and peculiar, but Charlie didn't notice. His ears had gone echoey. His hands dripped from the ends of his arms like melting wax. Only heavy. Got to turn over, he thought. Sick.

Charlie was just about to pass out when Sergei sprang excitedly on to the window ledge. He was racing back to report that he had followed Maccomo to the Riad el something, and that in the seconds between sneaking in and being chucked out he had glimpsed Charlie's parents – but he took one look at the pile of comatose Lionflesh and the groggy boy in front of him, and he shrieked.

Sergei knew what was going on. He had seen enough alcoholguys in the streets of London and Liverpool, enough humans unconscious because of the poisonous chemicals in their blood. But how come the Lions were in this state? He ran through in his mind what they had consumed. It had to have been in either the food from the café or the water.

He remembered the water boy. Only he, Sergei, having helped himself to water from a puddle behind the café, hadn't touched the bottled water. Only he, Sergei, was fully alert.

He had seen how close Maccomo's lodgings were to where the boy accosted them. He had heard all about the medicine the Lions had been given at the Circus, and how Charlie had given it to Maccomo to make him dull and dopey.

Charlie rolled over and groaned. In a split second Sergei was beside him, yelling at him, berating him, cajoling him. 'Wake up. Wake up. WAKE UP! Don't go to sleep! Come on, yer great twaggler, you can do it! WAKE UP!!!!'

Maccomo had put a lot of medicine into the water.

Charlie had drunk less than the Lions, and he had drunk the orange juice and the soup as well, which diluted the effect, but he had had enough.

Sergei stopped jumping around and yelling. It wasn't working.

So what else?

He thought. Why was Charlie more awake than the Lions, though he was smaller and therefore more susceptible?

Soup. Orange juice.

Spitting and cursing, Sergei leapt out the window again and snaked his way swiftly back to the marketplace.

Sure enough, in the corner where the detritus of the day's stalls was piled up, waiting to be taken to the dump, lay a lot of only slightly rotten oranges. Some children were going through the stuff, looking for anything good enough to eat or sell, but they didn't mind the scrawny cat who was trying to roll oranges away. They liked him actually. They laughed, and one little girl in a pink silky dress decided to help him. Sergei played with them, nudging the oranges, pretending to talk to the children.

Before long, a group of six skinny kids was carrying handfuls of oranges down to the old hammam, and throwing them in the window, because it amused the skinny cat. They were sad when he jumped in after the oranges and wouldn't come out again, but then the father of one of them came along shouting and wanting to know what they were doing out so late, so they ran off back to the marketplace.

Inside the hammam, Sergei was shredding the oranges with his claws and putting them in the Lions' mouths, trying to squeeze their great jaws together, trying to get some of the juice into them. He didn't much like putting his paws inside the great pink caverns of teeth; he didn't especially like the idea of one of the Lions waking up and biting his leg off by mistake, but he didn't at all like the idea of them just lying there asleep until Maccomo came back for them.

He shredded, he squeezed, he talked, he cajoled. 'Come on, come on,' he murmured. He went back again and again to Charlie, licking his face, squeezing oranges in his mouth. 'Come on!'

Twice in one day! he thought. Couldn't these snikin' creatures stay awake for half an hour on end?

But he was worried.

What to do? Should he carry on trying to bring Charlie round, or should he . . . maybe . . . go back to the Riad el whatsitsname and try to attract the attention of his parents?

But Maccomo was there.

Sergei stared at Charlie. His scraggy ears twitched back and forth and his whiskers drooped.

Suddenly he jumped on to Charlie's tummy, pummelling at it, his claws in Charlie's shirt, his paws pulling and pushing.

'Wake up wake up wake up wake up!' he caterwauled.

And Charlie did.

If he was surprised to find his mouth full of raggy bits of orange, he didn't say so. He just shook himself, threw up, and then stuck his head under the pump.

'I feel horrible,' he announced.

Then he saw the Lions, and remembered some of what had happened.

'It was the water,' said Sergei.

Charlie picked up one of the bottles, and sniffed it. He wrinkled his nose.

'We must have been pretty thirsty not to have noticed that,' he said. 'It's the Lionmedicine.'

'Thought so,' said Sergei.

'Which means,' said Charlie, turning a little green again . . .

'Yeah,' said Sergei. 'That snike. I saw him. 'E was waiting outside for you all to become totally comatose, then he took off with a lad from the town, so I follered 'im. 'E'll be back for yer. For all o' yer.'

'Is he there now?' cried Charlie. 'Sergei – look out of the window!'

Sergei peered out.

'No sign,' he said.

'We must get these guys awake and scarper as soon as possible,' said Charlie. 'Before he comes back – but where's he gone? Why would he risk losing us, after all the trouble he's taken?'

'It's not that simple,' said Sergei. 'Charlie –'

'What is it?'

'I saw . . .'

'What?' said Charlie.

'Er – yer esteemed mum and dad,' said Sergei.

Charlie stared at him.

'Here?' he asked cautiously.

'Here,' said Sergei. 'Here, and free.'

'Mum and Dad . . .' Charlie's face was flushed and he couldn't let himself believe it. Here? Now? Free?

'Yes, Charlie, Mum and Dad, Professor and Mrs, Doctor and Mr, Aneba and Magdalen – them. Yer very own parents. I am acquainted with them, you know. We shared precious moments in a rubbish tip, remember?'

Charlie's breath was coming a little short.

'Take me,' he said simply.

Sergei looked at him with great sympathy in his milky eyes. But he didn't move.

And, 'Oh,' said Charlie, after a moment.

'Of course,' he said, as he thought a little longer.

Charlie knew he had to sort the Lions out before he could go to his parents. The Lions were in great immediate danger.

But his parents!

For a second he let himself imagine seeing them, running to them . . .

And how good would it feel, if he knew he'd let the Lions down? Soon it would be getting near to dawn. If they didn't get home tonight, there would be another whole day for Maccomo to make his move.

Sergei was watching him carefully. 'You've brought 'em home,' he said. 'You've done what you said you would. You can leave 'em now, if yer choose to. Yer can do what yer like.'

'Thanks,' said Charlie, with a tight little smile. 'Thanks, but – you know I can't.'

Sergei shrugged. 'Come on, then,' he said.

Charlie looked round at the unconscious Lions.

'Got to wake them up first,' he said. Then he had an idea. 'Sergei,' he said. 'How far away are Maccomo's lodgings?'

Luckily for them Maccomo was still canoodling with Mabel when they climbed up to the balcony of his chambers. While they were clambering through his window, he was retreating with her to her private sitting room, with Aneba and Magdalen following at a safe distance, their nerves and muscles tense with the effort of being invisible to him. While Charlie was pocketing his last bottle of Lionmedicine, Maccomo was whispering to Mabel how the boy and the Lions were nearby and would soon be unconscious from the drugs he had fed them, and Magdalen and Aneba were desperately listening at the door, trying to make out the murmurings within. While Charlie and Sergei were shinning down to the ground again, Maccomo was still declaring his love, and Charlie's parents were sitting desperately in the corridor, their backs to the wall.

Magdalen was almost weeping. 'My sister!' she was saying, oh so quietly, over and over.

Aneba was for rushing in now and forcing Maccomo to take them to Charlie.

'And what will Mabel do?' hissed Magdalen. 'Am I to watch my husband killing my sister over my son? Or my sister and her boyfriend killing my husband? We must wait, and follow him back!'

Aneba dropped his head and thought quickly.

'We'll need disguises,' he said briefly. 'I'll go and find something. Stay here.'

'I'm going nowhere,' she murmured, misery all over her face.

Fifteen minutes later, Aneba was back with two burnooses, hooded robes he had found in the hotel laundry downstairs, and they tried to settle down to wait.

Ten minutes after that, Maccomo left Mabel's room by the other door, which led to the other side of the hotel, and an exit to a different street.

*

'They'd better have woken up by now,' panted Charlie as they hurtled back to the Lions and the hammam.

They hadn't. But they were a lot more responsive to oranges, prodding and cold showers than they had been. By the time Maccomo reappeared outside the hammam they were up, strong and furious, ready and waiting for him.

'Don't kill him,' Charlie said.

The Lions looked at him as if to say, 'Why ever not?'

'It's our nature, Charlie,' said the Oldest Lion. 'It is who we are.' It seemed the closer they were to their home, the wilder they were becoming.

Only the Young Lion seemed to understand. 'It's not Charlie's nature, though,' he said. 'Charlie can't let us do it because he is a human – a good human. Good humans don't like to kill – not even their enemies.'

The Lionesses looked to the Oldest Lion, who thought, twitching his whiskers impatiently.

'You are our friend,' he said finally. 'You could have left us in Venice, you could leave us now to go to your parents, but you are loyal to us until the end. Because of this, we will honour your nature, even though to do so we must deny our own – which may be a mistake. We will see. These matters must always be addressed when different peoples work together. We will honour you.'

The Lionesses channelled their disappointment into their anger, and when Maccomo sidled through the entranceway, with ropes on his back and a knife in his teeth, they were ready for him. There was no contest – a man who thought his prey was asleep and just needed tying up versus six livid Lions, a young boy mad as hell, and a sardonic, irritated streetcat.

The Lions pounced, and if it hadn't been for the promise they had made Charlie, they would have eaten Maccomo there and then. They knocked him about all right, patting him easily like a cat plays with a mouse, bruising him and terrifying him, and the Oldest Lion held him down with one magnificent unfurled paw, while Charlie tied him up. Maccomo was astounded. He couldn't believe what was happening. Charlie was shocked by the strength of the fight, but he was proud too. The Lions showed no feeling. They were just doing what they do.

'Hang on,' said Sergei. 'Give 'im some of this to keep 'im quiet.'

Charlie took the medicine bottle and said to Maccomo, 'Open wide.'

Maccomo didn't want it. He'd stopped taking it – it wasn't a hugely addictive drug but it had still been hard fighting the urge to sink into its lethargy. Now, offered it again, he looked as if he were more likely to spit. But then the Young Lion opened his claws and showed them, curved and nasty in the dim light. The trainer knew he had no choice. He glugged down the drug.

Charlie strapped him on to the Silvery Lioness's back,

face down and lolling with shock, horror and Lionmedicine. Then the boy scrambled on board the Young Lion, feeling again the warm smell of his fur and the ripple of his powerful muscles.

'You coming?' he called to Sergei.

'Not as such,' the cat replied. 'As in, not on yer nelly. Lions yer know are one thing, Lions yer don't are another kettle of *poissons*. I'll see yer back 'ere.'

'Sergei,' said the Oldest Lion, 'thank you.'

Sergei sniffed. 'Yeah, well,' he said, and began to scratch his bum.

So, in the darkness before daybreak, Charlie and the Lions scrambled out of the hammam, out of town, racing against the dawn across the rolling sand dunes under the crescent moon and the morning star. Branches of broom scratched at them and left their sweet scent in the air. Ahead of them lay the low, dim Argan Forests and Lionhome.

CHAPTER EIGHTEEN

'There's no more talking,' whispered Aneba.

'I know,' replied Magdalen, shaking her head. Then she looked at him.

'You're right,' she said. 'Come on. Let's just do it.'

They crashed the door open and burst in. Mabel was standing in the middle of the room – alone.

Aneba spotted the other door, flung it open, and cursed.

Magdalen shouted at Mabel.

Mabel took it calmly. Then when Magdalen ran out of breath, Mabel said, 'I am lying to him. He knows where Charlie is. He will take me to him tomorrow. I may have been a bad sister and a foolish woman but do you really think I am going to sit around and let him sell a boy! A Catspeaker at that! And my nephew!'

Magdalen was just about to go off on one, shouting that Mabel had never cared about her nephew before, and what, so, she wouldn't care about him now if he wasn't a Catspeaker? – but she didn't. She stared at her sister for a second, and then she burst into tears, and fell into her arms, saying, 'Really? Really? Will you really help?'

And Mabel said, 'Course I will, Mags,' which is what she used to call her when they were children, and made Magdalen cry all the more.

Aneba watched, smiling. Thank god for that, he thought. He knew as well as the sisters did that everything between them was far from resolved, but at least for now they could get on with rescuing Charlie.

'So where's Maccomo gone?' Magdalen cried, mopping her face.

'I know where he's staying,' said Mabel. 'He'll be back first thing. We mustn't do anything to alarm him or make him think I'm not on his side. Tomorrow morning he'll be back.'

'No way,' said Aneba. 'We've waited long enough.'

'Maccomo doesn't even know you're here,' Mabel said. 'If he so much as saw you he'd panic. He doesn't know Charlie is family to me . . . he thinks he's safe.'

'I don't care, frankly,' said Aneba. 'Where is he keeping our son?'

'I don't know,' Mabel insisted. 'He'll tell me tomorrow. He'll be back in the morning.'

Aneba shook his head in disbelief. 'Yeah, well, sweet dreams,' he said, and, chucking one of the burnooses to Magdalen, they swept out into the night. They weren't going to stop looking until they found their boy.

*

Rafi wasn't sleeping either. He had crossed over from Spain, and he was having trouble with the sand that blew about on the Moroccan roads, and camels that pouted and spat at him as he tried to pass them, and the herds of sheep that panicked when he tried to drive through them at speed. Five times he had fallen off the bike into a woolly sheepy pile. He wasn't hurt, but he was in a hurry. The Corporacy people kept on calling him, and he had given up answering because he had no further news. He had to get to Maccomo, and he had to get that sniking boy.

But he'd ridden all night, and he was nearly at Essaouira – he'd be there by dawn. It was incredibly cold riding at night, but at least there were no sheep and camels – though the moonshadows were strange, and it was hard to see the road ahead of him. There, for example – what was that? A group of six or seven shadows, or animals, or something, streaking across the road, out of one bank of low woods and into another, disappearing among the curiously shaped trees.

Rafi shivered, and roared on by.

When they arrived at Lionhome, it was dawn, and the sun was already starting to burn off the cold of the night. The sunlight sloped in shafts across the golden landscapes, casting long shadows from the spiky trees on to the dry grass and dusty paths. The morning was going to be bright and lovely. Birds were singing, and little invisible insects made crackling noises.

Charlie could not see the Lions' family. He could not see their home.

But they could, and as they grew nearer they ran faster, the Young Lion bounding along beneath Charlie like a – well, like a Lion that smelt his home.

Their home smelt them too. Suddenly, from the golden grass between the trees, golden heads began to rise, golden eyes staring. Then golden bodies, golden limbs stretching and coming to their golden feet, black whiskers twitching, ears going to and fro.

An immense male, shaggy and magnificent, stepped forward and stared.

Charlie's Lions stopped.

The Oldest Lion stepped forward, and flicked his ear.

The Other Lion swayed his head.

The Oldest Lion blinked slowly.

The Other Lion shivered his whiskers.

'Is that it?' whispered Charlie.

'I don't know,' said the Young Lion.

'Why not?' said Charlie. 'I mean, this is your place – these are your people.'

'Yes,' said the Young Lion, 'but . . .'

'But what?'

'I've never been here before,' said the Young Lion softly. 'I was born in captivity.'

Charlie gasped – he hadn't realized. But of course – neither the Young Lion nor Elsina had ever seen the wild.

'Oh, my word,' he said.

'Yes,' said the Young Lion. 'I don't know what it will be like. I'm so, *so* excited.'

Charlie rubbed his ears affectionately. He *knew* it would be OK. Challenging and interesting and perhaps difficult, but OK. And he knew that he couldn't know about it – it was wild stuff, to do with being wild. A human could never understand.

This knowledge gave him a pang.

It was just then that he realized all the Other Lions were looking at him.

Charlie glanced quickly at the Oldest Lion – whose job was it to explain? He was in Lion country now, and he had to go by Lion habits and Lion manners.

The Oldest Lion pulled himself up and shook out his mane.

'Brothers and sisters,' he announced, with a little growl of happiness, 'we have returned. Many of you will not remember us. Perhaps we have been forgotten altogether. We are your family. We were stolen. We have returned . . .'

As he spoke a rustling and whispering started up among the Other Lionesses. It didn't sound entirely friendly. But then a creature rose up at the back of the group. It was an old old Lioness, whose fur was thin and her limbs lean and weak. She came forward, calling a name that cannot be written in English.

'Is it you?' she said. 'My son? My son?'

The Oldest Lion did not seem so old after all as he bent down to lay his head on the floor before her. Charlie swallowed several times.

'Grandma!' shouted Elsina. 'Are you my grandma?' and she bounced over to the Old Lady, nudging and shyly kissing her, her tail flicking and her face a big lioncub grin.

The Old Lady stood on her thin legs and smiled.

After that, everything fell into place. The Lionesses moved slowly round to the group of staring Lions behind, touching noses here, baffing paws there. Elsina ran round and round in circles, and soon found some other cubs. In moments, they were larking and gambolling. The Oldest Lion and the Young Lion together and in turns started to tell the pride the story of all that had happened.

And Maccomo?

Charlie took him, unconscious, from the Lioness's back, and laid him out on the ground to pour a little more medicine in his drooling mouth. The Other Lions looked at him with curiosity – was he dead? He looked dead, but he didn't smell dead. Should they kill him?

The Oldest Lion said, 'He it was who stole me and the Mothers. He is our prisoner.'

'Lions don't take prisoners,' said a young Lion. 'You've been among humans too long.'

The Oldest Lion snapped. 'He is our prisoner!' he roared. 'We do not kill him, we do not eat him. We give him this –' here he gestured to the bottle of medicine

Charlie was holding – 'and we keep him prisoner. That is all.'

Charlie looked down at Maccomo, lying tied up on the dusty ground, half-unconscious, his eyes rolling, an idiot grin on his face.

Goodbye, Maccomo, he thought. Good riddance.

Then he looked over at the Young Lion. Much as he would have liked to stay at Lionhome, he had family and business of his own to attend to, and he could hardly wait.

It was hard saying goodbye to the Lionesses. It was harder saying goodbye to the Oldest Lion. It was almost impossible to say goodbye to Elsina.

The Young Lion touched his arm. 'Come on,' he said. 'Off we go.'

The run back to town seemed quicker – because it was light, and because Charlie knew where they were going. But in a strange way he didn't want it to end. He knew he was racing to his parents – but he knew as well that this was probably the last time he would cling to the Young Lion's golden back, smell his warm fur, share the adventure with him. The thought made him blink. He pretended it was just the air whipping swiftly past his eyes, but he knew it wasn't.

When they reached the edge of the dry, scraggy forest, the Young Lion stopped.

'You're on your own now,' he said. 'I can't come out there – I'd be seen.'

Side by side the boy and the Lion looked out over the great rolling dunes – part desert, part beach – to where the town of Essaouira lay on the shore below them, seeming to hover between land and sea.

'Yeah,' said Charlie.

'Mmm,' said the Lion.

Charlie thought perhaps he should just say, 'Bye, then,' and run off across the dunes.

The Young Lion was thinking he should just turn and stroll back through the forest.

They turned to each other, and at the same moment they cried out. Charlie cried, 'I'll never forget you, I'll come back and see you, you've been so great, you're the best and I'll never ever forget you'; and the Young Lion cried, 'I'll never forget you, Lionboy, any time you need me just send for me, you have been the best human friend a Lion could ever – no, you've been the best *friend* . . .'

They stared at each other for a moment, horrified by the reality of what had to happen, promising their eternal friendship silently, with their eyes.

'You could wait, and then when Mum and Dad . . .' said Charlie.

The Young Lion smiled at him. 'What's the point?' he said. 'We'd just be putting it off.'

Charlie knew he was right.

'Give Elsina a kiss from me,' he said.

'Yes,' said the Lion.

Then Charlie just turned and ran off across the dunes, and the Lion turned and ambled slowly through the forest, his head low. Neither looked back. They couldn't bear to.

Charlie was panting, sweaty-browed and dry-throated by the time he got to the gates of town. Sergei was waiting for him. He'd just had a spat with a man who had a stall selling leather slippers, and the man had thrown a bucket of water over him, so he was angry and spitting. Couldn't this guy see that he was a reformed character, a cat of integrity and purpose, not a cat to chuck water at?

Charlie wanted to sit a moment, catch his breath, find a drink of water, and make a plan. Sergei said they should head straight on.

'Just let me get my breath back!' panted Charlie in English, more to himself than to Sergei.

'I am not stopping you,' said the slipperseller, with a funny look.

'Not you,' said Charlie, with a grin. 'Sorry. Do you have any water?'

'Just dispensed all my water on a dirty cat trying to eat my slippers,' said the man. 'You want slippers?'

'No, thanks,' said Charlie – though they did look very nice, all different colours like flavours of sherbet: cherry, tangerine, lemon, pistachio, blueberry, blackcurrant and melon.

Sergei was giving him a fish-eyed look and squawking, 'Come on, boy! We've got to find them before that other bird notices Maccomo's gone and starts making a fuss! Come on! On your bicyclette! Time is passing!'

Only when the slipperseller began looking around for more things to throw at Sergei did Charlie pull himself to his feet and start through the shadowy arch of the gateway into the town.

Mum and Dad, he thought, and the thought gave him strength. It didn't matter that he was hungry and thirsty and hadn't slept since he couldn't remember when. He was on his way.

He'd had a chance to wonder where they would go, if they were here. He'd thought that they'd find out where he was, and go there. But how on earth would they find out where he was? Only Maccomo knew, and Maccomo had been dealt with.

'So where did you see them, Sergei?' he asked.

'The Riad . . . the Riad el something,' Sergei replied.

'El *what*?' asked Charlie.

'El I can't bliddy remember!' said Sergei. 'Anyway, it's not far.'

'Where?' said Charlie.

'Erm . . .' said Sergei.

Charlie looked at him.

'You know what riad means, Sergei?'

'Noo . . .' said the cat.

'Kind of . . . hotel.'

'Oh,' said Sergei. 'Um . . . Sorry.'

Well, they'd just have to find it . . . Charlie, with Sergei sort of following but looking as if he was just skiving about, walked as calmly as he could towards the Place Prince Moulay El Hassan, where all the cafés were, where he would buy an orange juice and, without attracting too much attention, get gossiping.

First he went to the patisserie and bought an apple turnover, a croissant and a little rice cake rolled in paper. The girl working there knew nothing about any red-haired woman or big English African man.

'El Omali?' said Sergei.

'Omali is a kind of pudding,' said Charlie. 'I don't suppose they're staying at the Hotel Pudding, do you?'

'Er, no,' said Sergei sheepishly.

Charlie walked over to the orange-juice cart and bought a big glass. The orange-juice guy had seen a red-haired woman and a big African man who certainly had a European look to him, but he didn't know where they were staying.

'El Arbah?' said Sergei. 'It's near here, anyway.'

Charlie just looked at him.

'Hotel the Four?' he said.

They went on to the café they had been to the night before.

'*Salaam alecum*, hungry boy!' cried the waiter. 'How were your kebabs?'

'*We alecum el salaam*,' said Charlie automatically. 'Big cup of milky coffee please and water.'

He sat down out the front, under a creeper dripping with dark-purple flowers, and began to eat and drink, stuffing his face and thinking: They're here. They're not far from where I am right now. They could just walk past. Stay calm.

The same beautiful tune was playing on the radio.

The waiter brought his coffee.

'I wonder,' said Charlie, loud enough for the other people in the café to hear as well, 'if anyone has seen a woman with red hair and a huge black man?'

The waiter's face seemed to be saying 'No', and various of the men in the café looked round, though they had nothing to say, to see who was asking. But Charlie heard a voice behind his shoulder, saying, 'Oh yes. The pale red-haired ladies and the black man-mountain? They are staying at the Riad el Amira.'

'Amira!' said Sergei. 'It was on the tip of me tongue.'

Charlie turned quickly. A swivel-eyed chameleon was staring straight at him from a branch of the creeper. He was bright green like the leaves among which he lay. No one else heard – who would listen to a small reptile when there is gossiping to be done? Anyway the people in the café didn't understand him, they didn't think chameleons could talk.

And Charlie was so happy that he didn't notice he had

been spoken to in Cat by a reptile. Or that the reptile had said '*ladies*'.

'Riad el Amira?' he said. The chameleon rolled one of his eyes to the right. 'That way,' he said.

'Thanks,' said Charlie.

His breath was coming short again. He was too excited. Too happy. Too scared in case it could go wrong again, even now.

He reached into his pack and took a couple of puffs on his medicine; he did some breathing exercises.

Then he leapt to his feet, flung down some money and, with a last wink at the chameleon, roared off down the street.

The waiter watched him go. 'Funny boy,' he said.

The chameleon blinked, and moved on to another branch, where his left leg and half his tail turned slowly purple, because they were on one of the flowers.

Charlie only had to ask three times where the Riad el Amira was. The first two people he asked were very helpful. The third, standing in the dimness of a doorway, was also quite helpful. He said, 'It's right here, you're on the steps.' Then he said, 'I knew you'd turn up, running after your mummy like a little baby. What, did you think I'd forgotten about you? Did you forget about me? Did you think I'd just go away? Well, I sniking well haven't, Charlie bliddy runaway Lionthieving Ashanti . . .'

Charlie was as shocked as you are. He was prepared for joy and reunion, not for his enemy. How dare Rafi turn up now, of all moments, and try to trample on his happy ending?

'Oh, shut up!' he yelled, and then he did something that always surprised him when he thought about it later. Overwhelmed with fury and not knowing his own strength, he just punched Rafi right in the face.

Rafi hadn't been expecting it either. He punched Charlie right back, and then he tried to grab him and get his arms round his chest. But Charlie was having none of it. He'd grown since he last saw Rafi – grown, grown up, and changed. He wasn't the same young boy whose parents had been taken away. He was a friend of Lions, a survivor of shipwreck; he'd escaped from a Venetian palazzo and helped a revolution; he'd rescued the Lions from a snowstorm; he'd travelled the sea and made difficult decisions and Rafi wasn't about to spoil his moment of glory. Never mind that Rafi was older and bigger, Charlie was cleverer and he was in the right.

He thrust his elbow hard into Rafi's belly, pulled away from him, and gave him a strong roundhouse to the shoulder. The hurt shoulder. Rafi winced, and roared with the pain. He lost his temper then, and rushed towards Charlie.

(A small crowd of cats, watching, mewed in alarm. Only one, with amber eyes, was silent.)

Charlie let him come, then at the last moment he turned, dipped and tripped him over.

He jumped on top of him, Rafi struggling and moaning. 'You can't just carry on forever getting away with things, Rafi,' Charlie hissed as he pulled at Rafi's leather coat, looking for the pockets. 'You can't just carry on helping yourself, as if the world is your toyshop. Some things, Rafi, are NOT YOURS!'

As he spoke the words, he found what he was looking for. Crumpled up and the worse for wear, but still itself – his mother's formula.

Charlie smiled, and shoved it in his own pocket.

Rafi took the opportunity to scramble to his feet, and for a moment Charlie was unsure what to do. Then he realized that he didn't have to do anything. Rafi was clutching his hurt arm, green in the face from the pain.

'You little . . .' he started to say, but then he just ran off, stumbling.

Do I follow him? Charlie thought. I should finish this off.

He didn't get as far as thinking what finishing it off might mean, because Sergei was there at his feet, mewing.

'What?' asked Charlie, still bemused and breathless. He'd fought Rafi! And won!

'Nice work, nipper,' said Sergei. 'But . . . erm . . .' He gestured through the archway.

Inside, the beautiful courtyard was full of people having their breakfast.

Among them was a red-haired woman, in clothes that showed she hadn't been to bed the night before, weeping over an untouched cup of coffee. Holding her hand across the table was a man, his broad shoulders slumped, his head gently shaking. You could see that he was saying kind and encouraging words to her, words he was trying hard to believe himself, and that she was not comforted.

All the air went out of Charlie's chest. His legs went weak.

'Off yer go, then,' said a voice.

He walked into the courtyard, his legs almost buckling beneath him.

He went up to the table.

He breathed deeply.

'Hello, Mum,' he said. 'Hello, Dad.'

POSTSCRIPT

Charlie stayed awake just long enough to eat another breakfast – the happiest of his life – and introduce his parents to Sergei. Then he slept for two days in his mum and dad's bed, with them sitting beside him, standing over him, stroking him, whispering in his ear would he like anything to eat, and hugging each other madly.

When Charlie woke up he realized he was five centimetres taller. Soon after, he met his new aunt, which gave him such a shock he nearly fainted.

He told Aneba and Magdalen everything that had happened.

They told him what had happened to them too.

The next boat back to London wasn't for two weeks. They couldn't decide what to do. Mabel thought they should stay there and have a bit of rest and holiday. Magdalen just wanted to get home – couldn't they go overland to Casablanca and back through Spain? Then back in England they could report the whole thing, find out what the police had been up to, get Rafi arrested. But

Aneba, now that he was here, was feeling the pull of Africa. Home in London might well not be safe, and meanwhile Ghana, he pointed out, was just the other side of the Sahara. They could get a truck, or some camels . . .

Charlie smiled.

But that was because he didn't know what was about to happen. He didn't know that what was about to happen would be worse than everything that had happened so far.

The End of Part Two

or

The Beginning of Part Three.